Nuptial Flight:
The London Vampire Conspiracy

John Michaelson

Burton Mayers Books

DEDICATION

Dear reader, this book is for you: fan of vampire fiction, conspiracy theorist, purveyor of all things odd and alternative, skeptic, father, mother, miscreant, NCA researcher, budding blogger, TV researcher, aspiring actor, human rights activist, hacker, Millennial, teacher, restless student, Christian, atheist, artist, bishop, micro-biologist, cult leader, accountant, club proprietor, systems analyst, trafficking victim, seeker of justice, nosy-parker, adolescent, virgin, drunkard, commuter on the early morning train, insomniac on their last dose of melatonin, friend, follower and person of a curious disposition.

I made several references to people, real and fictitious, in October's Son, and have toiled to bring you closure to many of the questions raised by a very stylized account of my life during a time I will refer to as 'The Dark Period'. Continue to read with an open mind, pray in your hearts what you want to believe, but above all read with empathy for the real victims in all of this, of which I am not one.

October's Son was about Sin; Nuptial Flight is about salvation.

Nuptial Flight: Nuptial flight is an important phase in the reproduction of most ants. During the flight, virgin queens mate with males and then land to start a new colony. One queen usually mates with several males. The young mated queens land and, in the case of ants, remove their wings. They then attempt to found a new colony. The details of this vary from species to species, but typically involve the excavation of the colony's first chamber and the subsequent laying of eggs which hatch into larvae, exclusively destined to develop into worker ants. The queen usually nurses the first brood alone. After the first workers appear, the queen's role in the colony typically becomes one of exclusive (and generally continuous) egg-laying. [1]

Not all ants follow the basic pattern described above. In army ants only males have wings. They fly out from their parent colony in search of other colonies where virgin queens wait for them.

---

[1] Adapted from: https://en.wikipedia.org/wiki/Nuptial_flight

Isaiah 1:17

CONTENTS

ACKNOWLEDGMENTS

Thank you to John and Richard of Burton Mayers Books for their continued support and patience. Without their probing emails and subtle reminders about missing manuscripts, October's Son and Nuptial Flight would not be in circulation today but no doubt stored on a hard drive somewhere, waiting for 'the day' when I could do everything on my own.

That day will never come.

I would also like to give thanks to friends and allies who supported and inspired me to tell my version of events, some of whom are mentioned in this book but with obvious name changes, in particular: The Donor, Jo, Djemal, Steve, Minx and Karl.

Thank you, truly, for releasing me from this burden!

Regards,
JM

AUTHOR'S NOTE

I've been described by my publishers as the worst type of author to work with: elusive, hard to contact, reluctant to speak publicly, and dealing in dark, uncomfortable and almost unpublishable subject matter.

Sadly that's been my life for nearly a decade.

In 2008 my life changed for good. In ***October's Son: The London Vampire Diaries***, published in 2014, I gave some insight into the changes my life went through and the physical and emotional journey that came with it during the first year. I wish none of it was real, and in many ways it had been edited heavily by my publisher to make it seem more fantastical than it really was, to match the 'genre' and attract a 'type' of reader. Perhaps this idea backfired, but trying to change people's perceptions about vampires cannot be done in one tweet, one blog post or one book. It will take time and patience for this to happen, both of which I have. This book offers a more accurate glimpse into my life as a modern day vampire hunter.

There was only one way to describe my life back then: bleak. And eight years on, as I write this now, I can still only see darkness and despair with an occasional silver lining. But rather than translate these feelings into abstract narrative and personify them into a dark anti-hero with super powers, I can only offer a placebo, one which is hard to swallow and will not cure the rot that hangs about London, or cleanse the cesspits of Europe.

When I gave October's Son to my publishers, it was in bits and pieces, a tangled narrative, enough to show my descent into the depraved world of a powerful few, mirroring my downward spiral as I was groomed by people I thought I could trust or help me explain my condition. I tried to end October's Son on a positive - if you can call it that - to create a sense of optimism; that I had been given access to the tools and knowledge that would rid the city of its Ant problem and eradicate an evil that hid beneath the façade of vampirism. And in many ways, after checking the proof, I even started to believe it myself – that there was hope.

Six years is a long time to reflect on my journey from being an arrogant estate agent to humble vampire-bashing anti-hero. Optimism, it would seem, is a dying virtue amongst cynics. I still live in a world of mistrust, where I question the legitimacy of everything I encounter. People, both physical and online, were met with instant suspicion and I found myself chasing shadows across London thanks to out of date and often incorrect information left to me by Michael.

Today's identities are not fixed but blurred between online personas and that of the physical person. People manifest themselves in tribes across several boroughs of London and amongst numerous groups and forums buried amongst the dark web. To counter this I have had to adapt and also share multiple identities, hiding what is valuable to me and working my way through the media hypocrisy (fake news phenomenon) as I try to change people's perceptions about modern day vampires.

The internet, my greatest weapon, my supposed antidote to the myths and lies that infect our culture, my democratic voice in a globalised village, has become nothing more than a hindrance, a distraction, a mere whisper deterring me from the physical field work I now find so much value in. I have had to rethink my entire strategy and approach to dealing with what I know to be true, and demystify the taboo of what I did to survive – take another man's life. My life, to this point, has been without reprimand for my actions and for that very reason I cannot help but feel that I am running out of time, that although I may be mentally condemned I have yet to be physically incarcerated.

No-one is above the law and one day I will have to be held accountable for my actions. Hiding behind a computer screen will not protect me which is why I have decided to come back out and fight. My appearances to raise awareness about the threats have been strictly limited and, in all honesty, have not been worth the risk, but I will persevere in the hope that one day some producer will wake up and take the topic of trafficking seriously. Perhaps if I didn't hide behind a mask that trust would be reciprocated?

Reader, please do not see this book as part of a franchise, where I introduce new characters only to have them killed off, or introduce new areas and locations in London, only to be explored in true sequel style; there are no map expansion packs as I battle on, to achieve nothing more than survival for another day, week or year. See this book as an insight in to my daily life; dip into the world of a man who never wanted to be a part of any of it – ever; a man who, up until 2008, never gave a damn about vampires, human trafficking, or mafia groups, because he was too busy making money and being selfish; a man who thought these types of people didn't really exist and that he would never come into contact with such people because he had a good upbringing, was well-educated and discerning enough to know the difference between right and wrong.

This book is far from linear and I have not presented exact dates, rather key episodic moments from my life, relevant insights into the highs and mainly lows, documenting the mistakes I have made over the years which are somehow all linked to the grand finale.

Sadly, truly, we are all affected by the content of this book. If you make it to the end of the final instalment (I don't plan to write more books) then I implore you to go and see for yourselves what is happening. Explore what is out there on your doorstep - and I don't mean by Googling it! Get away from the comfort of the computer desk or the armchair in the front room, put down your smart phone or tablet and get outside to observe the uncivilised side of man which has thrived beneath your very nose. Notice the resurrection of Neanderthal man 2.0, redesigned and operating under your very eyes; explore the dark side of our ancestry that we repress, but don't step too far inside the psyche.

Just don't carry on pretending that life is good for everyone. It really isn't.

I want you to read this book and feel compelled to take action. Without sounding patronising, I want you to rediscover and explore humanity, and support the non-governmental organisations (NGOs) who are trying to put an end to the horrors I have seen.

Be human again.

To you, dear reader, I confess the highs and many lows of being The London Vampire.

AFTER MICHAEL

When I left Michael's secret lock up in Camden for the first time, I remember feeling truly exuberant. My pockets were lined with cash and I had the biblical equivalent of a vampire hunter's guide to London stuffed in my jacket pocket; I was stupidly armed to the teeth, carrying small blades and throwing weapons which I had no idea how to use. My logical mind had been doused by adrenaline fuelled curiosity and I was heading straight back into the heart of London where all the pain began. The deep-rooted problem, however, was that I was still none the wiser.

If I thought that undergoing two near death experiences in a year was somehow a right-of-passage to the truth, then I was surely going to be bitterly disappointed. After all, Michael had chosen to abandon me when I needed him the most and no amount of money, weaponry or written word could substitute the touch of the master's hand, so to speak.

I found myself travelling by bus to an address in Warren Street, a busy exchange route on the fringe of Euston and the West End. By chance it had been one of the first addresses I recognised after scouring through some of Michael's handwritten pages. I might have easily overlooked it had the letters not been painstakingly stencilled across two pages; heavily imprinted were the words: Warren Street Hive, and a flat number. There were some other descriptions which detailed timings - a bit like the opening hours of a shop - and a list of names and phone numbers, all of which had been frantically tallied on the side.

On my journey in I had tried to dial each one of the numbers but all of them were out of service, which gave me little hope of completing any investigation pre-recce. An address doesn't just change, however, and I knew that by attending the premises in person that I could make sense of these obscure details myself. Possibly.

I got off of the bus beside the hospital on Gower Street and cut across to Warren Street Tube Station, to assess how busy the streets were. Light drizzle had been falling all morning and the streets were glossy and grey. There was no break in the clouds, everything in the street felt shaded from natural light.

I arrived outside a basement flat about halfway along the street. I spent several minutes passing up and down the road looking for somewhere inconspicuous to stand and wait and observe. I re-read the notes again in Michael's notebook and deduced, given it was a basement flat, that the address was perhaps used as a brothel. He wrote words like 'plague' and 'infection' and there was an illegible page which resembled a menu; denominations of £20 notes equated to minutes. From experience, I knew straight away that this attracted a certain amount of risk; a brothel in London could service up to 8-10 men an hour depending on how many women were working at the joint. In the UK, the law suggests that women can only sell sex on private premises with the assistance of a maid but this rule was regularly flouted by organised crime syndicates. But despite the danger, a brothel could also provide me with several lines of enquiry. And like any illegal business in central London which had a prolific turnover of money, I knew that a man or group of men were most likely to be in control of the merchandise, and if I was to wait around long enough – unnoticed – there was a chance that I just might see them leave and perhaps pick up a trail, if indeed this address was linked to an Ant hive like Michael had described in his journal. It was classic detective work, in theory.

As I stood and waited, occasionally dipping into a lank copy of The Metro, I considered how rather brazen I had been to set off straight for one of Michael's suggested locations. Michael was a man who had mentored me (or groomed me, however you want to look at it) into what I am today, yet he had always considered me reckless, rebuking me for going with my heart and not my head, which may have been one of the reasons why he chose to abandon me. I felt guilty, like perhaps I needed to spend more time reading and researching his material before rushing straight in like an amateur sleuth. Hindsight is a wonderful thing but it could not change the fact that I was standing on Warren Street, pockets stuffed with cash and silver, looking for a fight.

A man left the basement flat. He was late thirties, perhaps, with a beige rain jacket and thin hair that trailed down his face into some pathetic excuse for a beard. He glanced from left to right before crossing the road and walking in my direction. I held the paper steadily in my hand, watching him in the corner of my eye as he seemed to fix his clothes and re-apply a wedding ring. I concluded that he was not an Ant, just a naïve client eager to walk off his guilt round the block before getting back to work in the company of sordid memories.

Another ten minutes passed before I found that I had finished the newspaper, or rather skipped through the endless adverts and celebrity drivel. I couldn't focus. I was already bored, and since there was no coffee shop to sit in or pub to stand outside of and drink, I found myself pacing irritably back and forth on the spot like an agitated punter psyching myself up for a visit. In the end, I reasoned that there was nothing else to do other than go and knock on the door and enquire about what type of business was on offer. Weeks earlier, days even, I would have been petrified to even leave my house, yet here I was, acting on some mad hunch, fuelled by adrenaline and inspired by the writings of a madman.

I strolled directly across the road, opened the gate and paced down the stairs until I was face to face with a red door and a well-used buzzer. I pressed it and waited. I couldn't hear the bell ringing but I could detect movement. Then, by the window, I saw the curtain pull aside and a face briefly give me a once over. Having been qualified as a punter the door was unlocked and I was ushered inside.

The maid was in her early forties, perhaps Chinese – it didn't matter, her English was good enough.

"You book appointment?" she asked me.

"I rang some time ago. I was just passing and hoped that you might have some girls available."

"Follow me." She walked me to a small bedroom at the back of the apartment, past several closed doors. I could smell the scent of cheap air freshener masking cigarette smoke, microwave meals and sweat. I could also hear the washing machine as it approached its final spin.

"You sit here," she said, pointing to a sorry looking single bed whose only company was a tired looking bedside table with a half used bottle of baby oil, some talcum powder, a packet of tissues and a tea-light slowly suffocating in a red lantern, perhaps to add warmth and some degree of eroticism. She left the room and I sat and listened to the sound of doors being opened and the scurrying of feet. Seconds later, girls were brought to the doorway and paraded in front of me, like I was bidding on merchandise at some pop-up cattle market.

The first girl who drifted in spoke no English, just nodded at me with a smile hiding bad teeth. Her body was good and her hair long and golden, although I suspected she was originally red haired; the next girl was petite with curly black hair, her skin tanned, perhaps from the Middle-east, she said 'hello' and I could detect an accent - I knew little about accents at the time. The last girl was oriental, older and slightly plump with ill-fitting underwear; she said nothing, merely looked at me and nodded mechanically.

The display was over. The maid ushered them to stand in line and wait for me to choose.

In those minutes I had totally forgotten my purpose for being there. Michael's journal was clutched in my right hand like a psalm book I was about to preach from; my other hand was nervously clutching a set of keys I had pulled out from my pocket. The maid stepped forward and asked me directly if I had made a decision. I shook my head and asked for the names of each one. She huffed and pointed at each girl. The gangly red-head was called Daisy, the dark skinned girl Destiny, and the final girl was called Demi. I doubted any of it to be true. The only thing I was sure of was that none of them wanted to be there, which made me feel even more uncomfortable, and angry. So I stood up and said exactly that.

The maid stared at me with cold black eyes. "Can give you special price today: eighty pounds for half hour, cum twice."

I shook my head. "I'm not interested in them."

She muttered something quick and inaudible at Demi. She nodded and led the other girls out of the room. The maid looked back at me.

"How much for time with you?" I asked her, half expecting her to entertain my joke.

"Men like you cause me big headache," she exclaimed, pointing to the main door. As I walked back through the hallway I caught a glimpse of the holding area, a dark, windowless room with cheap cotton throws on the sofa and a small muted TV in the corner. She continued to pour scorn upon me as she unlocked the front door. "You give me tip!"

"I've got a tip for you alright." I considered impaling her there and then with all the blades in my pockets, just to see what type of mafia group would arrive to clean up the mess. "Learn some fucking manners and stop living off immoral earnings."

As my foot stepped back into the concrete basement, the door slammed and I heard her shout 'fuck you' through the letterbox. I stood there righteously for a moment, breathing damp, cold air, comprehending what I had just done. Part of me wanted to start banging on the doors again, but then I looked around and noticed, concealed inside the window, a small CCTV camera pointed right at me. I stared intensely at the red LED, looked away for a second and then glanced back at it and raised my middle finger slowly before making my way back up to street level. It was then that I realised I had just made several errors.

I crossed the road again, shielded myself behind a Range Rover, and waited to see what would happen. Not that I had really disturbed the Ants' nest, if it was even that. For ten minutes I waited until I saw a middle-aged businessman descend the stairs. He was a normal looking white male, about five-nine in height with shaved greying hair and a sense of arrogance about the way he held his head. There was no further reaction to my visit – my behaviour must have been atypical of sexually frustrated men who bottle it at the last moment.

Five minutes later a young looking male arrived on the scene, parking a shiny black BMW convertible a few spaces away from the house. He was in his late twenties wearing branded trainers that were so white that I felt dirty just looking at them. The rest of his sports attire included a figure hugging hooded sweater for Galatasary FC, confirming that he was most likely a Turk. Minutes later he emerged back on to street level, well before the businessman, and jogged back to his vehicle making calls on his mobile. I made a note of the registration number and watched him start up the car and drive away.

After another ten minutes of waiting around I decided to move on.

That was about as eventful as my day got. I went for a brief stroll down Tottenham Court Road towards Oxford Street but decided, halfway into my walk, that it was perhaps a step too far to enter such busy territory after months of solitude. So I hopped straight back onto a 29 bus towards Camden with the intention of revisiting the lock up that Michael had bestowed to me and returning much of the arsenal of weapons I was carrying. It was time to go back to the drawing board and rethink my strategy.

A VAMPIRE HUNTER'S JOURNAL

I had intended to spend the rest of the week venturing out to locations across London to build on the momentum of my new found life as a hunter. But in reality I was just a tourist with a map; little more than an amateur investigator trying to go semi-pro in a field I didn't fully understand. If I was about to spend my days, weeks, months even, pursuing leads and following supposed Ant trails across London, then I really needed to understand what I was dealing with.

From one visit to the lock-up in Camden I gathered together a collection of books and folders to read through during the cold and wet evenings. I also paid several visits to the local libraries, applied to join the British Library and browsed online book shops to try and explore the world I had been thrown into at an intellectual level.

Much of my initial research was regurgitated late at night onto a website I had paid someone to set up for me. Despite my flippant, cynical tone coming through a bit strong, I felt that by doing so I was discounting much of the smokescreen of vampirism that pollutes the internet and saving people lots of research from doing my own thorough investigation. During this time I also went about setting up several social media profiles and infiltrating vampire sub-cultures online to look at how people, mostly men, groomed individuals to take part in blood-letting activities and other perverse fetishes associated with the vampire sub-culture. There were also several badly made vampire documentaries on YouTube to watch through and that also inspired me to become proactive and add my own poorly produced content, even though I didn't have my own answers, firm evidence or access to the locations or resources that I needed.

And then there was the issue about Michael's notes. On reflection, his journals and diaries read more like the confessions of a mad man. Despite being a very articulate writer, Michael seemed to spew vitriolic monologues across several pages, all of which I decoded as nothing more than hate-fuelled rants, catharsis of his frustration and anger at his own piteous situation, mixed in with his grievances against modern society. Many of the entries were not always dated which made it hard to put his works into some type of chronological order or logical context; one journal may have been written several years before or after the other. Ironically, many of the older looking, more worn out journals seemed to be the most up to date, purely by the fact that news cuttings were sometimes stuck in, circled and dated. Many of these stories supported the same conspiracy-fuelled ideology about deaths, murders and suicides being linked to the behaviour of people who had been infected or influenced by Ants.

Michael loved his science and there was some convincing evidence and research done into the effect of parasites on human behaviour and I bookmarked most of these notes with small sticky tabs so that I could investigate it further myself. I even spoke with people across online forums about much of his research and condensed some of it into The London Vampire website.

Amongst all of Michael's writing across his diaries (this took me weeks) I found no reference to our encounters or the meetings we had.

Over time I slowly emptied Michael's lock-up of all its possessions and kept them safe at my address, feeling more settled that I had access to everything I needed in the comfort of my own home rather than hiding out at some mouldy, dark lock-up with a temperamental light fitting that I couldn't be bothered to fix. It also reduced the urge for me to go astray and venture out into the West End looking for trouble, like I had on the first day of discovering Michael's arsenal.

From my own research, and with the help of Michael's writing, there were some key addresses and areas of London that kept coming up. He regularly mentioned offices and financial buildings located across the city as bases, but it was unclear whether these organisations were controlling some type of financial arm of the Ant's operation or was deep rooted in the ownership of the buildings and organisations. An example of this was the offices at Longacre, which I ventured out to investigate in more detail. Geographically, the most intriguing thing I could find out about the place was the far reaching access of the building which made it seem like a central hub, however trying to gain access to the building or gain information about the companies and their activities was much harder. I made the decision to archive the location as a 'possible' base, even posting it online, and looked for more manageable targets instead: cafes, bars, private member's clubs, holistic clinics or home addresses.

Several other clippings and cuttings from London papers, like The Metro and The Evening Standard, and regional weekly papers like the Hackney Gazette, Ham and High, all detailed court proceedings and local goings on, but most unreported news was found on twitter and across Facebook pages and forums online. There was a whole community involved in investigating and discussing strange goings on around London and I decided I would try and infiltrate these groups to make contact with the opinion leaders. It kept me out of trouble most of the time.

There were some evenings where I read, with interest, some of Michael's more legible notes where perhaps he was more reflective having eaten some ice-cream, but I couldn't help but wonder that some of the content was deliberately misleading and in there to lead me off the scent of something bigger. The reality of the situation was that I didn't know Michael very well, despite being indebted to him (so I thought), but I did start to slowly understand how he worked and operated in London. That said, there was something exhilarating about sitting, a glass of wine in hand, trailing through notes and pages of delicate handwriting; the lyrics of a lunatic, I would often conclude, or a man whose sanity had been pushed to the brink and never quite made it back into the real world.

Days turned into weeks and soon months. I remained largely housebound, waiting for books to arrive from online retailers, and using the British Newspaper Archive, to make my own independent enquiries and follow up investigations regarding certain events. In many ways my task was a self-fulfilling prophecy; my own notepads were building up into a library of their own and I had a network of associates I had attracted from the web.

At times I felt like I was getting somewhere, like the moment when it felt like I had discovered a key suspect, a name repeated across several journals, only to then discover a newspaper article detailing the death of that very same person for legitimate reasons. I found myself reading obituaries with great interest, trying to imagine and piece together past lives of people based on a single eulogy or short verse left by a loved one.

The London Vampire website began to act as a distraction, a place to vent my frustration and counter the mix of lies caught up in the surface web. Vampires were not being presented as a collective identity threatening teenagers; the vampires were the teenagers. Vampirism had been given new life in popular culture, blurring the lines between TV drama, literature and film. People did not notice or care for the malicious, malevolent force operating under the guise of vampires – because that wasn't entertaining enough. It made me so angry. And so I set about trying to make videos and tweet about this lie, but to no great effect – I just didn't have the skills or the hard evidence to validate my experiences.

One evening, whilst reading some comments which had been posted on a video I had produced, I realised that I was at risk of losing all credibility in the online world. Here I was, barely a few months into trying to educate people about what was going on with regards to a malevolent force in London, and I was already losing face. 'Where's the proof? This is fake, right? You're crazy!'

What next? I concluded that I needed to be back in the field doing real investigative work, not waiting at home for the answers to come to me. Discover the truth, that was my unoriginal motto; so I left the website to stagnate and set out to find answers. That started with a visit to retrieve more journals to get more leads.

Weeks after being given access to Michael's lock up, I arrived in my car one evening to collect the last remaining items only to find my access to the workshop blocked thanks to another fire at Camden Lock. Thankfully the lock-up was not affected directly by the blaze but it made me realise that I was at risk of putting all my faith in Michael's work and not having any belief in myself as an investigator. That's probably because there were many moments where I felt like a lunatic.

It dawned on me a cold and wet evening that I was exhibiting all the characteristics of a lone wolf, and I considered that I was perhaps more of a danger to myself rather to anyone I might meet, human or antlike. The fact that I was clumsy and out of shape didn't help matters either; my new found energy and rigorous fitness regime before Michael's chilling revelation was now a thing of the past and my thirst for wine and spirits meant I had lost my toned shape and clarity of thought.

I prayed that an answer would come.

VICELAND

I came across a few interesting journal pages of Michael's one evening and felt compelled to investigate immediately. In heavily scored pen across a double page, he had etched the words 'Poppy Paedophile Ring' in thick red ink. If there was ever a cry for help from his journal, this was it. The pages following and leading up to it were incoherent, the ramblings of a man incensed by his own anger that he could not clearly express his disgust in words, but rather through heavy sketching.

I read over it carefully several times. He mentioned something about the axis of evil being between three points in Soho's red light district. The names of bars were mentioned and there was a very coarse looking diagram to show an approximate location of a base marked by an X. There were timings which I assumed were windows of opportunity – late, ranging from 10.30pm to 3am. No particular day was mentioned but a description of a black panther made me both laugh and take heed. All my other investigations inspired by the works of Michael so far had drawn blanks and I grew resentful at being indoctrinated by his misinformation. For example, a video recording I got developed from a reel of 8mm film was nothing more than a scrambled montage of London hotspots - I had to crowdsource on YouTube to seek information from the general public/ghost hunters in trying to help me solve a riddle. The majority of people who responded claimed everything to be some kind of elaborate hoax, a practical joke set up by me, but there were some people who were genuinely interested in my efforts to try and make a difference. Going forward, I realised it was probably best that I follow up all of his allegations and trails in person.

At the time of reading Michael's revelation it was half past nine on a Friday night. I figured there was no better time to go into the city and investigate. The weather was relatively mild which meant the streets around Soho would be fairly packed, making it far easier for me to blend in and investigate. I studied the journal again and memorised the key details of where I needed to be and what I needed to have to hand. I dug out an old Remembrance Day poppy from my dad's bedside table and took this with me to use when I arrived.

Since my dealing with Ed I had re-invested in a long, thick coat and had returned to the same local tailor, asking that the inner lining be fitted with a sheath for carrying large but delicate maps; I presented them with a thick cardboard tube which had an architectural drawing rolled up inside. I had armed myself with something much shorter than the sword once given to me by Michael. It was about a foot in length with a heavy edge, the same weight almost as a machete, just a touch sharper. It was tucked neatly away along with some rolls of cash.

It was raining when I arrived at Oxford Street but this did little to part the masses of warm bodies traversing to and fro between Soho's many side streets. I walked south down Wardour Street, past people queueing to be squished into noodle bars; the pub drinkers were spilling over the pavement along with smokers, choking and laughing at the roadside. The neon lights of the city got progressively stronger and more varied in size and colour as I approached what some might regard as the gay quarter of London. Soho's diverse epicentre of seediness consisted of: lap dancing-bars, nightclubs and sex shops; punters, drunk and sober, were sauntering out of one and into another.

I identified the three points on the map according to Michael, starting at the archway to Madame JoJo's. Looking south I walked towards Windmill Place only to cut through a small road towards the edge of Greek street, and that was my triangle, or axis of evil as Michael had so eloquently described it. The rain ceased and I found myself somewhere discrete to stand and watch and affix my poppy.

I watched as phone booths were being packed with fresh calling cards and I could soon see a pattern of street hustlers preying on single men as they travelled to and fro, beckoning them into their club to be ripped off. Perhaps this was what Michael was talking about, the scenes of men and women selling false promises to other men. I observed with interest before carrying out a more detailed investigation, trying to find anything out of place. I looked for the obvious signs first: solo, obscure entrances with one or two men stood outside it; open doors with stairs going up or, more often than not, down into some type of seedy basement area; adverts for massage by models written on bright card were common, juxtaposing the many reflexology businesses that looked legitimate, but there were enough reviews and forums online written by dissatisfied punters to say otherwise.

I must have been lingering for too long, traversing between each point on Michael's map, because a woman approached me, a black girl in her twenties with a very strong East London accent. She was dressed more for a night walking the streets than a night on the town: black trousers, shiny black trainers, a black bomber jacket and knitted Nike beanie hat.

She struck up a conversation like so:

"Having a good evening are we?"

"Yes thanks, just looking."

"You look like a man who is looking for something in particular."

"Not really."

"I can tell - you're looking for girls, right? You're looking to party."

I laughed and tried to ignore her. She laughed with me and walked beside me.

"What's your name?"

"John."

She held out her hand, most of which was covered by fingerless black gloves, but her nails were clean and neatly filed. "Nice to meet you, John. I'm Kadi." I shook her hand and she responded with a salesman's nod. "So what are you looking for, John? You look like you want to have some fun."

I shrugged my shoulders and looked around, seeing if anyone else was being harassed in such a manner. "I'm not really the partying type."

She nodded. "I see, so you are looking for girls then?"

I caught her eye and she smiled victoriously at me. I shook my head and said nothing.

"What are you looking for, John? I know some lovely girls who would be happy to party with you."

"Is that right?"

"Swear down. Black girls, white girls, Asian girls – whatever you're looking for, we've got what you want. Sixty quid, anything you want to do."

"Anything?"

"Whatever you're into. I've got some Sixteen year old girls that would love to give you a nice blow-job."

"Not really my thing," I said, now getting visibly annoyed by her crude, casual approach. I started to walk away.

"Come on, John. Just pop it in her mouth and release, no extra charge."

I found it hard to believe that such blatant, coarse bargaining could happen so easily in a London street in a supposed modern and civilised world. I began to shake. All I could see were men around me, one after the other, seemingly following one another in a line: window shopping, punting and probing each adult sex shop entrance. Then the feeling returned, a feeling I had not experienced in months, a tight gnawing at my chest, like something was prodding into my heart, urging me to bite – wanting me to feed.

"Maybe you like boys?" she asked.

I looked at her, expecting her to be laughing at her own joke. But she was not about to give up on her wretched and vile sales pitch, she remained resolute and looked at me seriously in the eyes - she wanted my business.

"Is she really sixteen?" I asked.

"You don't like the look of the merchandise you can walk away," she said. "You don't pay until you're ready to fuck."

"And I can do anything I want?"

"You can party how you want, baby."

I controlled my breathing and then nodded at her. "I'm a bit nervous. Never done this before."

She smiled and led me away from the main hubbub of Soho, down a small side street and beyond a more obvious knocking station which had a pink light above the window. She tapped on a black door and waited for it to open. A man looked at me as he opened it, studying my dress and looking for the woman's reassurance.

"He's here to party," she said as we walked right past him. "Second floor, John."

I followed her up; all the while I could feel the man staring into the back of my head as I climbed the narrow stairs. The house fell silent as the door was shut. I could have been anywhere. The place was in need of refurbishment - tatty wall paper and crumbling plaster - but I could hear people moving about the house; floor boards creaked and the patter of tiny feet ran from end to end above me. The first floor had a series of rooms coming off a hallway and at the end of it was a communal living room with black leather sofas. It looked more like a waiting room with plum coloured walls, 'menus' on a coffee table and muted pornography playing on a TV screen. I followed the woman up to the second floor but halfway up she stopped and turned to me and spoke.

"You're serious, right?"

I nodded. "Of course."

"Before we go any further I need to see some form of commitment."

She wants the money now, I thought to myself. Cunning. In hindsight it made sense, if she really had the goods promised then it made sense for her to take the money and disappear if things went wrong.

"Sixty quid was it?" I asked, staring at her outstretched hand.

"Sixty for straight sex or oral without. You want more, you pay more."

I frowned – the terms of sale were already changing from what she had suggested. Undeterred, I pulled out a roll of notes. "Here's a ton," I said. "She'd better be worth it."

The woman smiled. "Anything for my time?" She took the roll of notes and looked at me expectantly.

Begrudgingly, I took out another twenty and waved it at her. She went to snatch it but I pulled it away. "Show me the merchandise first."

She carried on walking and stopped in the next hallway. The doors had thin, painted wooden hearts hanging from the handle, except for the one we were stood outside of. She opened it and walked in.

Sitting on a bed and dressed in a thin lilac dress, a young girl, pale skinned with long brown hair, stared back at me with dark brown eyes. She didn't smile and she didn't say hello; she just looked down and brushed her hair aside so that I could see her shoulders.

"She's all yours. Do what you like to her."

"Are you sure she's sixteen?"

"Of course, baby."

The woman swiped the twenty from my hands and walked out of the room, shutting me in with the girl. My heart had ceased racing and I found myself trembling out of anxiety. I had vowed never to return to such places after the events and experiences of the previous year, yet here I was, walking along the fringes of hell, a mad man's notebook as my guidebook to the unholy and immoral underworld operating under the surface of London's trendy night-scene.

"Hello," I called softly to her. She tensed up and her shoulders flinched inwards. "Are there any more of you here?"

She looked at me puzzled. "You pay, half hour," she recounted.

I sat at the edge of her bed and studied her carefully. She was, at a guess, older than sixteen, but being used and abused on an hourly basis seven days a week had prematurely destroyed her youth and left her physically and emotionally scarred. I ordered her to stand up and turn around for me. She did so obediently and I scanned for traces of abuse: bruising, evidence of scars. "Lift your hair away from your neck," I said to her slowly, using my arms and hands to guide her. Dutifully she did so and I could see several downward scars from the base of her skull to the middle of her neck, like she had been deliberately cut or chained cruelly.

"I'm not going to hurt you," I assured her, standing up and walking behind her. In my mind I tried my best to toughen my heart and remain indifferent to her situation; whether she was a victim or not, I still had to be cautious that she didn't turn on me. There were no other noticeable scars or marks on her body and she smelled - if there is such a scent - perfectly human with an aroma of cheap body lotion. I lifted the edge of her nighty above her thighs and could see mild bruising around the lower back and inner thigh. "What's your name?" I whispered gently.

She didn't answer at first, just played mute and remained rigid, cold and shivering. I realised I was perhaps overwhelming her with questions. I sat back down and waited until she was ready to turn around. When she did I had another roll of money in my hand.

"I'm going to make you an offer," I said, "but I need you to tell me the truth."

She looked concerned. "Please, police no," she whispered fearfully. I shook my head and assured her I was not looking to arrest anyone, and that I was not with the police.

"I need to know if there are others working here, or if there is a room where bad stuff happens."

She looked at me, confused, not understanding, and staring at the money in my hand. I had paid the black woman her fee and it was unlikely that the girl standing in front of me would see any of that. A bond had to be repaid in most cases of human trafficking. "I can help you," I whispered. "I'm not interested in you. Where are others?"

She sat down on the bed and looked down. "Some girls working here."

"Young?"

She nodded.

"Younger than you?"

She paused and then nodded her head tearfully. "My cousin, she is just thirteen."

"Where is she?"

She looked concerned, worried that I might do something to her. The tears were welling up. I tried to reassure her that I posed no threat but she was cautious and protective about her cousin.

"You're from Moldovia?"

She shook her head. "Serbia."

I handed her the money and stood up. "I can help you. Tell me where she is?"

She shook her head again, looking down at the hundred pounds in her hand. "My cousin, Beatrix. I am Olga. On floor," she said pointing upwards. "They do very bad things on floor."

I nodded and thanked her, instructing her to wait quietly before I crept out of the room, shutting the door behind me without making a sound. The handles of other doors all had a heart hung from it apart from the one at the end. From the layout of the first floor, I figured it lead to another stairwell. I listened carefully for sounds of movement but could only hear the creaking of beds from closed rooms as men approached their climax.

I took the sword from my coat and held it out, ready to use. I opened the stairwell door. It was dark but I could see a glow coming from the top of the stairs; it drew me upwards. I tip-toed cautiously. At the top of the stairwell were two more doors, one open with a light on inside, the other closed with a heart hanging limply outside. I pressed my ear against the door and listened. I could hear the sound of low whimpering from a girl and a man's voice hissing cruelly at her. The girl sounded young, much younger than the girl sold to me in the room below. I gripped my sword, breathed deeply, and then burst through the door.

A man, late fifties, overweight, hairy and with thick designer glasses looked up at me. A girl was knelt in front of him and it was obvious that he had been busy pleasuring himself forcefully using her mouth. The girl, a scrawny mass of pale flesh and bones, darted to the corner of the room with tears streaming down her face. I didn't need to ask her age, she was a young teenager – no doubt. The man stumbled backwards in a panic, quivering, and talking gibberish about how 'sorry' he was and that he 'didn't know she was mine' even before I'd even said a word. His penis wagged below a tuft of coarse pubic hair as he struggled to dress himself and make for his clothes, a designer suit folded neatly on a chair. I knew instantly that he was not an ant, but nonetheless I deduced that he must have been part of this poppy project by the red metal flower attached to his jacket lapel, therefore he needed to be dealt with. There was no shadow of a doubt that he had been methodically abusing this girl and taken a great deal of thought and care in doing so. The girl was crying, howling into the sheets with horror as I continued to brandish the sword in his direction.

"I'm not here to hurt you," I assured her. She didn't speak, just shook her head and cried like a child; tears and snot ran down her face and her eyes were puffy. There were clear bruises on her skin and burn marks along her arm. I doubted that she even knew which country she was in; the likelihood was that she had been ferried from place to place, sold and resold to new gangs with a bigger bond placed on her each time, but I'll cover the trafficking process with you later. What saddened me was that she had at least ten years of slavery ahead of her.

"Beatrix, it's going to be okay!" I said assertively. She stopped crying and we stared at each other in a silent stand-off, my eyes searching from her to him, him to her. Nothing was said. I kept nodding at the girl until she became silent, wiping the tears away from her cheeks. A list of Slavic phrases and other customary sayings from Eastern Europe would have helped me greatly that evening.

I turned round, surprised to see Olga standing at the top of the stairs nervously. "I said to wait for me," I hushed. But her being there actually helped. "Take her to your room, and do it quietly. I'm not done here."

Olga quickly led Beatrix away to the room below with some clothes. They were both whimpering, both fearful that the man guarding the door might come for them. I hoped that he would because I suddenly felt a powerful wave of rage and loathing against the man staring at me, shaking in the corner. He had dressed himself in pants and was trying to button his shirt. Within a heartbeat I charged at him, kicking him in his gut. He cried out and hit the floor. I kicked him in the face, hard enough so that his glasses snapped in two, and then I rolled him over. He looked up at me, blood streaming down the side of his face and around his eyes where the frame had cut his skin. I dangled the sword above his genitals and goaded him to give me a reason not to castrate him there and then.

He began sobbing, howling for his dear life as I teased his pants aside with the cold steel blade and kicked his legs apart. He assured me he was a 'good man' and he had made an 'honest mistake' by using the girl's mouth as a sexual orifice. I reminded him that she was a child. He said nothing in his defence, just blurted out that he had paid for her not knowing her real age.

I delivered my own verdict with one swift flick of the wrist.

The man howled out in pain, writhing and twitching on the floor as blood started spouting out from his genitalia. The sight of blood seemed to stir some sympathy within me so I searched through his clothing and found his phone, dialled 999 and threw the mobile down at him. "Tell them where you are," I said, "and maybe you won't bleed to death."

As he spoke into the headset I heard heavy footsteps thundering up the stairs. The hired help had arrived. I ran towards the hallway door and waited until the man opened it. I caught him by surprise and kicked him hard in the chest, knocking him back down the stairs. It was a lucky shot for he was perhaps nearly twice my weight and a foot taller than me. I ran down the stairs, following behind him as he tumbled. When he hit the door at the bottom he stayed down, giving out a heavy sigh as I leapt over him. I kicked the remaining doors open to see other men gathering their belongings as their female victims screamed in the corner of each room.

"Get out now!" I growled, brandishing my sword like a lunatic. Each of the men grabbed their belongings and headed for the door.

I looked in at Olga's room and found her with Beatrix, and then I insisted that they both follow me.

Subsequent events seemed to unfold in seconds. I led them onto the street and set about winding my way through the narrow roads towards the nearest police station, which was Charring Cross on Agar Street. As we snaked between the crowds, my sword concealed, my heartbeat racing, I contemplated how I was going to deal with these two new girls I had rescued. I had no plan, not even a contingency, but it was my wish to help them and I was fuelled solely by adrenaline and righteousness. Suddenly a girl's voice called out after us. It was the black panther, the female pimp who had sold Olga to me only ten minutes ago. She ran behind me and grabbed my arm forcibly, saying that I had made a big mistake, calling me every name under the sun. I swivelled and head-butted her in the nose and watched her collapse to the ground. People gasped in the street and Olga and Beatrix began to cry again. "She can't hurt you anymore," I said to them both, breaking into a slight jog. The girls followed me tearfully, and that was when I noticed that they were barefooted.

There had been no more trouble as we finally reached the police station but there had been several witnesses. The duty officer buzzed us in and looked up at me in surprise as I burst in, the girls trailing behind me. I said that they were both victims of trafficking and gave the address of where I had found them. I also said they would probably find their paperwork there and that I had seen them being sexually abused on the premises. The officer stood up and asked for my details calmly.

The girls looked at me uncomprehendingly. I urged them both to stay with the police officer but they didn't look convinced. They shook their heads, wanting me to stay, but I couldn't – I had gone a step too far and was at risk of landing myself in a whole heap of trouble. The address I had just given the officer was the same address where they would find a castrated paedophile and a badly injured doorman. Then there was the incident with the assault on the black girl.

"I will come back for you," I assured then both, nodding and smiling as I began to leave.

Olga looked at me and nodded, cuddling Beatrix tighter as she continued to sob. I watched the custody sergeant walk through a door with a female officer in tow, calling after me. As they approached Olga and Beatrix I was already out of the main door and sprinting back towards the strand. I had broken into a sweat by this point, the type that seemed to cling to your skin and not let go. I knew that every square inch of the city was monitored by CCTV and I had to somehow make myself vanish.

I headed towards Aldwych where the student cafes and nightclub and campuses seemed to fuse into one giant strip of academia. I forced my way into one of the student union bars and went straight for the toilets, but not before helping myself to a new coat courtesy of a student engrossed by the girl he was chatting to. In the gents toilets I freshened up, folded my coat and placed it in a bag, withdrew a hat and tried on my new attire. The jacket fitted nicely and I found my way in the main kitchen. Two male members of staff looked up at me and told me I shouldn't be there. I ignored them both and carried on until I found the service exit that led onto a small alleyway. I looped back around until I was on the main road and hopped on to a bus, keeping my head low.

Two changes and a tube ride later, I was back in Highgate, tired, exhausted, and deeply troubled by what I had just done.

That evening was significant for two reasons. Firstly, it made me doubt Michael; not doubt him in the way that you don't quite believe all of what he says, but in a way that categorically discredits him as a man of sound judgement. I began to think that, somehow, Michael's purpose in giving me all his old journals was to throw me off the real scent, to send me on wild and dangerous missions across the capital until I got caught or, worse still, killed.

As I settled myself down to read through more of his journals, I grew tired of his ramblings and frustrated that perhaps I did not know how to crack his code, or if I was simply over-analysing each situation. Of course, the money and stash of tools were welcome gifts, but it did not really make life easier only moderately more comfortable; and what use was a pile of cash and weapons if I ended up in jail or dead?

The second reason why that evening was significant was because my own moral compass had been altered. Perhaps the events months ago at a sauna in Crouch End had not fully changed my perception about the seedy underworld that sits on the very high streets of London, seen but not acknowledged. Perhaps the sordid goings on advertised in every phone booth or in the back of local paper, classified ad on Gumtree or adult dating site was a way in, a gateway into the depraved and lucrative world of organised crime and sexual exploitation. I pondered whether I should even be chasing a new type of vampire that even I couldn't classify fully, but focus my efforts on a darker, tangible evil that permeates the fringes of modern society.

I would like to think that my exploits of that evening had somehow damaged the chain and cycle of some type of organisation, whether it be Ant related or not. Michael's journals had pointed out page after page of addresses and organisations of brothels, old and new, obsolete and invalid. Perhaps he was on to something. Perhaps his rants were somehow connected to the darker web of crime perpetrated by Ants, or maybe vampirism as

I knew it went far beyond the realm of just luring impressionable young men and women to join an evil elite club. Perhaps Ants were partly responsible for the significant rise in trafficking not just in the UK but on a global scale; harvesting food and goods in abundance, especially with increased migration from war-torn countries in the Middle-East.

I finished a whole bottle of wine that evening as I began to research the topic in more detail. I grew fascinated at the level of complexity that human traffickers and organised crime groups went through to conceal their trade in human flesh and I was amazed at how easily the perpetrators seemed to avoid being caught.

Whatever Michael wrote in his journals, whether true or not, did not disguise the fact that there was a greater, more palpable evil that could be tackled and possibly cleansed on my doorstep.

VAMPIRE 2.0

Wherever you stand on the argument about the pros and cons of the internet, you cannot deny that the web has changed the world we live in. Back in the early part of this decade, the web was my primary tool and sadly my greatest ally. But the relationship would be short-lived. Trolls – disinformation – rejection. How do you cope with it?

On reflection I realise that it takes time to build any sort of credibility and maintain a persona, and only seconds for it to be broken down. I learnt that the hard way. I have existed through a stream of social media accounts and now pride myself on a lack of blood and gore; my intention was never to promote but to prevent.

I must have read several books on investigative journalism and broke many of the rules to avoid bringing down good people. Even through hijacking other people's accounts, morally I am not okay about starting fires and running away from them. It took me a while, but eventually I realised that I had everything I needed to do the job and so my life as an online vampire hunter was short lived.

Michael never entered the online world and now I understand why.

Before long a whole 12 months had passed since my transformation. But in that year I felt like progress had been minimal. I had spent months visiting parts of London and documenting them with my own journals, a camera when necessary, and updating Michael's notes to try and link his ideas into some kind of coherent map. In that time, to stop myself from going insane, I had also started to forge links online. I connected with artists, amateur journalists and students on the web to discuss my findings with them. Having trawled forums across the surface web seeking information about London and its dark history, vice hotspots, trafficking, vampire groups, those interested in the occult, etc. I decided that I needed to build and maintain an online presence.

Michael's notes had been useful on some occasions. One of the golden rules he taught me was to ensure that you left a trail. I befriended two writers online who wanted to support my cause and promote my work. I agreed that a website dispelling the myth about vampires would be a suitable starting place and so in 2009 the London Vampire found a home online. In exchange for them hosting the web site I agreed to give them, as writers, creative control about how they presented my information. I was, to a large extent, immersed in my work and had found that working on a social media sites to create a presence of sorts very time consuming and ineffective.

Some of my early social media efforts, in hindsight, were sloppy and brutally trolled and ridiculed. Had I known that, during my recovery at home, the response would be so vitriolic I might not have ever bothered. So when the website went live I had directed my colleagues to create a contact page. The email queries ranged from the bizarre, the upsetting, the thoughtful, all the way to being downright odd and embarrassing. I ended up publishing a very small sample of these through an online magazine, purely because I didn't want this book to lose its aim – to tell people about what I do, not what I've done – and done badly.

Vampires, it seemed, were alive and well in popular culture and people didn't like the fact that I was trying to undo a myth and create a modern day definition of what a vampire is: a parasite that thrives off the misery of others.

At one point my colleagues maintaining the website told me that traffic was increasing and that I should let them tell my story. This was at a time when the genre was being revamped as sexy and young. True Blood, The Vampire Diaries and Twilight were flooding the entertainment market with books, films and TV adaptations. My writer friends wanted a part of that action and since they had effectively brought me to life online I agreed to their requests. But it felt wrong, if I am honest, to combat the nature of these stories with stories, especially since my story had no definitive ending.

When I read their initial interpretations of my story I decided to back away from the project. There were too many plot holes, elements that needed exploring and explaining in more detail. I did not want to contribute to the already saturated market and so I asked that any inkling of a story be put on hold until I was ready.

In 2014 I was ready, so I agreed to *October's Son* being published, a narrative account of how I came to be, but I am compelled to share with you what happened in those five years leading up to that moment. That is far more interesting, believe me.

ARE WE A NATION OF VAMPIRES?

In May 2014 I was contacted by as associate of Dr Emyr Williams, a Psychologist who wanted to learn about real vampires living in the UK. There seemed a natural expectation of performance from myself, that I might rejoice in such an article but I was very against the message such a report would send out. Do we really need to fetishize vampirism further? I thought not, and whilst I politely gave my view I intended to publish my own essay titled 'Are we a nation of vampires?' but thankfully some tabloid newspapers published the same soundbites from his article within a month and I felt that all I would be doing was fanning the flames on a pointless topic. It was another distraction that I didn't need.

The requests didn't stop there, however, for it appeared (years after maintaining an online presence) that I was some type of vampire expert. I think my ego was aroused and I started to consider responding to some of the requests; such as: taking part in the publicity campaign for a film: Abraham Lincoln, Vampire Hunter; or promoting the stage adaptation of Let the Right One In; or allow myself to be whored by a PR company and say nice things about the release of True Blood on DVD.

I did none of these things.

I am glad, because I felt I had passed a series of tests. This campaign was never about me, but about what I believed in. Now, before I continue with the story, I must confess that I am not perfect and that I did, eventually, take part in several interviews, but I have reflected on them later in this book in detail, explaining why I thought they were good opportunities.

Had I not kept my eyes on the prize, I may never have invested the time and energy needed to yield something from Michael's writings.

HIGH STAKES

Michael's journals had taken me nowhere except down a blind and furious path through some of London's most deprived and depraved areas. Since the night where I had castrated a paedophile at some illegal brothel in Soho, I considered whether this was really the life I wanted. So I withdrew from investigating street life for a while and set about finding the pulse of London's seedy but very high-profile nightlife.

Using several bogus online accounts, I had managed to identify a popular group of swingers and hedonists that arranged exclusive parties across London's most expensive boroughs. I joined some of the closed groups, merely as a voyeur like most of the other men and women, and started messaging them through Twitter. In particular I found the handle of one man/promoter who claimed to be able to meet the needs of any client and act on any party request that would culminate in some type of sadistic orgy. I made further enquiries. And when I had all the information, I cross referenced this with some writings of Michael that I had trailed through which talked about 'high society' and 'Sodom'.

The time finally came where I was able to identify two

or three 'targets' that I would base my hunt on. In many ways I saw this as the last shot; the rest of Michael's materials had led to nothing conclusive. His content was out of date, addresses had changed - either because the block had been demolished or rebuilt (being London, this was not uncommon) or the owner, tenant or licensee had simply moved on. In the best part of over a year I had used most of the money left by Michael to make enquiries; a year had amounted to nothing much other than a couple of risky situations where I put my life or that of others at risk.

It was hardly what I would call progress.

There were evenings, however, when I found myself considering whether I had missed some of his cryptic clues, and often I doubted whether I was intelligent enough to translate his sketches, maps or symbols; the very experience often left me feeling paranoid, dejected and looking into the bottom of a glass than out into the world. However, that was about to change.

The letters V or Q appeared most commonly in two of his journals. To this date I am still unsure as to whether they represent persons, places or objects since V or Q is often referred to in a location. For example, one extract from Michael's journals read: V often inhabits bar/s between the hours of 22:00 and 23.30; the exchange is subtle and VQ can be seen relaying orders to Ant.

There are literally hundreds of similar notes taken by Michael, which to him meant more than they did to me. V or VQ or Q is also, according to his notes, often transported, which suggests the use of a vehicle of some sort. My only lead to go on was that V or Q had a great deal of activity around the a particular postcode, which is the area around Mayfair and Park Lane. For me, this posed two problems, firstly the area is one of incredible wealth, but also known for being incredibly transient regarding the type of people who pass through. Indeed, the area is known as a hub for foreign investment and there is, to date, a competition to transform the area into boutique hotels, private members clubs, luxury apartments, art galleries, etc. All of these venues feature high security, and sometimes work to action these projects are completed under the cover of diplomatic channels. The other problem, and this is where my sceptical side creeps in, is that if I really believed Michael's magniloquence then I was effectively supporting the idea that the Ants were made up of a hierarchy; an elite movement who deem themselves as untouchable by regular people, the ultimate bourgeoisie. In my heart I knew that this couldn't be the case since I had found links to organised crime networks, and groups and forums operating under the surface web, all of which seemed to share the same ideology as the Ants and their desire to corrupt and feed.

It was a Tuesday night and I was surveying one of the addresses, a night club in Mayfair. It wasn't particularly taxing work, I was just watching from my car, noting who went in and who went out; recording taxi registration numbers and that of private vehicles, the number of guests and brief descriptions. My last dealings with Veronica had not been pleasant and I believed I would never find her again. However, imagine my surprise when I caught sight of her there. I experienced both dread and delight. I concluded that V must have stood for Veronica. The car she used was linked to a private hire company based in Knightsbridge so there was little chance of tracing it to an address unless I had access to the company's itinerary log, and I didn't have the resources to do such a thing.

I returned to this club regularly each night, looking for a pattern. Whilst Veronica was often delivered alone, or with the company of other soldier ants, when she left she sadly frequently visited restaurants and clubs that had waiting lists or were guest-list only. My gift of the gab for blagging my way in to such venues was limited, especially at the times of day she often arrived; there was always a burly man or two standing with an earpiece at the door, a centurion protecting London's wealthy. But on one occasion I was lucky enough to gain entry to Annabelle's, where she often visited, after ringing ahead and getting myself on the guest list. It was a coordinated effort with help via social media, about the only time it has actually worked out for me, which coincided with a time when the seedy adult party promoter promised to be at the bar.

The club was made up of several rooms, each with their own theme. On a Thursday night, the night in question, I made my way in and found the club to be full of men, mainly, in their late thirties or early forties. Women: models, dancers and paid escorts were also there and much younger than their male counterpart. There was a certain feel to the place if I am honest, a crucible of selfie culture, people who wanted to be looked at and adored whilst they traded idols. I was fine with that as long as I was able to maintain my cover and, no thanks to several visits to beauty salons and fine tailors, I hoped that I might pass for an arrogant bachelor. I anchored myself at the bar that evening, ordering spirits and studying the row of drinkers who frequently came and ordered cocktails or bottles of champagne. On my rare trip to the toilet I could hear men sniffing coke from the cubicles around me, anyone else taking a piss seemed indifferent.

After a couple of hours waiting around, knowing Veronica was somewhere in the venue, I became unsure as to what I was going to find and wondered if I had the balls to go looking for her. I ordered another whisky on ice instead, at the barman's suggestion. He became deeply enthused about each single malt he had behind the bar. Whilst telling me about the peaty notes or the honey tones, I found myself looking around every few seconds, longing for a glimpse of my target. I concluded that she owned a stake in the bar or there was a room, an area so exclusive that not even the bar advertised it to people. This was confirmed when I asked the barman if they often had private parties, intimate venue rooms - that type of stuff.

He smiled and stared at me, nodding. I mentioned to him that a friend and girlfriend of mine (lie) had attended certain parties in the SW6 postcode and that they were always looking for pre-party venues. I also mentioned the promoter's name I had been following on Twitter to see if that sparked any interest in his round, pale face.

"I think I know what you are trying to ask me," the barman said.

I smiled back at him. "I'm trying not to be so bloody obvious about it," I replied. "If you can introduce me to the owner or promoter of the club, then I'm sure that I can get an invite for you."

He beamed back at me with an over-enthusiastic smile. He offered me his name as Peter and told me to wait at the bar, saying he would go and try and get him for me.

By the time Peter's 'manager' arrived I had finished a fine single malt which left a rich warmth in my gullet and the extra level of confidence I needed to cover my terrible acting.

"John?" the man asked, extending his hands.

I regarded him: late-twenties, a crimson John-Travolta style shirt from the seventies beneath a tailored black jacket. "Nice shirt," I remarked, shaking his hand. "You must be...?"

"I'm the guy who books sex parties," he said laughing at me. I chortled with him and turned away, seeing if anyone was watching us.

"I don't recognise you if that's true," I added. "You obviously don't travel north of Oxford Street."

He nodded, rubbing the tip of his nose. "I recognise you though," he said overconfidently. "Are you a member of Equinox gym?"

I shook my head. I knew of it, a place where the wealthy would train privately if the wanted, in the very heart of Kensington.

"So, you want to arrange a party?"

I looked over at Peter who smiled at me whilst he was

serving glasses of champagne to two anorexic models.

"Possibly," I said. "My friend was hoping to arrange something in the coming weeks and he wanted a venue with a private room so that all the guests could arrive in fancy dress before he revealed the address there and then, you know, before it got public and went viral." I paused for a second and watched him nodding but he didn't seem convinced. "That's the problem with Facebookers and Instagramers: they can't keep their fucking mouths shut. You must have learnt the hard way, right? I mean, some of these parties you organise – you have to keep everything strictly hush hush, I imagine." He didn't say anything. Instead he turned and surveyed the women on the dance floor. "It was me who contacted you through Twitter the other day, asking about booking something."

There was another pause before he spoke. "Sure, I remember now. Problem is, John, I get a lot of guys saying stuff to me online – but they're not all legit though, you understand? Some of them are just fantasists, begging me to upload video snippets from parties, or share some pictures of the girls, and then all I get is a barrage of dick pics."

We both started to laugh together.

"The real problem," he continued, "is that people who contact me on Twitter usually don't have hot girlfriends to bring to these types of venues, they're just chancers, risk takers. That's not you is it, John?"

I didn't look at him, just shook my head and continued watching the girls. "I've got myself a great girl."

"I hope so." He drank champagne out of a glass like he was taking mouthwash, throwing his head right back. "If you give me some dates, I can let you know a time and a price. Hopefully you've got space on your guest list for one or two more."

I nodded. "Bring a blonde," I said. "In fact, why not bring two?"

He laughed. In fact, we laughed together at my own

misogynistic tones and a verbal contract had been made.

"Here's my card, John." He handed me a richly embossed business card, with thickly printed numbers across it. There was no name. I looked at him and he laughed back at me.

"I think you've given me the code to your safety deposit box." I studied it carefully, laughing at myself, considering whether my cover had been blown or I had just stumbled into a nest of Ants without knowing. The card was identical to the one given to me by Veronica months before. She was there, at the venue, and minutes before had most likely been with this very man before we got together and spoke. I looked up above the bar and noticed a camera looking down on us. Someone was watching, for sure. "Seriously, how will I get in touch?"

"Just show it to the doorman the next time you're in, let's say tomorrow night? That will give me time to investigate some options for you." He shook my hand. "But you must bring your girlfriend along," he said. "Like I said, I get a lot of single men trying it on. If your girlfriend's as hot as you say she is, you're definitely on for the party of your life! If not . . . well."

He shrugged his shoulders with such arrogance that I wanted to smash a glass in his face right there and then, but he had already started backing away into the crowd. An impossible challenge had just been presented before me: to materialise a loyal and stunning girlfriend in less than 24 hours.

At that moment I decided that I would go home and start investigating the premises in more detail and find out who put up the money for the club and who exactly this Chris character was really involved with.

I hailed a cab and asked that the driver navigate to Highgate via Soho. He looked at me like I was an idiot, but I wanted to look for signs, visual reminders about what kind of sordid city I lived in. I had to honestly challenge myself as to whether I, John Michaelson, one man, could make any difference to any of it.

The bar was actually co-owned by a Lebanese restauranteur who liked to socialise with a load of beautiful models and attend fundraisers. The other was some banker, an unknown entity. Chris had been tweeting that same evening, promoting an event he was attending at the weekend, oh, and posting a few selfies of him with fat lipped models he met that evening.

I must have been fuelled by adrenaline and coffee for the rest of the day, having had such little sleep. My mind was hyperactive, processing so much information, and at times I was worried that my heart might go into cardiac arrest at the thought of entering the lion's den. The strain I had put myself under during the past year was starting to take its toll and I didn't feel as fit as I was. I had started to put on weight and my diet contained hardly anything raw anymore – it was processed; high in fat, higher in sugar. That same day I left the house to try and rapidly enhance my look; the barber and beautician did their best, but my eyes were still a bit puffy and red and I needed to rest if I was to look my best. But I knew that wasn't enough – I needed a date!

Dressing in my sharpest suit helped take pounds off my waistline and when I got round to smoothing my hair back with product I must have looked closer to my age. Did I look like a swinger? Certainly not according to dozens of online forums, but I looked eligible and perhaps charming and audacious enough to attend sex parties across the capital. The only thing that was missing was a good looking girlfriend. My research online had yielded that this Chris character was known more internationally as a promoter/con artist but on a superficial level he seemed genuine in that he loved what he did. Images and links posted online pointed towards a man who surrounded himself with model types. I needed to hire out a girl of a similar calibre for the evening, which wouldn't be easy since I was looking at the best part of £300-400 to get someone to match the look, but that might not be enough to secure them for a whole evening. I also needed someone who could act, to buy into my backstory, so surely I was looking at having to pay double.

I was resentful spending Michael's money on such sordid expenses, fuelling the very black economy I was trying to bankrupt, but I was convinced that I was getting in with the right people, and I desperately wanted to get to Veronica.

I saw this as my last shot.

After much looking, I asked an escort to arrive at my house an hour before we left so that I could debrief her. I found her through some classified online ads and her profile was detailed with lots of pictures, many seemed genuine and not photo-shopped. She called herself Alissa. On the phone, during a micro interview, she confessed that she had attended sex parties before and that it did not faze her. Her spoken English was okay and that was the hardest part of the selection process out of the way. By admitting that she has already stripped away any inhibitions to engage in such folly, I found myself feeling prejudiced towards her; I had a feeling that we might not get on. It wasn't going to work, I told myself. There would be no chemistry between us, that was my worry, and I feared that Chris would see through my costly, cobbled attempt to get myself on one of his guest lists.

When she arrived, I realised that I should have scrutinised her personal stats a bit more and been more rigorous in my recruitment. She claimed to be Venezuelan, a 'South American Temptress' but she was actually of Eastern European origin, of that I was sure, and with her heels on she was some three inches higher than the five foot six description on her profile, which meant she dwarfed me somewhat. I led her into the kitchen and gave her the back story to follow for that evening: I was a writer looking to delve into the dark world of sex parties in the capital. She showed some degree of interest. She asked if there was anything else to do before we left, hinting at the services offered on her profile. I said I would see how we were for time after the meeting (I had paid for six hours) but I assured her that I was satisfied with her appearance and was more concerned that she could act in character for such a long time so gave her time to rehearse.

The cab arrived and we left for Mayfair. I was sat in the back for the best part of ten minutes in complete silence whilst the driver took us through Euston.

"What kind of things do you write," Alissa asked.

"Not very nice things," I said. "I write a lot about what goes on behind closed doors."

She nodded to herself. "Like true journalist."

"Yes, that's what I said on the phone to you, something a bit like that. Can you tell me about the party you went to?"

She looked at the driver who seemed too preoccupied to be listening. "There was one time," she began in broken English, "when I first became escort. It was with my friend and she asked me to come. She said man she knew wanted models and paid good money. I trusted her, my friend, so I went with her."

I was already dreading the meeting at this point. Her English was sloppy, often stop-start; I needed her to have a bit more oomph as she seemed to whine her last words up and down. "Where was the party?"

"Hampstead." She smiled like it was a good memory. "In a big house – I made lots of money that night."

"Were there many people?"

"There were twelve, maybe fifteen girls. We all looked – what is the word - glamourous and wore masks," she said, waving her hands about her eyes and hair. "They gave us champagne and offered cocaine before telling us to flirt with all of the older men - talk little, smile a lot, laugh at their jokes and then touch arms, hands, stroke face… We had man and woman telling us what to do and say. For a long time I thought to myself, hmmm this is okay, good money for nothing, but then a man took us all into a room and announced there would be a break for everyone to get ready."

"Get ready for what?"

"I didn't know," she replied. "My friend took me to a room and we all got into our underwear only. Someone went turning all lights off and only candles, red and yellow and white candles, lots of them, they lit them around the house. When we came back outside, men were also in their underwear only. And then..." she raised her hands up like that was the end of the story.

"Then what?"

"Then we start fucking."

It was a blunt, non-graphic account of what probably happened. Any hint at intellectualism from her had disappeared in an instant when she reduced her conversation to such coarse anecdotes, yet here I was trying to buy myself in to such a hellish sounding soiree.

"That's it?" I said, sounding disappointed. "It just turned into some masked orgy? You can't remember the names of men and women? What happened to the hosts? Where did it go from there?"

"Sure, I remember," she said, "but it was my first time. I was careful at first. I recognised one man I like and he took me to a room with another girl. Later there were two other men who wanted to take turns with me. But I knew the risks, and they were gentle with me. My friend was not so lucky, she was chosen by an older man with two others – he took her to some kind of dungeon."

I raised an eyebrow. It was certainly revelatory but most of what she had said was typical of what I imagined happened at these secretive masquerade events, from what I had researched anyway. The dungeon bit was the most unusual part of the story, but I guess all tastes had to be catered for at these types of events.

"Did you do any more parties like that?"

She half shrugged. "I did one more but I didn't like it. There were lots of men and not many girls and the house was not as nice. One of my friends got hurt when she was there and there were men who wanted to take risks – not use protection. I value my health," she said proudly. "Always use condom."

I was mildly reassured but I was starting to warm to her because of her honesty.

We arrived at the club and the bouncer's wearing hats welcomed us in without a second glance when I showed him Chris' card. I breathed a sigh of relief given I had brought a crescent-shaped, four inch metal claw into the club, for my own protection. I took Alissa to the bar and ordered a £140 bottle of champagne so that she could look like all the other starved models.

"I need us to look like a couple," I whispered to her as I topped up her glass. She laughed and kissed me tenderly on the cheeks. I then turned to see Peter, the barman from the previous night, watching me excitedly. I waved Chris' card and asked if he was in. Peter told me to sit at a table and he would ask him to come down shortly.

The music was darker that night, and much seedier. The R & B lyrics fought with hip hop beats, and the lighting seemed to be murkier. And it was hotter, a couple of degrees more so than the previous night. Alissa clearly felt at home, I watched her shoulders thumping upwards to each beat and her hair flick from side to side as she struck model poses. I started asking about her experience of being at such events and she mentioned that she had dated lots of wealthy businessmen who used to take her to such bars; British bankers, Lebanese restaurateurs, and Russian pilots. She clearly didn't have a problem doing what she did, not surprising given the rates she could earn in one evening.

About five minutes passed before Chris walked over to our table. He shook my hand, pleased I had returned and seemed delighted by my offering of Alissa. "Do I know you?" he asked her playfully as he kissed her on the cheek. She shook her head and looked at me with a smile, acting the part beautifully.

"So let's talk, John," Chris said, helping himself to a glass of champagne. "You're looking for a venue for an event."

"Somewhere secure and very high class," I said. "My clients don't want to give out an address, they want everyone to meet, be vetted and then get ferried to a secret location. They like it that way."

"I'm intrigued to know who your clients are," Chris said putting his arm around Alissa jokingly.

He was an embarrassing flirt, almost playing the idiot too well. "They're wealthy and they like their privacy," I said. "Your security on the door is a bit lax." I pulled out the knife and showed it to Chris. His mood suddenly changed and I feared I had jumped the gun. Even Alissa looked worried.

The smile had vacated from Chris' face. "Are you some kind of psychopath?"

"No, but you've dealt with my kind before, Chris." I was risking everything on my irrational behaviour. "I'm not here to beg for your venue, it's already been used by some of my clients. Veronica, she'd probably recognise a few of them."

I left it there, my words and her name, to hang in the air. Chris gave a nervous laugh, almost like he had been second guessed. I could feel sweat running down my sides. I'd blown it.

"So you know Veronica?" he said. "Why didn't you tell me that before? I could have just given you a good price there and then?"

"Because I expect loyalty, and I wanted to be assured that I'd get the level of service I hoped for. If Veronica's in, perhaps you can take me to her, and show Alissa and myself round some of the private members rooms, if that's not too much of a task for you?"

Chris nodded and asked us to follow. "Put that fucking thing away though," he said laughing. "You scared the crap out of me."

Alissa grabbed her glass of champagne and I took mine also. As he walked ahead of us, Alissa squeezed my arm and whispered in my ear: "Are you some kind of gangster?" She almost sounded intrigued, like my little power display gave her some degree of arousal.

"Something like that, but don't worry," I said, toying with her. "You're safe with me."

We followed Chris past the barriers and came to a thick door which was seamlessly integrated into the wall. He opened it, allowing us to see a row of stairs down into another basement room. Alissa grabbed my arm excitedly. I grew worried. This was really happening.

We came into what I can only describe as a den. The soft thumping of drums could be heard from the main dance area - somewhere above us and to the side. There were silk drapes, black and luxurious red with sequins, hanging from the ceiling; the sofas were built into the walls and there were several smaller cubicles dotted around a mini amphitheatre and several arched recesses; stone torsos of men and women were decorated in between granite reproductions of gargoyles which gave the venue more of a gothic meets burlesque appearance. There was also low LED lighting under each stair leading into the pit. Chris walked into the centre and addressed us both.

"This is the main performance arena," he said, spinning on the spot. "We get a lot of private parties held here, sometimes artists come and do a talk or musicians play a small intimate set to their celebrity mates."

The area was very fitting and immaculately presented. I looked at Alissa and she looked impressed as she peered into each of the cubicles.

"Is there anywhere else?" I asked Chris. "Anywhere else private where people can go from here?"

"There are some rooms next to the main office," he replied. He gestured with his head and led us past a small cocktail bar, and through a small archway that had pleated silk drapes either side of it. Lanterns were on the walls and obscure looking artwork, reds and silvers and whites shaped into wide streaks of madness across large canvasses. He came to a door that was almost hidden and stopped and looked at us both. "Veronica is in here right now," he said. "Did you want me to ask her to come out, or see the room first?"

I thought for a second. "I'll surprise her," I said. "Perhaps you can take Alissa back to the main club and look after her; I think she needs a top-up. I'm happy with what you've shown me. When I'm done I'll come back up and we'll talk about dates."

Chris gave a contented nod. He knocked on the door, popped his head inside and spoke to someone, mentioning that a guest was here. I heard nothing in reply, just watched as Chris opened the door wider for me and then took Alissa away.

"Don't go anywhere," I said to her.

Alissa played the obedient girlfriend brilliantly and gave me a kiss on the cheek. I watched her walk back towards the main dance floor with Chris, his hands already touching her back.

There are moments in life when you look back and think that it was all surreal, like it never really happened and you were a TV viewer of your own life. In that very moment, John Michaelson became the third person. I watched him boldly enter the basement office. He paused for a second before closing the door behind him and waited for the woman to turn from her paperwork and look over at John. When she finally did there was a long and painful pause; numerous chemical processes and exchanges took place in both their bodies; eruptions of gaseous emotions were taking their time to settle down. Finally, John stepped forward.

"Hi Veronica, how are you?"

"I was doing very well," she sighed, "but now that you're here I'm not quite sure how I feel about the situation."

I imagined that she might have access to a panic button or a mobile phone, but when I checked my own phone I saw that there was no service - we were totally cut off from the world. She didn't seem fazed by my presence.

"I'm not sure how I feel about everything, either," I said. "I'm fine by the way."

She cast me a wicked smile and I saw her teeth shine through blood red lips and snow white skin. Her make up looked less refined than when we last met but her nails, however, were gelled and pristine and looked like they could start ripping at my flesh if I said the wrong thing. I stood my ground and kept my eye on the door behind me.

"How did you do it, John?" she asked. "Ed was so much more charming than you, and stronger – more virile even, I should know. He should have ripped you to shreds that evening but he didn't. Somehow you managed to overcome him."

"I guess you underestimated me," I cautioned. "Maybe I wanted to live more than you thought. I didn't want to get sucked into your sick fantasy world, and I was ultimately worried about others having to go through the same pain."

"There's nothing made up in our world, darling," she said condescendingly. "We're survivors of this age. But you're never going to get a chance to find out, because you turned your back on our way of life."

"Yet here I am, scouring the pits of London looking for remnants of you and your organisation, whatever you're part of. You, alone, coordinating misery from a cell buried beneath an expensive looking front. Hardly the life of luxury you promised me is it?"

She looked at me and spread her legs out a bit further than shoulder width. "What do you want then, John? To take up my previous offer - to fuck me here and now so you realised what you could have taken so freely?"

She made my stomach churn. I pulled out my knife instead and took measured strides towards her. "You need to wash your mouth out for a start," I cautioned. I stopped a few feet away from her, pointing the dagger at her heart if she even had one.

"So, you really have become this lone warrior, slowly striking us off your hit list given to you by the old mad man, Michael. How are you getting on with those journals of his by the way, productive?" she started to laugh.

I hated feeling like the underdog, and just like our last encounter months ago, I felt belittled by her distinctive arrogance. She did that well, exuding such conceit, even in the face of death. She knew I was blinded by my conscience, which is why I found it difficult just to get on with the job and kill her, end it there quickly and run, but she was wildly enigmatic, and part of a bigger circle. If she was V and I killed her, then who was VR and how would I get to him or her? And if she knew about Michael's journals, who had given her that information? I started doubting everything again. Me discovering the club was just another system of control.

"His writing can be a good read," I said calmly. "Especially after a few drinks – you tend to ignore the typos here and there, but then nobody is perfect, right? We all have our faults." I stared at her for nearly a whole minute in silence. "You have a weakness, Veronica, and I want to know who he is."

She laughed again and started swirling in her chair playfully. "Why don't you just come over here and slip that blade inside, stick it wherever you like, wherever makes you feel good about what you're doing." She started undoing her blouse and pulled it apart revealing a pair of pert white breasts, no bra. She gripped them tightly in her claws and squeezed them together. "You want to ask about my partner, whom you naturally assume is a man?"

I didn't say anything. Was I being led along an elaborate hoax set up by Michael?

She continued. "You still have no idea about what you're about to uncover. If you make it out of here alive you'll incur nothing but a death sentence."

I watched her press harder and deeper with her nails until blood seeped out from where she had pierced the flesh. I was horrified and at the same time mesmerised at this sensual mutilation, the casualness of it all.

Red blood on white skin.

I deduced that she was an Ant Queen, she must have been. Surely this is what she was, pulling every dirty trick out of the book to try and make me succumb, to catch me off guard, to show her sadistic nature and repel me. That's when I turned just in time to see the door open and a man come lunging at me.

I managed to evade half of the blow as he struck me but I still felt myself tumbling to the floor. My head hit the edge of a desk and I could feel it sting as I wrestled with him on the floor. The man, who I had not seen in the club until now, clasped my shoulder with one hand and reigned down a heavy punch to my solar plexus, causing me to fight for breath. A fortuitous angle, as we struggled on the floor, allowed me a knee jerk reaction hard into his groin. I then pushed deep into his throat and pinched whatever sinew and veins I could find before rolling myself on top of him. My left hand struck him across his face before his hands grabbed mine.

Veronica was laughing at us, getting off at the two of us struggling for dear life. I managed to slip away from his grip and stand myself up, throwing whatever I could on top of him to keep him down: a computer monitor, printer, office chairs, but he still got to his feet. He made one last lunge for me but I kicked a swivel chair between us so that he fell forward. When I saw the back of his neck something switched inside of me and I thrust Michael's blade directly below the base of the man's skull.

He twitched momentarily and then crumpled to the floor. It was a surprisingly quick yet cold and uncomplicated death, and the only thing that stopped Veronica from laughing.

I scowled at her and for a second she looked scared, genuinely concerned for her miserable life. I was upon her in seconds, pinning her to the chair and holding the same bloody blade to her throat.

"Is this really what you want?" I whispered.

She looked at me and shook her head. "It's too late for me," she hushed mockingly. "I was like you once, but I've gone too far and you're about to do the same. Do what you must, John, but you must understand that you're about to unleash hell."

She closed her eyes, waiting for me to end her life. And that's when I paused. I realised that I still had a choice; I was in control. I hovered above her, unsure as to whether I was doing the wrong thing. In a year I had finally made my way into the darker, inner circles of this underworld movement but now, and only at that point, did I realise that I was about to descend a one-way path into London's unchartered underworld; there would be no escape.

Already a body of a man lay on the floor, a clean entry wound and thick red blood seeping out from beneath the man's skull. Veronica would be next, and then what? Where would my wrath end?

"Do it for me," I said. I grabbed her hands and wrapped them around the blade and held it to her throat. She opened her eyes, surprised perhaps that I had been so unpredictable, and in many ways I think that's why she chose to follow my instructions. With a cruel smile and almost parting thanks, she made a swift, sharp jab upwards and forced the cold steel deep into her throat. I stepped back in shock and watched her cough her own blood up across the office, over her white blouse and her milky white skin, a harlot drizzled in scarlet.

Veronica's blood started coagulating quickly, pumping slower and slower down her body until it spilled no more.

In death she had bought me more time so that, perhaps, I might go deeper and discover the identity of R. I checked my clothing to see if I had been splattered with blood and touched the back of my head. There was blood there, my own, but not a gushing stream of the stuff. I grabbed a hanky from my top pocket and wiped the edge of the table where it had struck, and then I surveyed the office and tidied up the rest of my prints where I knew I had touched things. I wanted to leave quickly, and was about to run out of the room when I saw Veronica's handbag beside her. I carefully opened it up and took out her iPhone and her purse. The phone was unlocked so I quickly turned it off and placed it into my pocket. Searching through the purse, I found nothing but a couple of business cards and some cash. No keys, nothing else untoward but most importantly - no ID! I took the cash and the business cards to examine later.

There was a key inside the lock. I took it out and used it to lock the door behind me from the outside. It would give me enough time to head back towards Alissa, make conversation with Chris casually and then leave as quickly as possible before people realised something was up. I had to assume there would be others in the club.

When I got to the dance floor Chris was all over Alissa like a rash. He was joined by two other glamourous looking blonde girls. When I walked over to them I could tell that they had been taking cocaine together, and Chris was kind enough to finish the bottle of champagne I'd ordered, freely offering it to the other girls. I approached the barman and ordered a double measure of scotch for myself.

"How was Veronica?" Chris asked.

"She seemed troubled," I said. "Then a man came by - he was pretty pissed, and she said that I would have to see her another time. They started arguing quite badly as I left." I sipped my drink, almost finishing it in one. "I came back up here before things got nasty. I hope she's okay."

Chris seemed indifferent. "She's always bringing back clients to this place," he said. "There's a whole load of them who live around here, the super-rich. She's always arranging stuff, but there's always a problem with the venues she organises or the merchandise that she brings in."

I thanked him for the information. "You need to leave me with your number so that we can stay in touch regarding the party I want to organise."

"I've already given Alissa the details," he said coolly.

Alissa smiled at me and held up an expensive looking piece of card. It had an address written in silver ink along with a date and time on the back.

"Alissa is an amazing girl," he said. "You've landed yourself a good one there. So I'd like to see you both at a party I'm throwing this weekend. I think you'll really enjoy it."

I nodded and then beckoned her over.

"You look stressed," she whispered. "You need to drink more and party."

"The party is back at my place."

She looked at me and giggled. I mentioned that I liked to honour contracts, and that the meeting I had come for had been a success. Then I whispered instructions in her ear: "Tell him we're meeting friends at Gilgamesh in Camden tonight and that he's welcome to come and bring his friends, but that he'll have to make his own way there. Then sigh in his ear and mention that we can't wait to meet him at his party and that you hope to see more of him in particular, winky face ...." I held her closer. "There's a bonus for you if you can get us out of here in five minutes, and I'll happily pay you for an all-night rate when the party comes around if you're happy to go along with it."

She didn't acknowledge me directly but simply

straightened my tie and told me to get her coat from the cloakroom and settle the tab. I did so, and whilst at the bar I noticed a doorman prowling across the club, clearly looking for someone. I avoided eye contact but I knew that something was up. I still had the key to Veronica's room in my hands and I prayed there would be enough time for me to get out safely with Alissa.

Peter smiled at me as he presented the tab. I threw down a roll of notes (Veronica's money) and tipped him generously, saying that it would be great to see him at one of the events Chris runs at some time in the future. He didn't stop smiling. I felt like calling him a fucking moron, telling him that he should not seek pleasures of the flesh, but use his real talents to get away from the superficial life that so many people aspired for. But I was hardly a shining beacon of righteousness myself. So instead I just smiled back.

I had insisted that Alissa turn off her mobile when we first arrived at the club. As we left, I told her firmly that we were never at the club. We hailed a cab and I gave a controlled sigh of relief as we got in the back of it and were driven away.

"That was fun," she remarked once we were a couple of blocks away. "I like your friends."

"They're not my friends," I insisted. "They're more acquaintances I've met along the way." I asked the taxi driver to drop us off half-way along Park Lane. Alissa looked confused but I explained to her that I needed some fresh air and time to walk off a cramp.

Several other couples were meandering through the park at that time of the evening, despite there being a chilly breeze. The moon was full and shone brightly on us both on what was a clear and crisp night. Despite moaning about being cold, Alissa cuddled up to me and continued asking me more questions about what I did for a living. I fed her the same story as most people, saying I was a property developer and project manager for several new developments happening across the city, which meant scoping out buildings and businesses that had potential to be bought out or redeveloped. She queried why I had told her I was like a journalist and I explained that there was a lot of interest in the club by foreign investors and that I needed to speak secretly to one of the owners. She gave a satisfied smile and held my hand for the rest of the walk as we headed towards Edgware road. I told her that I was hungry and so we slipped into one of the many Lebanese juice bars, I then informed her that it was okay for her to use her phone again.

I had just bought us both an alibi.

As I ate and drank I watched her playfully swipe her fingers across her phone, posting social media updates across several accounts. "No mentioning where we've just been to," I said. She looked a lot younger in the bright light of the restaurant. Her hair and make-up was still perfect and she had a model's pout. She caught me looking at her. I apologised but she just smiled, saying she quite enjoyed being enjoyed.

I ordered a taxi from Edgware Road and we arrived safely back at mine. Alissa walked with me to the door and I let us both in. I checked the clock and it had been nearly five hours since Alissa arrived at my house and the contract had formally begun.

"We have an hour left," she said matter-of-factly.

I nodded and withdrew my wallet to give her some more cash. "And you did a good job, so here's your bonus like I promised."

She took my money - or rather the money I had taken from Veronica - and placed it in her bag, then she leant in and gave me a slow kiss on the lips. "How would you like me?"

"You can sleep anywhere you like," I replied. I would have been a hypocrite to take advantage of her, given my poor reputation with women in the past and the crusade I was now embarked upon. She looked at me confused, like

I had offended her or not found her attractive enough, which wasn't the case at all.

"You want me to choose a bedroom?"

I shook my head. "No, I want you to rest here. I've enjoyed my evening with you and I need to do some work now."

"But you've paid for me."

Any other call girl might have been grateful and ran out of the door but I sensed that she had genuinely found the night fun in some bizarre way. Had she known about the chaos that had ensued minutes after Chris took her away from Veronica's office, she might not have got in the taxi with me at all.

"You were amazing," I said. "And still are. I would be happy if you stayed the night, but I'm not going to ask any more of you."

It was late. She checked her phone. There was little, if any, point of her leaving my house to make her way home at such an hour. I had the space and the privacy to offer her a little luxury and I think she liked the idea of having company.

"Okay, I'd like that."

I showed her to my father's bedroom, the best room in the house with use of an en-suite. I then locked up and sat in my attic room with a large glass of scotch and enjoyed the feel of it in my throat. Staring up at the moon through the skylights, I reflected on the events of the evening before I started to notice the bruises across my body. I was mad on many levels; mad to have gone to the location knowing my cover could have been blown from the night before; mad to carry a knife around London; mad to have paid several hundred pounds for a high-class escort to accompany me to the club and pose as my girlfriend, with just an hour's rehearsal time, and madder still to not even have enjoyed her like most hot-blooded men would have done.

I stayed awake at the prospect of her coming up to my

room of her own accord, for genuinely wanting to be with me – that would have been different; I secretly craved to be desired again by women. But that was not the end goal, and sadly not the case. I meditated, trying hard to focus on my role and purpose from now on – I was at a crossroads.

I withdrew the business cards I had taken from Veronica's purse and wrote down each name. I had not come across any of them from deciphering Michael's rants, and none of the cards told me anything about that person: age, address, occupation – there were not even emails, just six digit numbers. I considered they may have been pin numbers perhaps, safety deposit codes or extension numbers for a larger company; they may even have been dates of birth but that would have meant that one person was born on 070603, meaning he was well over a hundred years old. What I needed was expertise.

Veronica had denied me answers in death but by offering up her own life she had given me a sense of closure on one level and bought me time to explore new avenues. The woman I held partly responsible for my torment years ago, the woman who had tried to orchestrate my death on the roof of St George's Hotel, was now locked in the basement of a club in trendy Knightsbridge, soaked in her own blood and cut out from an evil network I still knew nothing more about.

Nursing the bump on the back of my head, I must have spent much of the night running through the scenario again and again, but at some point I must have fallen asleep because at sunrise I felt someone sitting at the edge of my bed.

I woke with a start, but was quickly assured when I saw Alissa present me with a cup of tea in her hands. She placed it on my bedside table and asked if I would join her for breakfast. I said I would and watched her walk away in my father's dressing gown, not the prettiest of images but I was comforted that she had felt safe in my home.

She was swiping her phone screen back and forth whilst eating cereal when I came down the stairs to join her. She mentioned something about not having any juice and keeping a fridge like a dead person, keeping only jars and bottles. I laughed as I sat down to join her. We talked some more and reflected on the events of the previous night. In particular, I asked her what she thought about Chris. She was very perceptive.

"He was a dick," she said casually. "Perhaps you didn't notice but he had his hands all over me like I was some kind of possession."

"I did notice," I said. "But in that scene a lot of the girls seem to like being idolised by rich men. You took drugs with him?"

She shook her head. "I had a friend who got with someone like him; she ended up relying on the stuff and being taken to dark places. One day she disappeared for nearly four days. When we found her she had so many drugs in her system and had slept with so many men that she got really sick. She moved back home where we hoped her family would look after her, but she never kept in touch." She shook her head in frustration and put down her phone. "I should have done more to help her."

"Hard to when you're moving in the same scene."

Alissa nodded. "You know, John, I don't want to be an escort for the rest of my life but it's hard to break the cycle, especially when I meet nice clients like you who pay so well."

"You can't journey through life living with regrets on a daily basis – it'll drive you insane eventually." I smiled, realising she didn't know the deeper, darker truth about my actions and my motives. I should have been stronger and told her not to worry about being my date – that I had a business card and an address and that I could always find someone else. "About this party Chris is organising," I said. "I don't want you to go if you're uncomfortable with it. I'm not even sure I want to go myself - I'm curious more than anything. But in truth, I'm trying to hunt someone and I don't think he's even going to be there."

"A hunt?" Alissa seemed intrigued. "Who are you hunting, John?"

I shook my head. "A very nasty bunch of property investors, and I wouldn't want you getting hurt. I quite like you."

"I can handle myself."

"I'm sure you can, and I could use your experience to tell me what to expect at events like the one he's organised." I held up the invite and looked at the gold writing upon thick embossed card. I had searched their social media accounts and found that the party we were invited to was a genuine one – 14 couples and about 16 single women were promising to be in attendance at a secret venue (we had the address). It promised, on the tweet, to be one of the wildest yet.

"So, do you still want to book me in?" she said expectedly.

"What's your fee for the night?"

"The same as last night; and your bed was very comfy so I would expect the same offer extended. But perhaps you can get some food in next time and we can eat a proper breakfast in the morning with real coffee and juice."

I agreed. I was sold on the idea of having her with me again, if not a little hesitant about the whole thing. Chris, whether he was part of a larger conspiracy or not, might have changed his mind if he had seen the mess I'd made in the club office.

Alissa left after breakfast. She gave me a gentle cuddle on the doorstep and I watched her leave. I was the one with regrets that morning.

For the rest of the day I trawled social media and checked the night club website, including its Facebook and Twitter accounts, to see if there was any report of a closure, any hint of a crime, any mention of foul play, but there was none; there was no chatter across forums about a police incident in that area of London, and no radio reports: nothing. It was as if their bodies had just been removed without fuss.

By lunchtime I was going stir crazy so I headed down to Knightsbridge by cab and asked to get dropped off by a Lebanese restaurant within walking distance of the club. There was nothing untoward, and that same feeling of madness crept back, the feeling I had experienced initially after getting sucked into this world; that feeling that there was a darker, deeper protection ring in action, and with it came that feeling of dread. I was dealing with an organisation I didn't understand that could somehow usurp the authorities to suit their own needs and exercise their own justice system. My heart had pains.

I stayed in a coffee bar for hours until the club opened for business, just to be sure, and that's when I knew for sure that a cover-up had taken place. With another lead terminated, my next investigation would be the party I had been invited to.

A voice inside my head told me it would not work out well for me.

THE VIP SEX PARTY

It had been four whole nights since the incident at the club
and the gloriously unsatisfying end to Veronica's life. And
in that time there was still no talk of foul play, attack,
suicide, murder or anything untoward at the club I had
attended with Alissa. Life carried on.

Alissa had confirmed by phone the day before that she
was still available and looking forward to the night. I
wanted to back out because I was afraid of the unknown.

There is only so much online reading you can do about
events, ploughing through images, amateur videos and
reading sordid accounts of what type of stuff happens at
parties like this, some of it written by hedonists, first-
timers and even fantasists, but nothing can prepare you for
actually attending and visiting such an event.

My fortuitous meeting with Chris had allowed me to
bypass a humiliating process of profile vetting and
scrutinising by the people who organised such events. I
had Alissa to thank for allowing us to queue jump what
could have taken years of work. Now I had to maintain
my cover which might mean joining in with the
proceedings. I was not comfortable about that idea.

I treated myself to a hair-cut and other facials,

manicures, even tanning and waxing salons to look the part. My best suit seemed cheap so, with the help of some branded tailors in Bond Street, I acquired a made-to-measure suit which took pounds off my middle and made me look taller.

Everything had to look right, even the masks we would wear. I had never been a fan of masks or seen the point, but when I tried on a very burlesque style, black mask I did get a certain pleasure from securing a degree of anonymity, and in some ways it allowed me to demonstrate a type of confidence I had not enjoyed before. I guess you could say that my attraction to masks began here, and it would also become a symbolic metaphor for my struggle. I also ordered a matching one for Alissa in red and hoped that she would like it.

Alissa arrived at my house that evening looking like a film star. She told me she had invested some of the money I had paid her into the dress she wore, a silk robe with gold sequins, and a pair of Jimmy Cho shoes she bought on eBay - they were the best I was told. The clutch bag and other jewellery had been gifts given to her by other clients over time.

Arrival at the party was set for 10pm. It was 8.30 and she was talking me through the procedure over a glass of chilled Sauvignon Blanc. She explained that we would arrive and be put into a holding room and encouraged to mingle. Not seeing everyone's faces was part of the eroticism of the event. Drinks would be served and, at roughly midnight, the groups would be split in two and everyone would strip down to their underwear. It sounded like a public school boy's wet dream but I had also researched on forums that this procedure was common.

The taxi arrived and I checked that I had everything ready. I didn't take anything sharp with me this time, something I would later regret, but I did conceal contingency items and spare cash cards should the worst scenario occur.

Alissa didn't talk much on the way down, but she seemed more excited than I did. I put it down to the fact that she was conditioned somewhat, used to meeting strangers and engaging in sexual activity with them, but I couldn't help but feel numb in my skin, like I was heading straight out of the frying pan and in to the fire.

"Did you tell anyone where you were going tonight?" I asked her.

She shook her head. "My friends know what I do but I don't tell them where I work anymore. Partly because they disapprove, and partly because I now only work with men like you."

That's what I didn't want to hear. She was naive and still considered me some beacon of good amongst the seedy world we were about to enter together. "You can change your mind," I said to her. She shook her head.

The car pulled up outside a grand four storey townhouse in W1. I tipped the driver generously and held Alissa's hand outside of the town house. The invitation in hand, I rang the bell and we waited. A minute later the door opened and a girl dressed in full burlesque outfit and mask welcomed us like we were old friends, taking the business card invitation from us.

"So nice to see you both," she said. "The party is gathering downstairs. Come this way."

The house was every bit as decadent as you would expect: large gilt mirrors with gold frames, expensive rugs, fine works of art, many of it probably original; and then there were the sculptures and ornaments from different cultures, perhaps hinting at a well-travelled owner. She beckoned us into a lobby that had doors leading into an open plan living area and that was where a number of other party members had already gathered in pairs. It was like a scene from a Kubrick movie: candles everywhere, red light, soft seducing vibes of music permeating the walls from built in speakers, silver champagne buckets everywhere, women in long dresses, sequins, thick and bouncy hair styles; the men were more intimidating – tall, assertive with their women, openly groping their buttocks and breasts as they spoke, some had booming voices and were perhaps already high on cocaine – a silver tray of which was placed like an offering at the end of one of the sofas. I grabbed a drink for Alissa and myself and stood in front of some phallic art work, watching the couples watching us.

"I thought there were going to be loads more single women," I mentioned to Alissa.

"They tend to arrive fashionably late," she explained. "I think to build anticipations and arousal in the couples."

"How does this compare to previous parties you've gone to?"

"It seems very high class," she whispered. "Try to relax and enjoy yourself."

It was easier said than done. I was in a room with nearly thirty strangers, engaged in some primitive ritual with some hand selected elitist couples, satisfied that they had passed the selection phase and would get a chance to literally feed their primal desires.

We must have been stood for ten or fifteen minutes when another couple approached us. The man was of a similar build to me, smartly dressed but with a short but well maintained beard and styled black hair. He introduced himself as Rob and he wore a red, devil type mask with lots of sharp black pagan symbols around the edges. I shook his hand and gave my name as Charles, why I will never know, but having a mask seemed to give me more impetus to lie. Alissa gave her real name and shook hands with a very stunning blonde with thick, curly hair and a red dress; she introduced herself as Jess and started gushing over Alissa's clothes, commenting how amazing and sexy she looked. It was shallow small talk for most of it and gave her an excuse to casually fondle her. I had little to say to Rob, other than ask him if he had been to a party before. He recalled vividly the last party he went to which had been organised by the same group of people, and I could see Jess and Rob getting off on their own trashy descriptions as they reminisced about the number of beautiful people who had been eloping so openly in front of other couples.

"Sometimes, once you've cum," Rob said candidly, like I actually gave a shit, "you can just sit down and relax with a drink and watch two people going at it until they both cum in front of you. Then it gets you in the mood again, and before you know it you're rock hard and someone else is asking if you want to spend some time with them. Next thing you know you're being led by the hand and end up having sex again with beautiful strangers – it's just amazing!"

"Sounds delightful," I muttered. Of all the myths and traits I'd researched about vampires, there seemed to be this obsession that they were all, in some way, sexually hyper-active. I had researched the effect of parasites on the human body and found that increased risk taking was quite common amongst those infected; if indeed you could pass the parasite on to another host through bodily fluids then it made good sense to do this through sexual activity. Parasites had evolved into perfect survivors.

I entertained Rob with a few anecdotes of my own that I made up on the spot, about an after party I allegedly attended in Ibiza at a club owner's house, and then one at a country manor on the outskirts of Rome. He sounded impressed and I had somehow attracted the interest of a few other couples who now surrounded us. Gazing at us with pouting lips and statue poses, and all wearing masks, we must have looked like giant chess pieces.

Alissa had been accosted by two more women who also complimented her on her looks, and slowly I found Alissa being pulled away from me. The time passed quickly and I noticed a change in the atmosphere, almost like the lighting had dimmed or something else was slowly deepening the mood. Perhaps it was the fact that some couples were now engaged in some real flirtatious courting, parading up and down the room and gently stroking each other as they passed, like an electric charge was being strengthened. Even I was touched and stroked by alluring women; the masks failed at hiding any sense of inhibition. I could see men's mouths and lips pulled back and alpha displays of teeth, their chins raised, chests puffed out.

At quarter to midnight the lights dimmed even lower. Then a man, fully dressed in pagan robes of black and purple silk - and wearing a gold mask - came into the room, followed by two surgically enhanced women in gold nylon swimming outfits. The night, I thought, surely couldn't get more bizarre than this. A hush descended upon the room. I remember his words well.

"Ladies and gentleman," the voice said, smooth as it was deep and pronounced. "I would like to welcome you to the first underground movement or our alternatively themed sex party. As you know, at your request, we have tried to make things a little bit blacker for the devil in you all."

His head dipped slowly and I could see that he was surveying the room, looking for a reaction to his wickedness. Chris was still nowhere to be seen and I felt like grabbing Alissa there and then to make a run for it, but the women had her now, their hands tenderly locked around her arms and wrists.

"Let us remember what it is like to have no barriers," he continued, "and no boundaries other than these four walls. Let us reconnect with the spirits, go back to what it was like to walk the plains of the earth and feel no fear, to take what is ours without judgement, and to feed our innermost desires. Let us not resist temptation!" He turned to the girl next to him and ripped the bikini from her chest. "Let us not ask forgiveness for our sins of the flesh." She barely flinched as he roughly squeezed her breasts and clawed his nails down her chest all the way to her naval, leaving feint red lines. "Take what is yours, my brothers and sisters. Take what I offer to you; consider it a sacrifice, for we shall make our covenant together. Succumb to the pleasures of the flesh, and satisfy your thirst – feed and drink double portions until you are refreshed and your energy lines are realigned." He looked around at the other girl and grabbed her by the hair. "Kneel."

She did so willingly whilst he held the back of her head, occasionally tugging her to show everyone that he was in control and unapologetic for his actions. Kneeling on the floor she looked up at him, and then the man pulled aside his tunic and withdrew his penis. He aggressively tapped it across her face and around her mouth. There was an uncomfortable silence in the room but I could also sense men, like the one stood next to me, were getting off on what we were witnessing, a precursor of the violent sex acts that were about to follow. The whole event now seemed less like a sex party I had read about in online forums and more like a dark mating ritual outside the gates of Gomorrah – things were getting very severe.

The man addressing us, now clearly hard and proud of his phallic display, continued his rant with his penis in her mouth. "The women will now depart company momentarily," he said. "The feast is about to start. Prepare to satisfy your hunger, my brethren, for the night's entertainment is about to begin."

He pulled the woman's head away aggressively with a sharp twist and pushed her to the ground, then he turned to leave and the women obediently stood and followed him out. I was half expecting a round of applause, but instead the rest of the women started to leave the room. Understandably, some of them looked reluctant to do so, including Alissa. She looked over at me as she was led away by her newly made friends; I gave a reassuring nod, although I couldn't promise her anything other than a glimpse into the pit of hell.

The doors closed and then Chris, the cocky-cockney organiser of this sick event, appeared unmasked in the room like some gameshow host, adjudicating the occasion. He was loud and crass, running on adrenaline perhaps and high on cocaine, insisting that it was time to 'buff up'. I despised him. He pointed to a clothes rail that had been wheeled in and asked us to hang up our designer suits. Men eagerly started stripping off and slowly it dawned on me where I was. As the shirts came off I saw that most of the men had the same tattoo. Perhaps it was a coincidence but two crescents seemed to sit on most of the men's hips or left shoulders.

There is no stranger sight than that of a candle-lit room filled with men dressed only in pants and wearing masks. To say I felt uncomfortable was an understatement but nonetheless there I was, my chest puffed up trying to make myself look presentable, believable even, that I really belonged there. Several of the men were erect which made for uncomfortable viewing and there was a disturbing silence, like the whole house was somehow soundproofed from reality; the house was metres away from a busy London street with thousands of pedestrians walking by in droves, swarming between tunnels and busy side streets.

Chris looked around at the group and was satisfied that proceedings could begin. I didn't acknowledge him; my mask gave me the anonymity I truly desired. He took out his phone and appeared to check some picture messages and then he busily started typing a message. We waited, like gladiators in our black and gold masks and bronzed (some oiled) bodies. To say I had a complex would be true given the types that these parties attracted: the model and athlete, many of whom had been hand selected by their social media photos.

There were two loud thumps at the doors again. We all turned to see them open and the same two women, who had been abused by the mysterious man in the tunic, entered and both were now fully naked. Following them were the rest of the women, now only in underwear and their masks. The candlelight gave the illusion that their skin was tanned and there was a rich scent of cherry as they paraded before us. I grew nervous, waiting for Alissa to come through; surely I would recognise her – we had matching masks - but I didn't see her. Many of the women were new, different to those who had gathered, perhaps the ones paid to be there and entertain the men or join in with another couple. It was unclear. I moved aside, trying to see where the women had come from but a woman blocked my path, she was short but very curvy, wearing black lacy underwear and a bust that was definitely not her own. She spoke to me in a thick European accent, asking if I was ready to have a good time. I half ignored her, searching the room for Alissa until the door was closed and I was locked in, held in a Sodom-themed prison where, it would appear, anything was about to go down.

"I'm looking for my partner," I replied coyly.

"Don't worry, baby," she said. "We're all here to have fun and let go." Her hand slid down my pants and she gripped me firmly by the balls. I backed away, nervous and somewhat violated by her crude advance. Beside me, the man who was eager to perform already had a woman on her knees and was thrusting himself into her mouth like a savage. The sound of heavy breathing and muttering suddenly grew in volume and I felt like the place was closing in around me, suffocating me. It was vile. Disgusting. I broke free of the woman who had somehow wrapped her scented arms around my neck and started pacing around the room searching for Alissa. She definitely wasn't there. I looked back towards the other side of the room to see Chris slip out of a door. I decided to follow.

He didn't see me emerge but I could sense him climbing the main stairs of the house. I wanted to call out to him but I didn't, instead I trailed quietly behind him, grabbing a solid object on my way up which happened to be a phallic stone sculpture. It would have to do. The 2nd floor was quiet and lit only by candles. The doors were all open and I sensed that Chris had gone one floor further up. Nonetheless, I checked the bedrooms before I followed and saw that each one was elegantly prepared for some kind of fetishized party: silk sheets, red drapes, and pillar candles of differing heights, black towels, lubricant, and a variety of condoms. But on closer inspection I found more metal trays on painted bedside tables. There were drugs, cocaine, brandy and razor blades – and there were also other metal instruments, types I recognised from Michael's stash - sharp daggers with glass handles, crescent knifes with hieroglyphic symbols. I took one and slipped it into the back of my pants, thinking it might come to some use.

I heard creaking from the room above and continued on my way up, silently ascending the wide stairwell. Sure enough, I found Chris making final touches to a room on the top floor. Large black curtains were drawn and the whole chandelier light fitting contained real candles which were burning softly. The bedside table had the same set up: drugs, condoms, razor blades, poppers, brandy but no knives or blades. He turned round and caught me looking at him, my hands held discretely behind my back.

"Sorry, mate," he said, "I'm prepping this room for one of the VIPs, you need to re-join the main party downstairs. How are you finding it?"

I took the mask off my head and stared at him until he realised who I was. "I've lost Alissa."

He laughed cockily. "Yeah, I imagine a lot of men showed an interest in her. I know I would happily give it to her."

"She's not in any of the rooms up here," I stressed. "So where else can she be?"

"Listen, you should be thanking me that I invited you here. It's only because of her that you made it on the invitation list. To be honest, I was quite pissed and forgot

I even gave it to you. We have a system where we go on photo applications and, no offense, but you would've been a no if it weren't for her."

"None taken…is Veronica here?" I said, knowing that I had watched her die in the office at the club. I was looking for signs of a reaction, an understanding of what he knew about her. He simply shook his head. That's when I knew that he was just a humble errand boy going about the house, making sure the party was in full swing.

"Haven't seen her since the start of the week. I had a few guys asking after her, though. She used to be quite popular at these types of events. Used to hang out with Rameses quite a bit."

"Who is Rameses?"

He gave an annoying scoff. "I'm kind of busy, John, to answer fifty fuckin' questions. Rameses is the guy dressed up who starts the ceremony off. This is *his* party, the whole concept and theme came from him. Sometimes, with Veronica, he used to start the party in front of everyone, some little ritual they had."

"So tonight is Egyptian themed?"

"No, something to do with new moons – all mystical and shit. It's always linked to the fucking moon."

It explained the tattoos. I realised that Chris had told me everything I needed to know, however, I needed to find Alissa. I approached him quietly. "Is there a basement in this place?"

"Can't you just enjoy being liberated and go fuck someone else?"

Without thinking I swung the blunt object over my head and into Chris's face, sending him crashing to the floor. He gave out a small grunt as I stood over him but he was unconscious. I dropped the object and picked him up off the floor, heaving him onto the bed. I decided to make him look as natural as possible, so I stripped him down to his underwear and lay him face down on the middle of the bed, sprinkling cocaine over his lower back.

Why? I'm not sure; perhaps I hoped someone depraved would come and sodomise the guy, to show him what it would feel like to be at the receiving end of such debauchery. My attention then turned to finding Alissa before something terrible happened to her, inflicted by the power-crazed, moon worshipping misogynist by the name of Rameses.

I passed no-one else on the stairs. As I entered back into the main room, where men and women had been reunited only minutes before, I witnessed an orgy that I simply cannot and do not want to describe in full. Bodies were strewn across chairs, across several laps, on top of sideboards, draped over furniture; mouths and all types of orifices were being opened and pummelled aggressively, and all I could hear was the slapping of skin against skin, and all I could smell was sweat mixing with richly perfumed oil. I couldn't control my breathing, focusing only on door at the other side of the room and finding Alissa. But I was intercepted by a thin, bare-chested woman with dark shoulder length hair and erect nipples, asking if I would spank her whilst she gave a stranger a blowjob. I stammered, spluttering something about needing the toilet, and then pushed her away to carry on my search.

I made it through the door and closed myself off from the sexual carnage. I stood listening to my heartbeat drill inside me. My body was perspiring – the house was so hot –and my hand and arm was shaking from where I had swung it with such force at Chris. I kept breathing and managed to calm myself, focusing on the surroundings. I saw a stairwell leading to a basement lit by red candles. This was where I figured Alissa must have been taken.

I tiptoed, descending silently, spiralling downwards into a corridor that was much cooler and darker, lit exclusively by more candles. Expensive looking sofas filled the hallway in between three closed doors. I tried the first door, opening it silently, and peered in to see two men loudly having sex with the same woman. I could tell it wasn't Alissa so I moved back into the hallway to try door two. Door two was locked. I listened carefully but could hear nothing so I moved on to door three.

The room was colder with artificial light coming from more stairs below. There was another level beneath the basement, recently renovated perhaps, one of London's new mega-basement type designs, perhaps a heated pool, gymnasium or cinema room. I hoped it would be the latter. But the second basement was not a pool but some kind of industrial kitchen, used for entertaining. I approached cautiously because I could hear movement and voices, chanting softly.

With each step I took I had to pause and let my heart catch up. Despite the temperature being cooler, I found myself sweating more than ever. Another step, this time close enough to smell the bodies of several men and women; they were huddled together around a table as I peered round the corner. They didn't notice me and I couldn't see what they were doing because the main kitchen light was switched off. Candles were lit in some kind of ritualistic ark on the ground and that's when I noticed that the flooring was covered in blood, and that's when I knew. I pulled the knife from my pants, switched on the main light and came into view, shouting at them to stop what they were doing.

The pack froze. It was like disturbing wolves from feeding on a carcass. The naked group of men and women turned and moved aside, their masks still on, and I could see the pinnacle of their sick fetish: Alissa's mutilated body lying on a metal work-surface. Their mouths were all saturated with blood and each pair of eyes, nothing more than glossy black pits, were staring back at me. As I struggled to draw breath, I counted perhaps eight or nine people. But the oldest man at the back, the one dressed in a gold and purple tunic, the man who started the proceedings, was glistening in crimson.

Rameses, if that was really his name, cried out. "This man has no place here!"

His voice was just an echo in my head. All I could focus on was the glazed look of Alissa's eyes, washed over and drained of life. Two large cuts had been made beneath her neck, and across various pressure points on her body there was evidence of deep piercings; some of the wounds were still pouring out blood. The floor was the industrial type, constructed with tiles and drainage channels, nowhere for the blood to stain as it would be washed down the drain. It was a perfect set-up for such activities, buried deep beneath the surface of an expensive city pad. Rameses repeated what he said, as if giving an order to have me forcibly removed.

One man started walking towards me, his blood stained mouth turned down into a scowl as he stretched out his arms to restrain me. Within a heartbeat I had thrust the crescent knife up into the man's throat, twisting sharply as I felt my knuckles hit his neck. He stammered back and started choking, his own blood now a fountain spilling out across the floor. The group became unsettled at this and I could see a couple of the men and women reach for knives and other blades that were kept in the kitchen. I didn't have time to think. All I could do was focus on getting to the man who I believed was the cause of all this, the man adorned in gold and smeared in Alissa's blood. I ran at the group with my hand and knife raised, forcing them to pack together in one corner, then I herded them towards the stairs. One of the women was armed with a long ceremonial crescent-shaped dagger - the one probably used to slay Alissa - and started waving it in my direction. I grabbed her wrist, swung her into the wall and twisted her arm behind her until the tip of the dagger pressed between her shoulder blades. I gave a hard push and she started screaming until she released her grip, then I kicked her to the floor. I picked up the dagger and my eyes fixed on Rameses. I watched him back away towards a small service elevator, only big enough for one person or a trolley of food.

As I went for him another man leapt on top of me from behind. We fell to the floor and I desperately slashed his arms with the knife but he didn't flinch; he held me at bay whilst the rest of the crowd escaped upstairs. The fight lasted no more than a few seconds. He had me pinned down, his hands pressed into my throat, nails digging into my scar. I writhed wildly until his naked, coarsely-haired torso slipped away from me. He kept shouting and chanting at me in another language and then threw me back to the ground. The sting of cold tiles smacking against my head and the feeling of warm blood on the floor must have brought me to my senses because I remember giving two short jabs to the man's ribs before he let go of his grip and rolled away from me. I somehow got to my feet and pulled a heavy food mixer off the work-surface and dropped it on his head – it kept him down.

The kitchen was suddenly empty. I saw the lift doors close and a woman ran up the stairs screaming like a banshee. Before I chased after them, I stared over at Alissa's body, praying that she might still have some life left in her. On closer examination it was clear that she was dead, drained of so much blood that her body already felt cold to touch, her life-force had ceased dripping off the stainless steel and was slowly clotting in pools. I stroked her forehead and whispered my apologies. She had died because of me, because I asked her to come with me. Why her? Surely they must have been expecting me and Chris had obviously mentioned my name to someone, or described my presence on the night that I disposed of Veronica. Could he be such a good liar? I felt stupid and anxious for even following him up the stairs, knowing that he may well have been part of a distraction to lead me away from the group, to lure Alissa to her death.

I was such a fucking amateur sleuth and now people were dying again because of me.

Killing Alissa, I deduced, must have been all about revenge.

Time was running out. I rushed up the stairs from the basement to find all the rooms now locked, the people probably barricaded inside. The lift had stopped at the next floor up. I ran faster to see if I could catch a glimpse of Rameses leaving but it was already empty when I arrived. He had gone. I only had one ritualistic knife in my hand and my arms and chest were now covered in blood. I did what I could to wipe it away but my body still dripped with sweat. I caught a glimpse of myself in the mirror, somehow my mask had stayed on but that didn't hide the fact that I looked like a raving loon. I had to get my clothes and get the hell out of the place.

Entering back into the drawing room in a state of mild panic, where the mass orgy was still taking place, only a few faces turned to notice me walk back through. I slipped into the cupboard where our clothes had been kept on a rail and began searching for my belongings. As I did so I could sense someone approach behind me. It was the woman from earlier, the curvy brunette who had asked me to party with her, except I could tell the offer was no longer valid. Luckily I turned quickly enough to parry her away and direct the knife into the door frame. I grabbed her by the arm and pulled her into the cupboard. It must have looked kinky because no-one seemed to bat an eyelid as I wrestled with her inside. She was surprisingly strong and caught me off guard with a head-butt across the ridge of my nose. I fell back into the rail and pulled many of the suits to the floor. She went for me again and I kicked out at her, catching her just below the knee. She fell, scratching at me with her nails, tearing at my arms and legs as I desperately tried to subdue her with half punches. We wrestled some more and she spat at me, hissing like a wild cat. Eventually I connected my knee powerfully in her ribs and then punched her in the head until she was limp. It was not my most gracious of fights and not something I like to boast about but I felt no compassion or sympathy for anyone left standing in the house that night.

"We will kill you, son of Michael," she whispered, panting for breath as I put on trousers that were too long and a suit jacket that was too tight. I told her to go fuck herself as I picked up some shoes and exited the cupboard, locking it shut. As I emerged back into the party, people were staring at me.

Rameses was standing at the main door, now adorned in a black and red gown but still with his gold crown and eye piece, pointing over at me with a dagger in his hand. Two burly looking men were either side of him.

"Seize this man!" he scowled.

I made eye contact with him one last time, praying that I would never forget the sharpness of his eyes or the tone of his voice. I would avenge Alissa, but not that night. I turned on my heel and ran to the opposite door – I had to get back to the outside world.

I imagined that the front door would be locked and my intuition was right, who would commit murder at home without securing your own front door? Plan B: the front window. Georgian windows are usually made up of large sheets of glass, but these ones were made of tiny panes, which made smashing each one a stupid idea. Thankfully I was able to prise one of the windows open. I made it out onto a ledge and then jumped over the wrought iron railings and onto the pavement before I was snared back inside by two pairs of arms.

I was free again and alive, just. The sting of landing on cold slabs sent splinters up my shins and had it not been for the adrenaline, keeping me moving, I might have collapsed into an agonising heap and succumbed to the pain.

I ran as fast as I could, checking the pockets of the coat and trousers I had taken. I found a locked iPhone and some cash. I ditched the phone and kept what little money there was inside; it was all I needed to get home.

I stopped at a payphone and gave the police the address of the house, citing that a murder had taken place and a gang of men were desperately trying to dispose of the body. The operator tried to keep me on the line but I hung up and limped away towards a taxi rank. I sincerely hoped that the police would arrive and follow up my claim but I didn't stay around to wait and see for fear that I was being hunted.

A new line had been drawn in the sand. A new level of depravity had been discovered, and my worst fear was confirmed: that people operating under the guise of vampires were very much alive and well and committing murder in the pursuit of fulfilling a blood fuelled fantasy. Michael was right and I had been wrong to doubt him. The situation just got a heck of a lot more serious.

Walking through the door of my own house, I locked it and stood gaining my breath in the hallway. The old antique grandfather clock ticked faithfully and I was able to regulate my heartbeat, but every time I gained some degree of clarity I started to think about Alissa and my heart began to ache again. She had said before we left for the party that she trusted me and had not told her friends about where she was going, probably because they would disapprove. I had funded her, encouraged her to act her part in this deadly game and she had paid for it with her life – cruelly.

I sat on the stairs and pieced together the moments from that evening. In the time the women had all been taken out, to the time I had ventured upstairs and back down again, and then disturbed them in the basement, I figured that fifteen minutes must have passed. In fifteen minutes Alissa had been lured down into the basement then stripped and slaughtered by a pack of animals. I was responsible for her being there and the guilt was like a cold knife twisting into my soul. But did they even know she was with me? The more I thought about it the more I realised that it was the perfect revenge for Veronica. It made sense that Chris was a recruiter; his age and profile gave him access to locations where hundreds of young Londoners would trail the club scene looking for fulfilment. The more I thought about it, the more I believed I had missed an opportunity to damage their supply chain for good. Chris had probably groomed many young men who had selfish aspirations to wholly indulge themselves and live independently of morals; the draw of seedy, no-strings fun was probably the pinnacle of self-actualisation for such lost souls. And the girls, spilling into clubs from the age of 18 up to their late twenties: impressionable, easily impressed by material wealth and naïve about the dangers lurking beneath their feet, in front of their very eyes - they must have seemed like easy pickings for such a disgusting man; for such disgusting men.

I prayed that I would get an opportunity to reach him another time. Meanwhile I had to prepare myself for a visit; I had to assume that they were coming for me. I changed out of my bloody clothes, bagged them up and then showered before patching up my cuts and injuries, and rubbing arnica into all of my bruises. I left most of the lights on in the house and sat myself, armed with an array of knives, in the study, adamant that the battle would be brought to me that evening.

Thankfully the battle never came to me that night.

SEVERED

Life after the events of that evening changed for the worse. I became a recluse; I barricaded myself in the house and didn't leave for fear of reprisal. I saw myself as a burden to the world, as a danger to any sane human being I came into contact with. People I grew attached to either died or went missing. It was a sad fact.

I never received a visit from the police about my 999 call, or a visit from a group of pissed off vampires after my bloody assault at their party. They didn't need to; I was psychologically wasting away, surviving on little sleep and a diet of microwave meals and red wine. They had won.

The doorbell rang one wintery morning. I snapped out of my trance like state and approached the front door with caution, a knife concealed in my dressing gown. When I got to the porch I could see a courier waiting for me with a small package.

"Mr Michaelson?" he said through the glass.

I nodded. Every previous courier I had encountered normally just shoved a package in my hand and demanded a digital signature, but not this man – he looked like he gave a shit that he was delivering to the right person, and that I needed to take the package from him. The man was young and gaunt looking with greasy waves of brown hair hanging beneath a cap. He stood there like he didn't know what he should be doing, like his script didn't include ad-lib encouragement or stage directions.

I opened the door. "Who sent me this?" I took the box, signing for it with an X.

"Can check sender on back." He turned and wished me a pleasant day. I watched him jog down the path and get into his van; it had the same logo on the side of it that had been embroidered on his polo shirt. I made a note of the company and the registration number and then returned inside.

I prepared myself some tea and toast whilst I thought about what the package could be. I was already super cautious about getting items delivered to my home address and used a private mail box for most of my deliveries from eBay and other specialist sites, on the advice of Michael. In fact, as I watched the kettle boil, I realised that I hadn't even ordered anything recently, which is why I struggled to find the courage to sit and open the package straight away. Eventually, with tea in hand, I took a seat in the dining room and started to carefully open up the parcel.

The white box wrapped up inside brown packaging paper was sturdy with neat lines and it smelt clean, like it had been sprayed in disinfectant; it was wrapped in a thin strip of cellophane. I got a knife to pierce the edges and that was when I first noticed the smell. It was not offensive, neither was it pleasant, but it did have the nostalgic whiff you get from visiting a butcher's shop on a summer's day. Inside the box was a layer of red tissue paper, more cellophane, an ice pack . . . and a hand.

I stopped breathing for a moment when I first saw it lying upon a pack of white mesh, the type used to absorb excess fluids and smells that you'd find in polystyrene packs of meat from a supermarket. I felt sick and ran over to the main window to see if anyone was parked outside, watching, anticipating me to start running out the house and screaming for help. Instead I paced about the hallway frantically trying to collect my thoughts.

It was gruesome and gut-wrenching, and a stark reminder of the type of industry I was now working in. I collected a chopping board from the kitchen and some disinfectant wipes and cloths. I also donned a pair of latex gloves from under the sink and collected some tongs and tweezers so that I might examiner the hand and inspect the remaining contents of the box carefully.

The hand was stiff and I was half expecting it to be clenched, holding something that I might need to prise apart to reach, but it was relatively flat. The hand definitely belonged to that of a male. The skin was pallid with blemishes and minor sun spots. The hairs along each finger were short but thick, and greying, suggesting that it belonged to an older man perhaps. The nails had been smoothed down and finely polished but were not cut short, rather they protruded enough for them to collect all manner of grime and dirt beneath. I used some tweezers to scrape along the inside of the index finger (it was a left hand) and placed the dirt/debris on a small white plate. I considered that I might take such samples to a laboratory - if I ever got my act together - or even invest in my own microscope, though the type I needed could not be bought at your local superstore or on Amazon. The biggest giveaway clue I found was a wedding ring of sorts.

I examined the stump where the hand had been cleanly severed from the arm. It appeared to be neatly done with no sign of damage or tearing around the edge, even the bone was not jagged, which suggested it was cut with a fine rotary blade at high speed after death. But then I was no expert, and much of what I had deduced was from trawling online forums. This was a professional job done by people with clear intent: to scare the crap out of me. I knew of only one group of people that would want to antagonise me in such a way, and given the amount of disruption and poking around I had done of late, this was a clear message for me.

I suspended my examination of the hand and went to my computer, searching for the number of the courier company. I found their details online and rang the central office, informing them that I had just received a shipment and needed details of the sender. When they asked for the barcode I could not give them that information, since there was none, and then when I gave them my address they said they had no record of a delivery being made there for that morning, or any morning or day of that week. The courier and his van were not legitimate. As I remained silent on the phone the woman asked me what the box contained. I told her it was nothing of any use and politely ended the call.

When I returned to the hand I paid particular attention to the ring. At first glance it appeared to be a wedding ring but as I touched it I realised it was loose and could be easily removed. Using my gloved hands I slipped it off and examined it in more detail. I laughed somewhat when I saw the very symbols used to represent the Freemasons, for I suspected straight away it was some type of wild goose chase, a deliberate hoax designed to steer me right back off track; the Freemasons were long time sufferers of every conspiracy theory known to man. I had already discounted their involvement months before, not from trying, but just because I didn't believe that human trafficking and murder was high on their agenda.

I kept the ring secure in a small box and took pictures of every finite detail: close ups of wrinkles, birth marks, the stump, and even the colour of the hair. Then I sealed the hand in a freezer bag and put it into the fridge and out of sight.

I spent the next few hours researching on the net whether cadavers had been found in London recently missing appendages. There were several cases of body parts being fished out of the Grand Union Canal over the years, but most of the time they were linked back to a person and an investigation had been successfully carried out, or the parts belonged to young women, prostitutes who met a grizzly death, or men or children of African descent who were somehow victims of voodoo. But there were also anomalies, tales of people fishing up just the hands and feet of children and the elderly. But why send body parts to me? And why a man's left hand? I uploaded the pictures to my computer and searched frantically for any missing clues. The hand had not been clenched nor was it pointing in any direction, it seemed almost prosthetic when looking at it on a screen, but someone had made sure it was delivered to me the way it was intended to be: quickly and freshly. The remaining contents of the box had been a combination of cellophane, disposable ice packs and brown packing paper. Even under my very basic UV lamp there were no cryptic messages or symbols warning me to back away. Despite my best efforts, the only thing I concluded was that I would make a terrible detective.

I focused my efforts on finding other clues. The writing was in thick black pen and block capitals, no obvious clue, so I took a sharp knife to the remaining tape so that I could deconstruct the box fully, and that was when I noticed some hair trapped under the packaging tape. I removed the strip carefully using tweezers and held it under a day lamp. It was coarse, almost orange and of two-tones, and that's when I realised that it was not the hair of a human but of some animal, most likely a dog or cat, I hoped. My trail really did end there. Without the help of the police or an experienced forensics team, I had no leads. The sender must have known exactly that.

Sitting down later with a large scotch, I thought about what this meant for me in the long-term. I had felt assured at one point that Michael or whoever he worked with was looking out for me, that my home had remained a safe haven and I would be protected, but now I started doubt my future in Highgate. My dad was still missing, and unreported by myself to the police. The guilt had already consumed me months ago that I had not actively investigated his disappearance, but there were no other people affected by his disappearance and there was still, I hoped, a small chance he could turn up. I was adamant that the hand was not his: there was no scar and no wedding ring mark that matched the details.

The next thought that went through my head was how to dispose of the hand. How do you get rid of a body part that is not yours? I felt guilty to be even considering ways of disposing it! But I had no intention of keeping it. It was one of the hardest decisions I have ever had to make. There were grim forums online which talked about slowly dissolving body parts in caustic soda, then burying it deep underground; some fantasized about blending or even slow cooking it and then drying out the bones to grind into a powder – black magic. I felt genuinely sick to think that people actually fantasised about such things.

The canal seemed an obvious place to dump a body part, but I wanted to eliminate any risk that the hand could point back to me, so to speak, as the perpetrator of that person's untimely demise. Slow cooking and digging would keep traces of DNA on site and I was keen to ensure that no trace of this hand existed in my home beyond the next day. I started to panic, and so I decided that the hand needed to disappear that very same day, and quickly. I would have to leave the house after all.

I opened the fridge and placed the hand carefully back into the box, grabbed my car keys and got into my car after checking the road for any sign of police or cars with people sat waiting inside. Satisfied that I had no company, I started the car and headed north towards the M25 – to somewhere sparse and obsolete. Little did I know that my dress rehearsal would prepare me for something a little more sinister and self-afflicted in months to come.

THE DONOR

I arrived back home later that same day to find that a hand-written message had been forced through my front door. I didn't read it straight away for I was still a little shaken by the events from that morning and had been on edge since disposing of the hand somewhere in the Hertfordshire countryside. Every car that had followed me back into London, I believed, was a potential threat and I hated the feeling of guilt from my actions.

I checked the house to see if anything had been touched before sitting down in the lounge where I poured myself another stiff drink. I opened up the note and read it. I was unsure who had personally delivered the message. Simply put, it read:

Dear John,
It is time that we got acquainted. Meet us at the Romans' rest place, where Kings also gather. 9pm.
The Donor

My heart raced as I read it. The Donor, the man Michael had talked about and proclaimed as his financier, a man he hinted as being my secret ally who had taken a deep interest in my struggle, had finally sent me a direct message. I hoped. But given the most recent gift earlier that day, a decaying hand disguised as a parcel of meat, I had to remain sceptical that it was even from the man himself and not a false attempt by Ants to extract me into an unknown location so that I could suffer a similar fate. But then I reasoned that this was less likely by the fact that the location was not clearly stated in the note – I had to guess the location of my murder first.

Something cryptic, something Michael would have said or written down for me, had been delivered like a message from an old friend who wanted to catch up but knew people were on to him. Certainly the writing was different, not thin and scrawling like Michael's, and neither did it match the bold black capitals of the box, which I had also disposed of.

A message from The Donor . . . finally. My spirit was lifted somewhat by the fact that Michael might actually be there with him. Had I passed a test? Were my efforts being monitored once again?

I knew the location had to be based around central London, and somewhere not too far for me to travel to by public transport. According to Michael, the Donor was an elderly man, an academic who loved London and everything it stood for. I went straight to my computer and Googled the key words: Roman Rest and Kings and London. A range of restaurants based around London popped up, so I removed the 'rest' from the search and tried again. It was pretty obvious from that point. The results talked about ancient Roman sites across London; there were some links to King's College, and an image of a disused Roman Bath located on Surrey Street. Incidentally, the motto of King's College was translated as 'with Holiness and Wisdom', and if I was going to find any of that then I was sure it would be from the Donor, and what better place to meet him than there.

I was adamant there could be no other place.

I checked the map and explored the bus route I would take, and then I calculated the time I had to get there. Assuming that the meeting was also some type of initiation test, I packed some essentials into my coat and left to arrive in good time.

A crisp breeze blew along Kingsway as I gazed up at the night sky. I had taken the bus to Bloomsbury and could have travelled all the way but as I mentioned before, I always prefer to walk the last part of my journey, any journey in fact, because it gives me time to acclimatise to my surroundings, to check out the building and any people adjacent to the spot where I was about to investigate. At 8.55 I had arrived on the street and saw nothing untoward, neither did I see much movement in the baths. Rather than stand idly and attract attention to myself, I decided to do one final loop of the area to time my arrival at the entrance to the baths dead on 9pm.

At 9pm I stepped down into the basement and tapped my knuckles against the glass. When no-one answered I gave the door a slight shove and it opened. I checked I had my belongings, which included a large eight inch hunting knife, concealed in my jacket pocket, and then purposefully entered the bath. To my surprise there was not one person waiting to greet me but four, all stood in a line.

I could tell that they were all familiar and at ease with one another just the way that they stood in some type of hierarchical order. And I could tell straight away that one of them was a doctor or some type of medical researcher by the way that he had his sleeves rolled up neatly and how his skin looked starved of sunlight; the two younger members, both female, were harder to place initially, but the smartly dressed man in a blue suit with slicked grey hair was, undoubtedly, the wealthy donor who had arranged such a meeting. There was no sign of Michael.

"Good evening, John," the man said. "We're glad you got our message, one of our simpler ones I must admit, but cryptic enough for you nonetheless."

I didn't' say anything to any of them; I just gazed at them suspiciously. I had anticipated the Donor and one other, perhaps, but not four. All the anticipation and excitement had thrown me and I somewhat lost my manners, including my ability to speak calmly. I stared down at what remained of the Roman bath pit; it was empty and the room was cold.

"I suppose it's a pleasure to meet you," I said eventually. "Does the Donor have a name?"

"Not today," he said, coming forward and shaking my hand. "The Donor will do just fine. You must be wondering who the others are and why I invited you here. I hope it will all start to become a bit clearer." He spoke with smooth melodic tones, like he had been enjoying a fine wine after eating a gamey pre-theatre meal somewhere nearby. His hand felt very warm as I shook it and he was incredibly charismatic. But I remained suspicious.

"I'm curious," I said, pausing awkwardly like I had forgotten my line. They all stared and smiled at me.

"That's one reason why you're here," he continued. "And at least that's one thing we all have in common." He stood beside the man with glasses; he was in his late twenties perhaps, pale skin, arched nose, jet black hair. "This is Karl. He's a researcher here at Kings College."

"Researching what exactly?"

"Tropical diseases," Karl replied.

"And this young firecracker," the Donor continued, pointing to the girl wearing a dark red sweater who looked barely a day over eighteen, "is Minx."

I stifled a giggle and gave a smile instead. "And what do you do?"

"IT specialist," she replied. I couldn't detect whether she was being genuine or sarcastic since my impressions of IT workers were radically different to what I saw in her.

"And this is Jo," The Donor concluded. "She's the brains."

"It's nice to finally meet you, John." She stared at me with dark brown eyes. She wore a long, blue cotton dress and a tight fitting cardigan that seemed to show the edge of her bones. She pointed her hand at the floor. "You won't need the knife in here, John, so if you can put it on the floor it will make us all feel a bit more relaxed."

I shrugged my shoulders and sheepishly placed two large knives on the ground. "Nice venue," I remarked, trying to change the subject. "You must have some connections."

"You could say: it's not what you know but who you know, right?" the Donor replied. "But you didn't come here because of the choice of venue."

"True, but having contacts is no clear substitute for knowledge."

"Indeed, and this is why we've invited you here tonight. We'd like you to join us."

"Well, I was rather hoping *you* could give me some knowledge before I decide to do anything."

"In time, John, you will discover everything you need to protect yourself."

Already he was beginning to sound a lot like Michael: no straight answers, talking in prolonged riddles and old fashioned sayings. I didn't know if that was a good thing or not, most likely the latter, but I *was* assured that the people stood before me were genuine, real people. "Okay, so let's talk about Michael," I said, throwing the idea out there.

The Donor nodded. "In truth, John, before you ask us, we don't know where he is. Shortly after your last encounter with the Ants, Michael spent time supporting and rehabilitating you at home and then he just . . . disappeared."

"He didn't mention anything to you?"

"Not a thing. He didn't even leave a note, and Michael liked to write."

I felt cold for the first time that evening. Here I was in

the company of Michael's 'friends' yet I was the only one to receive a message of any kind from him before he went missing. I found that odd. I started to feel a bit uneasy at being sat on a chair with my knives on the floor. "That's very like him," I said.

The four of them smiled as I said it, but I daren't tell them about the letter. Not yet.

"It is and it isn't," The Donor assured me. "You see, John, he was part of our cell. And typically, when a member dies or disappears, a cell carries on regardless; it doesn't stop to pick up the pieces or advertise for hired help, it keeps on going until the job is done. But we believe he's still out there which is why we need your help to find him."

"So you broke your own rules and made contact with someone outside of your cell?"

"Not exactly," Jo interjected. "Quite simply we're continuing our investigation, of which you were a part of it. We've hit a dead end and we're out of ideas. You were the last person to stay in contact with Michael, so we've invited you here to ask for your help."

I didn't say anything. It was plausible that Michael was part of this group, but for me to go in and recklessly start telling them what I knew bought me no leverage to find my own answers. "I haven't seen him since he saved me. That's why I started going out again on my own, to see if I could find him."

"Yes, you certainly like to get out there and start stirring up the nest," the Donor remarked. "Funny really - especially since you knew which areas to go and start investigating. We can only assume you had help."

I shook my head. "I was hoping you might be able to tell me where Michael is, which is honestly why I came. I've been feeling very left out regarding your little meet ups ever since Michael told me all about you," I explained, referring specifically to the Donor. "But he didn't tell me anything about a larger cell, meeting in basements in central London like some AA rehab group. Now, as I'm here, I feel it's only fair that you give me some answers."

"Answers will come," The Donor explained.

"Oh quit the bullshit!" I snapped back at him. "That was Michael's favourite line. You invite me here, asking where he is, and expect to give nothing in return. I want in, whatever it is you do as a group: a scientist, a hacker I assume, and a girl who lost someone dear to her, and then you, the money, the man who makes things happen with an unclear motive whilst playing a round of golf in between investigations. Meanwhile, I'm rummaging around London desperately seeking answers after being discarded like some loose end. But now I've obviously caught your attention again . . . so, either you're genuinely at a loose end or you want someone to do your dirty work again, which is what I believe Michael was getting me to do all along, using me as a puppet, grooming me to attack and to kill people who may or may not have been so bad. And then he left, because he could no longer give me answers, no longer bare the guilt, or a plan went wrong, or something else. Fuck, I give up – please tell me."

There was an uncomfortable silence in the room. Eventually the Donor nodded. "Not a bad deduction," he said. "But if you want in then you will need to trust us and take a giant leap of faith."

"How do I do that? I'm a man of little faith."

The medical student, Karl, piped up all of a sudden. "You can start by giving us another sample of your blood."

I began to laugh. "How much do you want? All of it?"

I saw a glimpse of a smile in his face and took a calculated risk that he was being sincere. He removed a small vial from his top pocket. "All it takes is a little prick." He pointed to a small table which was covered by white muslin cloths.

I looked over at Minx and Jo. "And what do you want from me, my bank account details?"

Jo didn't say anything, looking over at Minx and The Donor instead. Minx started communicating to me, speaking in technical tongues which I decoded as saying that she thought my website was shit and full of inaccuracies. I thanked her and explained that I didn't solely manage its content. She then said that, regardless of whether I did or not, it had damaged any credibility I might have in the future but that, if I let her, she could help cover up any of the gaping holes in my web security. I thanked her politely.

"I use several aliases," I assured her.

"Yes, and I know each and every one of them." She then proceeded to tell me each and every fake account that I had set up. I felt a bit embarrassed, and stupid to assume that I had any leverage at all on these people who had called *me* in for a meeting. I was in the Roman bath of a top university, where kings gather, trying to convince a rich professor (if he was even that) that I had the experience and skills needed to join their cell and do whatever it was that they did, only better.

I walked over to the chair, removed my coat and sat down. Things certainly weren't going to plan.

"What is it you want to do?" Jo said plainly, her voice very matter of fact and controlled as Karl walked over and started rolling up my sleeve.

"I want to end it," I said.

"End what?"

"This constant feeling. This sense of emptiness and worthlessness I get when I reflect on how my life has changed and I think about where it's heading. I want the feeling of guilt and dread to end – to wake up feeling revived and positive, not resigned to the fact that I have a secret I cannot share with anyone. I want to find out the truth, what really happened to me and who the hell these people are behind it all and why the fuck they chose me."

She walked round to join me and watched as Karl started to draw blood. I barely noticed the needle go in because I was focused so hard on Jo's eyes as she listened to my story. Only then did I realise that her hand was on my shoulder. There was something quite magnetising about her; I had felt it before during my first encounter with Veronica, but Jo seemed to have a degree of charm and warmth that Veronica lacked. Her hair, light chestnut in colour, fell in wonderfully straightened strips that hung just above the shoulders; her face was thin but her lips and eyes were rich and full of life. I longed to be in the company of a woman like her and sat obediently until Karl had finished taking blood and placed a cotton swab over the vein.

"Why the blades, John?" she asked, holding one up and looking at the inscription. The Donor and Minx set about inspecting it also.

"This is Michael's," The Donor confirmed, looking down at me suspiciously.

"He gave it to me."

"You won't need these types of things at our meetings," Jo said. "We're going to help you control and channel that anger in other ways."

I reflected for a moment. "How did you know that I've been busy messing things up, stirring up the Ants' nest, so to speak?"

"Messy is a good word," she remarked. "There has been all kinds of chatter floating about the dark web talking about this rogue London vampire hunter who goes by the name of John Michaelson."

I shook my head, never hearing that term before. "I'd hardly call myself a real vampire hunter."

Karl stuck a plaster on my arms and then asked me if he could have a sample of my hair. I nodded, asking if he could style it at the same time, but no-one seemed to laugh at my pathetic little jokes. This was deadly serious to them and I was losing credibility quicker than I had been losing blood.

"What are you going to do with that?" I asked him.

"I'm going to run some tests, see if there's anything we can do to help you. Minx can access your medical records. And then if there's any blood left, I'll drink it."

I started to laugh, thankful that he was human after all. "And then what?"

"And then we'll call you to arrange another meeting, providing everything checks out," answered Jo.

I felt disappointed that I had travelled all the way for such a short briefing. The Donor handed me my coat and I rolled my sleeve back down. "Are you going to shove another letter through my door when you want to hook up?"

My phone suddenly started ringing. I looked down at it: anonymous. Then I saw Minx holding her cell phone. "Keep your ears to the ground, and don't do anything too stupid," she said.

I watched them line back up in hierarchical order as I stood and put my coat back on. It felt like a dismissal more than anything else and the anger started to boil inside me again, but luckily I caught Jo's eye as I left and she gave me some hope that they genuinely did care about my wellbeing and might be able to help. Maybe. I was too embarrassed to ask for the knives back, perhaps that was part of the test? Either way, I desperately thought of ways to seem useful. Before I left I placed my hand in my pocket and withdrew Veronica's iPhone. I explained to them how I got it (left out the assisted suicide story bit) and said they might have more success than I would accessing the data and learning a bit more about the secretive network I thought I was fighting. The one that I believed we were fighting.

Minx gave me an approving nod.

I left the baths and in my frustration I powered down to the river and looked over at the lanes of busy traffic. How good it would have been to just leap in front of a lorry and end it all there, the great anti-climax of meeting the Donor, my weapons laid down, blood sucked from my veins, and a short back and sides from the medic student. But then I found comfort in the thought that I was no longer alone.

I might yet get a chance to put things right, I thought, and a fire started to burn inside of me again; in a city which seemed darker than ever I had to remain positive and fan what little faith I had into flames.

STUDENT UNION

Two days after my meeting at the Roman baths I got an email to my main account from Minx. She wanted to meet with me and asked whether I would object to visiting her at the LSE campus near The Strand. I replied and agreed to meet with her later that day at around 6pm. She mentioned that the phone I had given them had proven to be very enlightening. I was somewhat jubilant when I read her last line, to think that I had somehow impressed them on my first meeting.

As I prepared to leave that afternoon, there was a knock at the front door. I didn't move, just stopped and listened. The knock came again, louder this time. I slowly walked into the hallway but I was reluctant to open the door because two well-groomed police officers in their mid-forties were stood in my front porch blocking out the light. I plucked up the courage to greet them both, staying as calm as possible.

"Are you John Michaelson?" one of them asked. He had thick skin and thin eyes, with a voice that seemed to resonate from deep within his chest. I stared back at him and glanced over at the other officer, a taller, more athletic looking version of the man asking the questions.

"What's this about?" Both of them pushed their warrant card against the glass and asked again if they could come in and talk with me. I stammered, asking to see the cards again, not knowing what a real or fake card would even look like. "Have I done something wrong?"

The man assured me that it would be more appropriate if we spoke inside. At that point in time, I figured that if they were both Ants posing as police officers then there was not much I could do: two of them, prepared and with the element of surprise, had me on the ropes. I beckoned them both in, walking backwards so that I could keep my eyes on them. They looked at me for guidance and I ushered them through to the living room so that I could be the one who shut the door on them.

I sat down on the sofa; they took a chair each. The colour seemed to drain from the room as one of the men started speaking. "I have some very bad news about your father."

I felt a small pop in my heart, like the pressure had finally been released after months of unknowing. I breathed deeply and then pushed my palms tightly together. "Is he okay?"

"Officers were called to an address in Islington late last night. When they arrived they found the body of a man we believe to be your father. We're not treating his death as suspicious."

I sat there, jittery with emotion and rage. Found the previous night at an address nearby? It didn't make sense; my father had been missing for months, albeit unreported by myself, yet suddenly he appears at an address in central London, a short cab ride away - dead.

I shook my head and spoke out loud. "What the heck was he doing there?" The men didn't answer me straight away. "I mean, he didn't have a flat or a house around there," I continued, cautious of what I was saying.

"It wasn't an address directly linked to him," the officer countered. "The flat was rented out by a third party. I can give you more details if you wish?"

"Where did you think your dad was?" the other officer asked.

I paused and considered my response very carefully. "On a business trip somewhere. I mean, he's retired, but he's always going away on short breaks with friends, or doing some consultation work. In truth, he wasn't the best communicator - it's just the way he was . . ." The taller officer remained silent, watching me react to the news. "How did he die?"

"The coroner concluded that he suffered a cardiac arrest: a heart attack. A paramedic was initially called to the address but I'm afraid he couldn't be revived."

"Who was he with?"

The man looked slightly uncomfortable. "He was with a young woman. We believe he may have been paying her for personal services."

How undignified, I thought to myself, to wind up dead in a prostitute's flat. I thought about the scenario and couldn't help but suspect foul play; it was just too perfect a death and so very fucking ironic.

"Did he have any possessions on him?" I asked. It was an odd choice of question, but in my mind I was already preparing to undertake my own investigation into his death.

"Just his wallet, his passport, house keys and the clothes he was wearing."

"Can I see him?"

The other officer looked at his colleague. "We can arrange for that to happen, my colleague will leave you the details of the coroner at The Whittington Hospital."

I nodded and thanked them, realizing I should probably be in floods of tears after being told of such sad news, but instead I just sat there in silence for most of the time, my leg jigging up and down.

"Can I ask when you last saw your father?" the officer asked politely.

I thought about how to respond before lying to them both. "A few days ago, perhaps . . . He was a private man. He would disappear for days at a time, sometimes I might not see him for a week or so, and then he'd tell me he'd been away on business. I'm only staying here temporarily, you see, whilst I sort myself out, look for a job. Now I don't know what I'll do."

The officer assured me that I could contact someone specialised in bereavement counselling and then informed me about the procedure regarding death certificates. It was a very short and formal delivery of bad news. When I had asked all my questions and answered theirs, I set about planning my next steps.

I requested the exact address where they found his body. The officer wrote it down on a piece of paper and then left it with me. Then both men stood and walked towards the front door.

I followed them out to the porch, watched them get into a police car and drive off. They had left me with a slip of paper in my hand, an address scrawled in pen. My gut reaction was to get myself down there and look for answers right there and then - I didn't feel like grieving - but I was conscious of meeting my so-called new ally, Minx, at the LSE café in the Strand later that evening. The visit to the address would have to wait.

By half five I was in the center of London, dazed and confused as I navigated the busy crowds piling towards Charing Cross Station and Leicester Square. It had started to rain which was good, because I had started crying unexpectedly and the cold droplets masked the emotions which I could no longer control. I struggled to remember what my father looked like and on the journey down I had been trawling through childhood memories looking for something positive to remember him by. I struggled with that, which made it even sadder to mourn him. He was an absent father.

I was early for my appointment with Minx and stood beside the abandoned entrance to The Strand underground station, reflecting on the day. Part of me hoped it was some grave mistake, but I conceded that the police forensics officer would be able to make a clear distinction between a passport photo and an empty cadaver lying naked at an address in Islington. I suddenly had a thousand questions in my mind; I was eager to trace his last known whereabouts, to somehow access his secret life. Suddenly I took more of an interest in him than at any point in my life; now that he was dead he became more valuable to me. That's when I first properly cried. I felt guilty that I hadn't pursued his disappearance, that perhaps I might have found him in time to warn him; his death was linked to my investigations and a painful consequence of my probing into dark worlds. Furthermore, the fact that he had died angered me because I never really learnt about the full sordid details of his life from him first hand - I would have to find that out in ways which might not be 100% true.

But I was really crying because I had no love for him. I felt less human than ever.

After I had cleared away my negative thoughts, it was time to meet at the agreed venue. I didn't see Minx when I walked in so did what most students were doing, sat with a coffee and tapped frantically on my phone. Minutes later Minx joined me at the table along with Karl.

I looked at them both and smiled. "Good evening."

Minx smiled for the first time. "It's good to see you, John."

Karl also had a smile on his face. "We've got some good news."

"I could do with some of that," I replied.

The two of them looked at me in my glum state. I was really terrible at hiding things it seemed. "I'll explain in a little while. I'm here to listen to what you have to say."

Karl began. "You'll recall, I expect, that we believe that the cause of everything is linked to and heightened by the presence of parasites."

"It was one of Michael's theories," I recalled.

"And from your own experience, you recounted to him something about removing a parasite from Ed's heart."

The hairs on my neck stood on end at his words. I thought I had been in a state of delirium through my injuries. Michael must have told them everything about me; I felt like I was some living experiment to them, that I had been put through a series of tests and was about to learn the results. It made me feel even more vulnerable.

"I was beginning to believe that I had somehow imagined the whole experience," I said. "Up until that night you're referring to, I had not been myself. I was more like a shadow of my former self, drifting in and out of consciousness. I was deprived of sleep and physically and mentally exhausted. Michael knew this, yet he did nothing to help other than lead me into danger and pry further." I looked sternly at them both. "The more I think about it, the more I begin to understand that his intentions were unlikely to be genuine, or for my own good, which explains why he left me. Something went wrong. Yet here I am - nearly a year later - and you're looking at me like I should be excited about what you're about to tell me. I barely know you both yet you know more about me than you're ever going to let on."

I took a long sip of my coffee and tried my best to control my anger. Minx and Karl said nothing. "This whole Michael experience feels to me like it was always about recruitment rather than finding a solution," I added. "You were all using me, watching me try and get to the people above. He didn't give a shit about my well-being."

Karl leant forward. "I would say you're ninety percent right. He used you to get to the Ants but not with the intention of you dying, that's why we think Michael went missing. He did show some concern about you initially and he wanted us to back off when he realized how close you were getting to the source. Then after your fight with Ed the trail suddenly went cold, everything just stopped and . . . now we're using you again to pick up the trail."

"And why is it so important to you?" I asked. "You're

a bright medical student with your whole life ahead of you. Why take an interest in all of this shit? People die because of them, the people I've been chasing. People have died because of me."

Karl nodded, prepared to take me on. "About two years ago my brother died mysteriously. He was twenty six and had been working as an investment banker when he decided to take himself out for a walk one night and leapt to his death from London Bridge. I refused to accept that his suicide was stress related and began my own investigation into his work life and new circle of friends. The deeper I dug, the more I discovered that he was into dark things; I'm talking the basics at first - private bars, strip clubs, pornography, recreational drug use - but soon he started attending secret parties and meeting new groups of friends that no-one knew about. He was hopping between forums on the dark web, trading in all sorts of stuff. At first I thought these were swingers' events or some shit like that, but it was something much darker and more secretive, like a smaller, sinister version of the Freemasons but on steroids."

I laughed at his comparison. "And let me guess, Michael suddenly appeared out of nowhere and made you believe there were vampires running around London."

"No, it gets worse than that. Whilst trying to get close to this group, I snuck myself into an exclusive member's only event, trying to find answers by tracking down key individuals. Suddenly out of nowhere I got a shooting pain in my lower back. I thought nothing of it at first, but then when I got home and checked my pockets I had a card saying I had been given a gift." He remained silent.

I shook my head. "What do you mean? What did they give you?"

"Nothing tangible, but when I undressed I saw that my back was red from where I had felt the initial pain. Being a medical student, I could see a small lesion synonymous with a poorly delivered hypodermic needle jab. I got my friends to examine it the next day and then I took a blood test. It was confirmed that I had been infected with HIV."

I remember breathing out hard when he delivered the news. "And you think that HIV was the gift? A little present to say, 'fuck off - don't get involved in our world'?"

"Precisely."

"Was it clear who it was from? Could you not have just been infected before that night and just not known?"

"That's unlikely - I know my body well, and I work as a researcher at the Centre for Tropical Medicine. I study viruses and parasites for a living, so please don't patronise me."

I apologised. "I'm just doing what Michael would have done, question the obvious. I'm sorry, that's awful."

"HIV is manageable, but then there was something else I noticed about my blood; I was infected with about a dozen different parasites."

"Is that even possible?"

"It shouldn't be, no – not that many. Arguably, some could have been picked up from a western diet. I fell ill soon afterwards but because of a relatively quick diagnosis I was able to cleanse my body of them."

"And you survived. Which is why you wanted to test my blood, you wanted to see if I'm still infected."

"I'd already done that once before; when Michael was tending to your wounds he brought me back a blood sample and the same pattern was there. I gave him the remedies and - by chance, somehow - you managed to pull through. He was right about you being a stubborn bastard. It's still a bit of a mystery, given that you were technically dead for several minutes, but anyway, here we are, reunited."

"Happy fucking families. And now you're about to give me my results."

He nodded. "All clear."

I sat back. It was a relief to hear. On reflection I had felt better for the first time in months and months, but at the same time I felt even more detached from society, and removed from this dangerous world I was a part of. "I don't know how to feel about that. Do I have HIV?"

He shook his head. "You're lucky, which is why we're all here I guess."

"So if I was still infected then . . . we wouldn't be having this conversation."

We all sat in silence and sipped our coffee, acknowledging our own journeys and why we were all at the cafe, brought together through a series of unreal circumstances. That's when I saw an opportunity to share with them my feelings and talk about my dad. I just started blurting out the events from earlier that day, about my dad being found dead and explaining to them when he'd actually gone missing. They were surprisingly sympathetic, which was nice because I had no-one else to share it with, and I found the experience instantly cathartic, bursting into tears again before affirming how angry I was about the whole situation.

"I have my suspicions," I said. "This was foul play, of that I'm sure, but I'm too fucking paranoid to investigate it officially. All I've got are some contact details of a grief counsellor, a number for a coroner at the morgue and the address where he died."

"Did you make a note of the number of each officer's warrant card?" Minx asked.

I shook my head. "Should I have?"

Karl interjected. "Even though we've been doing this for a while, we don't know how far the trail goes with this. It could just be a very hardcore group of sick individuals, carriers of the virus who feed to keep the hunger at bay and control the spread of the virus, but it could also be a pandemic, something we know is happening on a larger scale but we can't prove. These people are well connected and have money, so you need to be careful, John, because if they can get to you they will, but not before taking you to the brink of madness."

I couldn't look them in the eye for I felt ashamed of myself for being pulled along, following a string of deaths and debauchery since my infection. "Right, so that might explain a few things," I said, thinking about the recent hand in the package delivered to my house. I didn't tell them about that. "They're trying to call my bluff, or provoke a reaction. Killing a parent is going to make anyone, especially me, more reckless, almost suicidal – they just want me to erupt and do some crazy shit."

"Don't be so hard on yourself. If you'd still been infected then you probably would have done something even crazier. The level of influence parasites can have on the human mind is fascinating but also, in some cases, a complete mystery. Just remember that one of the ways that the parasite travels from host to host is through transmission of bodily fluids."

"Like biting, or having sex," added Minx. "Even attacking someone and exchanging blood – whatever the parasite needs to continue its life cycle, it will do."

"So where should I go from here?" I asked. "I want to help you guys, but at this moment in time I also want to avenge my father."

"Give me the address," Minx instructed, "and I'll look to see if I can find out whom the apartment belongs to. You might want to swing by in person and see for yourself, but it's always good to do your research first."

"I think I will. I was going to go there today if we hadn't have met, but that would have been a bad idea on reflection."

"And then when you're done avenging your dad, you can help us track down Michael," Karl added.

"What did you find at his flat?"

The pair shook their heads. "We don't know where he lives," they answered in unison.

I looked at them in total disbelief. "How can you not know?"

Karl leaned forward. "When we said we're part of a cell we were being deadly serious. Minx can find most stuff out through hacking and searching through databases, etc. but Michael was old school – he didn't even use a fucking computer or a mobile phone. The man is an analogue ghost living in a digital world. He cannot be found."

"Then I guess I can be of some use after all." I recounted my first chance meeting with Michael, when I followed him from Highgate to Macklin Street in the West

End over a year before, and described to them the flat and its surroundings in detail.

"We should tell the Donor and ask him what to do," Karl said cautiously.

"Are you serious? If I'd known you didn't know where he lives I would have told you straight away when we first met. After the past couple of days I've had I'm prepared to go there right now with you both. If he sees that I'm with you he won't go crazy at me."

Minx was more cautious. "We should at least let the Donor know our intention."

"That's fine, but he's literally ten minutes from here. You'll both be with me – it'll be okay!"

I recalled momentarily Michael's stark warning that he had issued to me: he threatened my life if I ever went near his apartment again.

"You must have seriously spooked him," Minx said. "Well done for tracking him down. It sounds like he had every reason to deter you from knowing more about him."

They took inspiration from my story and I managed to convince them both that we should go straight to his apartment, despite each of them having reservations. I argued that I was not part of their cell and effectively my own agent, which meant I could do what I liked. That's the way I sold it to them; they either supported it or not. Deep down I felt mildly euphoric that I might be able to see the man again. I asked what they thought we should do if we found him.

"Perhaps I'll speak to him," Karl said. "He probably still thinks you're infected, so we can't expect him to be a kind and sincere man. If I tell him that you're clean, he should be fine with us all being there."

I wanted to tell them both the truth, about the letters and the hideaway in Camden, but I was still mildly suspicious of them both - you could say I had trust issues - and wanted to keep the cards close to my chest until we got to Michael's flat. For me, this was also about seeing how much I could believe their motives.

Minx finished her coffee and then studied me for a while before speaking. "I know it's hard, John - with everything going on right now - but you're going to have to trust us. I promise that later tonight I will try and get you the details of the person who owns the flat where your father's body was found."

I nodded. It was a fair deal: I take them to Michael's flat, and in exchange they give me intelligence on my dad's last known whereabouts.

FINDING MICHAEL

Macklin Street is just another non-descript road in the big city: narrow, grey, barely used by cars, and easy to miss. It is hidden by bigger attractions like theatres and more popular eateries around the immediate vicinity, notably Drury Lane; it would be easy to walk right past the street. Yes, I remember clearly the day that I followed Michael there and all the details came flooding back me as we approached the tower block.

Winter Garden House was an ugly sixties-built wedge of flats and it was hard to tell if the block had windows because the architecture was so dark and grey. There was an area to the side which was kept locked where all the bins and rubbish were stored, and one main, secure entrance to the communal area where the lifts and stairs were.

Minx and Karl were with me, searching for clues and inspecting the local cafes before we tried the main door.

"I can't believe that you never knew where he lived," I commented.

"It's one of the Donor's primary rules: don't disclose any personal details or anything incriminating about yourself."

"Good rules. But you must have come together somehow?"

"The Donor brought us all together," Minx replied. "He probably does know where we live, but the rest of us certainly don't."

I looked at them both, asking if they knew each other's details. They shook their heads. "It's just a shame that the rules for newcomers are a bit different. You guys seem to know everything about me."

"Not everything," Minx assured.

We lingered around the main entrance until someone left the block in a hurry and didn't check that the door was shut. Karl held the door and Minx and I stepped into the foyer. The floors were dirty, despite the lingering smell of disinfectant - you could feel it in your chest when you breathed in deeply. I saw the door leading to the stairs and the alcove for the lift shaft.

"What floor?" Karl asked.

"Maybe the third," I said. "I'll know when I see it."

Karl and I got in to the lift and Minx took the stairs. It all came back to me; the memories of Michael making me face the corner, stabbing the edge of his blade into the middle of my neck. The lift stopped on Level 3 with a loud shudder and we got out. Minx joined us and we looked around, but it was obvious straight away which flat was Michael's: the one which didn't have a working light above it, an old green door with tarnished brass locks and scuff marks around the walls. I felt sick looking at it and steadied myself against the wall.

"You're sure it's here?" Karl asked.

I nodded. We didn't really have a plan of action, unusual given how organised they had seemed initially as a group. I told Karl that I wanted to be the one who knocked and walked over to the door. I called back to them, "Stay out of sight – I don't know what kind of mood he'll be in."

The pair nodded and dipped out of view. I gave

three loud knocks.

At first I heard nothing, just an emptiness that seemed to occupy the whole floor; there was stillness, like all the residents were in hibernation, buried inside their flats. Then I heard movement, the faint shuffling of something or someone from behind the door. I stepped back. After a while the shuffling stopped and I stood, my heart thumping in my chest, for the best part of a minute, waiting. Then I heard keys and the sound of shuffling grew louder. Suddenly I began to panic – what if Michael kept true to his word? I half expected a sword to be thrust through the letterbox door or a silver dart fired at me as it opened.

Keys turned in the lock. The chain rattled. This was it – Michael was at home. But as the door opened I did not see a man, assertive with silver hair and piercing green eyes staring back at me with contempt, but an elderly lady, perhaps in her early eighties: frail, vulnerable – not even English from the way she spoke with a raspy voice.

"Yes?"

For a moment I didn't know what to say. I just stood there, staring into the glazed expression of a frail looking woman. "I'm looking for Michael?"

"Who dear?" the woman asked politely. Perhaps I had misjudged, got off at the wrong floor, but the flat had the same layout, the same orange and brown wallpaper. It had to be the right place.

"Michael," I said again. "He lives here, or at least I thought he did."

She stared at me and her eyes softened. "Yes, there was a man before me," she said. "But he's not been here in a long time."

"Do you know where I can find him?"

She shook her head. "No dear, but there is some mail for him, I kept it for you just in case he ever came back. Perhaps you want to come inside and have a look?"

I asked her if she was sure and the woman laughed.

"If you were here to mug me, dear, you'd have been in and out by now. I don't think you're that type."

I laughed and followed her into the living room, shutting the door behind us. The locks were all still there, including several large sliding bolts. I hoped that Karl and Minx had heard the conversation and would show some degree of intelligence and wait for me quietly outside whilst I investigated. The smell of the flat was very different, somewhat musty and putrid for want of a better word, like being in an unclean canteen on a piping hot day; the central heating was on full and I felt like removing my coat. I instantly recognised the layout of the living room area and kitchen: the Formica work surfaces, patterned wallpaper and even the wooden table had remained the same; I had sat at it with Michael and drank tea in that very room. It was just how I remembered it, apart from the shelves – they no longer had boxes of keys, or piles of books, or anything for that matter. They were empty. The walls, which had displayed pictures and maps and newspaper cuttings, showed differences in tone and brightness from where they had been removed.

The woman was busy rummaging through a pile of letters and envelopes on the kitchen surface. As she did so I noticed other details about the room. The freezer was still there and the kettle, a faded blue plastic type, remained; but there was no radio, no TV, not even a sofa. It was as if the woman sat on a solitary chair and did nothing all day long. It was certainly no way to see out your last days. I also noticed that the window was sealed shut with gaffer tape. Nothing in this room gave her any sense of identity or any taste of life outside; nothing appeared to give her purpose.

"Here it is, dear," she said, handing me a pile of letters. I flicked through them and read the front of each one. One said Joseph Edwards, the other John O'Connor; most of it was junk mail or promos from banks - cheap mailshots - but there was one letter, handwritten, that made me shiver and I held my breath: FAO John Michaelson.

"This is addressed to me," I said out loud.

The woman continued to hover about me, pottering around like old people do. I then realised that I was sat on the only chair in the room. "I'm sorry, I'm in your seat."

"It's okay, dear," she said. "You won't be here long. Better open it then, just in case the man comes back."

I nodded and opened the letter. It read:

Dear John,

You are a fool to have come to try and find me. If you are reading this then you have learnt nothing. You are the catalyst for all of this mess. If you find my flat empty it is because I have moved on, sought a path of solitude, one where I will not cross paths with the likes of you or any of the liars you now work with.

If you are here on the advice of someone else, then know this: they want you dead and they will kill you. Make no mistake, the beings you are hunting are godless, they are not wired like sane men, they cannot empathise, they cannot reason what is beyond the thirst, and what comes from within the darkest pit of their soul dictates their every move.

Seek the Donor, but beware for you will see a glimpse of the devil.

Michael

I folded the letter up and lay it on the table.

"What does it say, dear?" the woman said. "Is it from your friend?"

I didn't say anything, just nodded reflectively. I looked down at the floor and at the woman's feet. Her shoes were small and her feet seemed to be tightly compacted into them, and her legs were thin and dry; cracked skin and blisters . . . and bloodied beneath thick denier tights. I looked back up at the women, just in time to see her swing a knife at my face.

I held her by the wrist just before she covered me in lacerations, but before I could call for help her other hand suddenly locked around my throat, crushing my windpipe. I looked into the woman's eyes and could see nothing but evil burning down on me, the whites of her eyes glowing as I thrashed about on the chair trying to get up.

"You will never learn," she hissed.

I managed to stand up. My hands gripped her forearms so tightly that all I could feel was solid bone and sinew holding her radius and ulna together as one. Her nails were slowly sinking into my skin and her body clung to me like a limpet on a stormy headland, and I felt her hot breath on my neck and the sweat that poured down it. I found what little courage and strength I had left and used it to charge forward, knocking her off balance, but she countered this by falling back and using my momentum to direct me into a wall. By the time I had rolled back onto my front the woman was at the kitchen draw again, pulling out a meat hammer and throwing it at me. The misconception that this woman had been frail, slow and vulnerable was about to cost me my life. She lunged at me again holding another knife and I batted her hand away, then I moved around her so that when she swung again I could grab her arm and pull her off balance, but not for long.

"Your friend is dead!" she growled. "We took him away and bled him dry."

I continued to parry her blows, hoping that she would lose energy, but she became more agitated which increased her rage and strength. In what little space there was I could do nothing but start to throw objects at her, starting with the kettle - sadly it was empty. I got to the table and pulled it between us. And as she went to go around it I picked up the chair and swung it forcefully at her. It caught her dead in the centre of the back and for the first time since her assault began I saw her buckle. Her bones may have been calcified but they were also light and brittle. I hit her with the chair again, sending her crashing to the ground, and whilst she was down I gave one more downwards blow until she stopped thrashing about and started to twitch intermittently. The chair was now in pieces. I kicked the knife away and quickly ran to the door, signalling for Minx and Karl to come and help me. They came rushing in and locked the door behind them.

"What the fuck!" cried Karl. We watched the old lady writhing on the floor, a pool of blood seeping slowly out of a deep head wound. The veins in her neck were hardening and she was choking, garbling something, her breathing laboured. Minx went close to her as if to help.

"Don't fucking do that!" I screamed at her. "She tried to kill me."

The three of us stood around her and watched the woman die, gasping for air and breaking into involuntary spasms whilst splinters of wood seemed to soak up the blood.

"You need to come clean," spat Karl.

"Read the letter for yourself!" I howled back at him, pointing to the pile of mail. "This shit's fucked up! I should never have come back here looking for answers – he warned me not to. This is all my fault, everything is my fault!" Without thinking I walked over to the kitchen units and started searching. "Do any of you have the capacity to do forensics?"

"John, it's quite fucking obvious how she died!" Karl snarled back at me.

"I'm not talking about her! I think Michael may have been using this place as a base, that he never actually owned the place. We need to tear this place apart."

"Well you can start by putting some fucking gloves on!" he shouted, tossing me a pair of latex disposables.

"John's telling the truth," said Minx calmly, showing Karl the letter, "if it's even from Michael."

"I recognise the handwriting – it's him!" I declared.

"I thought you wanted a forensic point of view," Karl said. "Do you have other stuff of Michael's we don't know about – copies of his handwriting?"

I wavered. I wanted to tell them about the lock up – about the hundreds of diaries and letters he had written, about his final farewell message to me, but I still didn't totally trust them both. "Just believe me for once," I said.

There was nothing much but tea bags and glass jars of dark honey in the cupboards, so I grabbed one, I'm not sure why but I just did. The fridge was dirty and empty of anything but jams, marmalades, dark coloured pickles and lard. The rest of the drawers were full of odds and ends: screws, batteries, tape, measuring ribbons; a jumble of assorted items that had no use to anyone except a crazy old lady perhaps. As we stood and thought about what to do, the chest freezer started wheezing again. Then I remembered Michael's deadly confession, about his fiancé that he claimed to have murdered by accident years before. I stood and stared at the dirty cuboid sat in the corner of the room - and then slowly walked over to it, prepared for the worst. I lifted the lid, noticing that it was packed full of black bin liners and heavily iced over. I struggled and fought to pull one of the packages out. Using a wooden rolling pin as a wedge, bashing away the thick ice, a bag finally snapped free. I lifted it, resting it on the floor; it was heavy, like pulling out a large joint of beef. Slowly I pulled the black plastic off and then collapsed beside it when I saw what it was: a woman's shoulder, freeze dried white skin, the occasional mole, shrivelled up but with clear evidence of where it had been butchered. I had half expected a body, but to be folded neatly, lovingly laid to rest perhaps, not cut into portions.

Minx covered her mouth with her hands. "What the fuck is going on?!"

I couldn't explain. I thought they may have stumbled across death like this before, but they behaved like amateurs, both of them. At that moment I felt incredibly betrayed by Michael, realising that I truly knew nothing about him at all, and then I began to contemplate Michael's warning about the Donor.

"We need to check the bedroom," I said out loud. I looked over at the old woman who had now stopped choking. She was pronounced dead by Karl, who had managed to calm himself somewhat. "We need to refocus and look for clues. I think she was just a messenger. You might want to stand back a little. Soon she's going to combust."

They both looked at me like I was crazy. "It's not a fucking TV show, John!" Karl snapped angrily.

They did not know what I had seen. I carried on towards the bedroom. I had to force the door open. As it burst open the smell assaulted my sinuses. My eyes started watering, and in the haze all I could see were the bedsheets, covered in dried blood stains and ridden with bugs crawling over what looked like faeces or rotten food, it was hard to tell. The carpet appeared to be moving, and I realised that it was either fleas, ants or flies. I quickly slammed the door shut again and checked the toilet next to the bedroom. The basin was putrid, coated in slime, and the toilet was overflowing with shit. I nearly vomited as I pulled the door tightly again.

I heard Karl and Minx arguing in the living room, clearly talking about me. I ran back in and shouted at them both. "We need to leave now! Don't get bitten, there's fucking fleas everywhere. Minx, quickly take some photos. Karl, grab some more of those jars. We need to wipe down what we've touched."

I picked up the letter and tidied up anything else that could incriminate me. Then I opened the front door and started wiping down my prints from the handle. I beckoned the pair to follow me out.

I could hear Minx whimpering and saw that Karl's hands were shaking as I led them down the stairs towards the main door.

We emerged into the fresh air and took long deep breaths. I signalled for them to follow me, to try and look normal and avoid unnecessary attention. Even I didn't know where I was going until I saw a bar two streets away. It was busy inside but it didn't matter. I led them both to a table in the corner and bought us all double shots of brandy and a sweet mixer.

Minx was the first to speak. "Michael could be one of them."

I hadn't wanted to think about it seriously until that point. "We certainly can't rule that out – I'm still not sure what happened back there, but I wasn't prepared for it." I could feel the cut on my neck from where the woman had pushed her nails into my throat, narrowly avoiding any veins.

"We should have thought things through a bit more," Karl added, handing me a small antiseptic wipe and a plaster. He winced as he downed the brandy neatly in one go. "Fuck! She died like she was fucking possessed. I've never seen that – I just . . . I can't stop thinking about her face."

"She was somebody once," I added, "and eventually someone's going to know that she's dead, and we have to get ready for that. There will be cameras."

Karl suggested ringing the Donor for some advice. I was reluctant to, and questioned whether he could be trusted. Minx convinced me otherwise. Karl also affirmed his loyalty to the man with no real name who we knew nothing about. We debated about what we would say, but I felt like I had little choice in the matter. They were part of the cell, I was just a casual add-on hoping to get included, although I had now jeopardised that for sure.

As they made the call, I went to the bar and ordered some neat vodka for us all. When I came back I told them what to do: "Check your legs for bites, and rub this into your shins."

Minx asked me what I had seen in the rest of the flat. I explained to her that there was nothing but death and decay. I was surprised that I hadn't questioned the smell before, but then the doors had been tightly sealed, some with gaffer tape. The sensation of alcohol evaporating on my legs was cooling, but the rest of my body tingled at the thought of being re-infected with parasites.

"I need to see the pictures again," I said. Karl was reluctant to allow Minx to show us what she'd taken on her phone in a public place, but Minx knew that I needed to talk through what had just happened. I think we all did. We started scrolling through the images on the smart-phone, looking for clues.

The woman was lying crooked on her back across the floor, her limbs contorted. Her hands were clenched into a fist and her face was pulled back into a type of pleasurable grimace.

"What are you looking for?" she asked as I zoomed in and out of the frame.

"Anything," I said. "Anything that can help us make sense of this fucking madness." She hadn't taken as many pictures as I'd hoped, but the resolution was good and I was able check details. The flat was practically bare but there were two details that bugged me. Firstly, how she stayed alive on a diet of water and honey, if that's what it was, and how the flat had come to be inhabited solely by her.

"Is there any way to see if the flat is owned by someone else?" I asked.

"I can run some searches on the electoral roll and I'll make enquiries with the council, or rather get my friend to hack in."

"Karl, what can you tell me about honey?"

He looked at me oddly and thought for a while before he spoke. "It's antiseptic . . . a natural source of sugar, made by bees . . . what exactly do you want me to say?"

"We don't have much to go on but-an elderly woman just attacked me with a knife in her home whilst I was reading a letter addressed to me. I'm as confused as you are." I handed him the sample jar. "Do something with it, run some tests, it's all we've got to go on."

"Did you notice the name of any other people on the mail?" Minx asked.

I recounted the names to her and she wrote them down. Once we checked ourselves that we were free of bites, I told Minx to delete the pictures from her phone. "There can be no trace of us visiting that place."

"Too late for that," she said, almost suggesting she knew more than I did about how phones store data.

"We have to think about the CCTV footage in the communal hallway," Karl remarked. I agreed with him, it may be hours, days or even weeks before the body was found, however, if she was an Ant then there might never be a body to be found. We hatched a plan to try and get access to such video. Minx suggested that the Donor could help us with that.

"How confident were you in thinking that you knew Michael?"

"This changes everything." I remember Minx saying, like she had experienced an epiphany. "You're starting to make me believe that he might be part of the whole problem we're trying to deal with?"

"I think it makes perfect sense," I stated. "No one I have met seemed to have a far greater knowledge of the problem we are all investigating. What bothers me the most is the fact that the freezer in his flat is full of body parts, allegedly of his fiancé…"

"How do you know this?"

"Michael confessed . . . he said he kept her preserved, although I don't know what to believe anymore. She was fucking butchered and portioned up. I can't help but think that this is all some greatly engineered lie: a sick game. Every single clue he left me has led to nothing but death and disappointment, and I think it's deliberate – I think he's playing us off one another, trying to keep us apart. And if it's not him then someone else is using him as an instrument against me."

"Against us!" confirmed Karl. "We need to seek advice from the Donor and Jo."

"We need to lay low for a while, stay away from places you'd normally frequent, just in case," cautioned Minx.

I explained to Minx that we needed to agree on a PGP encryption service between the three of us, just to make sure no-one could intercept our communications. She agreed to that and so did Karl, reluctantly. I then told them to make their way from the pub separately, and at different times. I mentioned that I hoped to hear from them again, even though I may have just ruined any chance I had of being part of a team.

Karl left first, leaving Minx and myself drinking another brandy in each other's company.

"How much more did Michael tell you?" Minx asked. I looked at her and knew that she had cottoned on, seen through my lies. "He told me loads of stuff. He gave me all of his diaries, and he wrote to me specifically in a letter giving instructions about how he wanted me to deal with it all - to carry on the fight, to try and make a difference." I finished the last of my brandy. "The problem now is... it just seems like a load of bullshit."

"Why, just because he wasn't where you thought he would be?"

"It's more than that," I explained. "He said he was moving on but that I shouldn't. He said that I should continue his fight."

"Why didn't you tell us this?"

"Because I'm having issues about whom I can trust. My dad's just turned up dead and I find out that none of you guys actually know each other. You're all filling me with confidence."

"I think he's still out there somewhere, John. He could be in real danger."

"Then the woman in the flat must have been lying, because she said Michael was dead, that they had bled him dry. I'm not sure what to believe. There were days when I found him so convincing, and others where I grew frustrated with him; I wanted to punch him, to secretly follow him around and build a clear profile of who he really was, but I didn't, because he struck the fear of God into me. And with good reason, too – he nearly killed me once. He's not a man to underestimate."

"You should leave town," she said out of nowhere. "All of this seems to be coming back to you. That woman looked half dead, like she'd been stuck there waiting for an opportunity to kill you, or Michael. I'm sorry we even went along with the idea of looking for him. I should have been stronger and talked you out of it." Minx deleted the last of the images from her phone and read some text messages. "We should have waited. This is why it might be a good time for you to just disappear. We'll get in touch online when things are ready."

"How will I know that things are ready?" I asked. "What the fuck *is* ready?"

"You'll know when you're ready. At the moment, I don't think you are – I don't think any of us truly are."

I understood what she was saying but I also began to doubt her motives, it felt like I was being put off my crusade against the Ants after everything that had happened.

She left the bar shortly afterwards and I stayed for one more drink.

PAYING THE FERRYMAN

Two days later, the day I had booked to visit my dad at the morgue, I was awoken by the doorbell. It had barely reached half-past seven in the morning. Clambering downstairs I saw another courier's silhouette through the frosted glass of the front door, this time a member of Royal Mail's workforce. I prepared myself for the worst. The courier produced legit documents and I had to electronically sign my name. Then he handed me a letter. The envelope felt expensive, like it had been made of the finest card. As the courier walked away I made a note of the registration number, just in case.

I read the letter over breakfast. It was from an organisation calling themselves the Association of Accountants – the professional body my father had been a member of for many years, or so it claimed. It was sent in condolence at the loss of a 'great man who will be sorely missed by his peers.' There was a number for me to ring, a contact person and an address in Aldwych where the organisation was registered. It all seemed legit, apart from the fact that I had told no-one about my father's death, apart from Karl and Minx.

I showered, got dressed and made my way to the local

morgue at The Whittington Hospital where I could see my father in person for one last time. The letter remained in the back of my mind and I examined it once more on my journey.

There was a small waiting area with a drinks dispenser and boards recommending counselling services as I waited near the main reception. A young porter helped direct me to the morgue, which was a building outside the main hospital area, reached by a ramp and some sharp turns. Inside there was a room where the coroner greeted me and asked me to sign the relevant paperwork before he explained the process of viewing the body.

He left me to gather my thoughts for a couple of minutes and then came back to escort me into the main viewing room. As I was shepherded in I could see a large glass screen, behind it the body of my dad lying under a thick purple pall cover. The coroner shut the door and asked me if I was feeling okay and still wanted to go ahead. I suddenly felt a wave of sickness, realising that my father was inches away from me, stone cold under a layer of fabric. I nodded saying he could pull back the cover whenever he was ready. The coroner was very professional and assured me that everything was going to be okay, he did this while expertly folding the sheet back to reveal the top part of my dad's torso.

I drew breath when I saw his grey, lifeless body lying still but there was something wrong with it straight away. Even the coroner noticed it when he looked over at my father's face; two tarnished silver coins covered each of his eyes.

I remember him apologising profusely, like he had been pranked by an embittered colleague. "I have no idea how they got there," he said, quickly removing them to reveal a pair of sunken grey eyelids. He went to leave the room, clearly agitated that someone had gained access to the room without him knowing in such a short space of time.

"Let me see those coins," I called out to him. "I think

this might be someone trying to send a message to me."

He gave them to me and I studied each one. One was an old ten pence piece, the other a coin from another country. "I'm going to hang on to these," I said.

"If you'd like to file a complaint I will need to see the coins," he explained.

I shook my head and turned my attention back to my father. "It's not your fault. Can I see his hands?"

The coroner rolled back the cloth further and I was able to inspect his hands closely, moving in front of the screen which I wasn't really supposed to do but given the incident I didn't think it mattered. Both hands were finely manicured and there was no sign of cuts or bruising to the arms or wrists, which ruled out the idea that my dad had been brought to his place of demise under duress. I checked his face, lips, and even looked over and through his hair. In fact, I showed little sympathy or respect for someone who had lost a father, rather I must have looked like a fraudster looking for clues, about to whisper 'where did you hide all the money?'. I found what I was looking for on his neck, a small bruise just behind the left ear – you could be forgiven for thinking it was an old burn mark or a birth defect. Lower down the back of the neck was a small horizontal cut which could have been used to draw blood. It was enough to convince me that my dad was involved with the Ants in some way, and that his death was certainly foul play. At that moment I decided that a visit to the flat where he had died was again top of the agenda. I had to begin my own investigation into why he went there, and perhaps find a way to close this loop once and for all.

"I'm sorry," I whispered softly in his ear. I placed my hand on his cold forehead and reflected on many lost years in silence, and then I told the coroner that I was ready to leave. He rolled the pall cloth back up and escorted me out of the room.

I walked back through the main hospital. I was so

angry that my life continued along this dark meandering path; I saw no end in sight. Even in death my dad had offered me no sense of closure. Michael's letter was right – I was being taken to the brink of madness. What I was experiencing was part of a string of events inevitably leading to something much more sinister that I couldn't even begin to comprehend or explain.

The two coins were tapping together in my jacket pocket whilst an image of the burn mark behind my dad's ear lingered in the back of my mind. I contemplated whether it could have always been there, that I had simply never paid him enough attention to notice any birth marks or scars. The crux of it all was that I still didn't know my father any better, even in death.

Before I left the hospital I passed the chaplain's office. Normally I would never have thought about stopping to read the notices, but instead I found myself looking at the pictures of the volunteers who gave up their time to work in such a place, full of misery and suffering. The photos were poorly taken, and printed on black and white copy paper, but I felt paralysed, like my body was subconsciously seeking spiritual nourishment. I looked at the main door to the chapel to see that it was closed; however when I turned to start walking again, a short, elderly lady was staring up at me. I jumped, because I didn't see her coming from anywhere, and after my encounter in Michael's flat I was now extra cautious of anyone older than sixty.

"Are you okay?" she asked.

I nodded, smiling back at her. She spoke with a delicate Irish accent and her eyes were kind and sincere. She brushed past me and opened up the chapel. I turned and watched her.

"You look like you've had a busy morning. I'm about to have a coffee, would you like to join me?"

How could I refuse? I nodded and followed her into the chapel and towards a small office where she went to fill up a kettle. I asked for her name. She introduced herself as Sister Eileen. When it was clear that she was from the Roman Catholic Church I explained to her that I did not belong to any denomination, or any religion as such, and that I didn't want to waste her time. She laughed and explained that it was fine, that I didn't need to be religious in order to grieve for a loved one, and that God was compassionate and cared more about having relationships with us.

I hadn't told her I was grieving, which made me even more intrigued. Before long I was sat on a church pew, a cup of hot coffee in my hand and a shortbread biscuit, recounting to her in detail what had happened, months of cathartic anger slowly being released. "Is this confession, what I'm doing now?" I asked.

She shook her head and smiled. "The Lord knows what's in our heart, and he understands our intentions, and he knows what your soul needs," she said. "You might think you're a bad person, John, but you are still a child in His eyes and he loves you. Forgiveness is not reserved for the righteous."

I explained that I was not seeking redemption and that I deserved punishment for my actions. I was seeking guidance; I didn't know where to go.

"The two are linked together. People drift away from God all the time because the path is narrow and the wider roads seem much more appealing. We can sometimes see the path to redemption but the route there often means we are asked to risk everything and turn away from what we know. Death merely reminds us of our mortality, and that we still have time to seek forgiveness and change direction. Above all, His love is unconditional and comes freely to those who seek him."

I can't fully remember how long we talked for, or what exactly she said to me; what I do know is that it was one of the best coffees and chats I'd had in years, and I didn't want it to end. She did things I didn't ask her to do, like reassure me that my actions were rational, she challenged my dark mind-set without even asking about my past, and she prayed that I would trust God and lay my burdens upon him. Above all, meeting with her made me realise just how lost I was in a material world, and how man's biggest sin was to pretend that he could make it through life without any help.

From that moment I started to understand my own limitations. But despite her assurance, and prayer, I knew that I could not sincerely ask for forgiveness until I had avenged those dear to me. I was too proud. But I guess God knew that, too. What helped was knowing that I was broken just like everyone else and could turn to him in my darkest hours.

She prayed for me before I left and I felt like my soul had been nourished. There is still a long way to go before my heart is healthy and full of love and kindness and compassion, but I left the hospital with something I had been missing in a long time.

Hope.

BACK INTO THE FURNACE

I got home and dug out the address the police officers had given me relating to my father's final whereabouts. Minx had emailed me some information by this point, warning me that I was dealing with a group who ran several brothels and escort services out of posh one bedroom flats in and around London. They were not, as she described, the most dangerous type of criminal gang, but they had enough contacts to make life difficult should I continue to be reckless. I kept the coins retrieved from my dead dad's eyes in my pocket, grabbed some cash and ran out of the door.

As I travelled on the bus, I kept thinking about how at peace my dad had looked. It made me jealous. I questioned whether they had really found him like that or whether his face had been contorted in fear, and that the people at the mortuary had somehow taken hours to fix his expression to look content. Either way, the fact that his eyes were covered in coins was significant. In olden day England, it was common for people who worked in accountancy (or any job as it happens) to have two coins placed over their eyes so that they could bribe their way safely into the next world. I had robbed him of that privilege.

Islington was relatively busy when I arrived that evening. Buses and cabs continued to stream across the main road and coffee shops and restaurants were swelling up with punters eager to chat and flirt and get pissed. On my way to the apartment I had passed several phone boxes, many of which were starting to get plastered with adverts offering hotel visits or a massage from a 'new girl in town', this accompanied stock images of girls bent over in a particular fashion so that the numbers conveniently covered their private parts. It was prime hunting ground for any man looking for a quick release and there was certainly no shortage of choice it seemed. All the ghouls came out at night, even in trendy Islington.

I got to the flat and surveyed the immediate area, looking for any signs of danger: men loitering or patrolling a particular stretch of road in pairs, alleyways leading to dead ends and possibly death, gargoyles ... in truth, I didn't know what to look for anymore. I laugh as I write this because I feel that many of these signs occur on every busy street corner in London. However, you have to remember that I was meddling with organised gangs of criminals. I just needed to be bolder and trust my instincts.

I found the address and pressed the buzzer firmly for about five seconds. There was no one looking over my shoulder as I heard the door buzz open. I was let in without anyone asking for verification. The flat was on the top floor and the communal stairs were narrow but in relatively good condition compared to some apartments I had visited during Michael's wild goose chase era.

I came to a door and held my breath as I knocked on it gently. A young Asian girl answered. She was wearing a blue, thick-knitted cardigan and designer black thick-rimmed glasses. She didn't look like a working girl, yet she beckoned me inside without batting an eyelid and led me into a room. It was kept tidy with a double bed, clean towels (rolled up) and warm lighting; it was certainly one of the more high-class establishments I had been to during my investigations. I pondered whether the very room I was sat waiting in was the one my dad had died in. I heard footsteps approach.

I made sure I kept my head down, staring at the floor as the door opened, realising that the woman entering the room was very likely to be the woman my dad had paid to visit. I felt a sudden chill along my spine, a dreadful premonition that history was about to repeat itself. And when the door closed and I looked up, I knew that my own dark history had come back to haunt me.

She stood there looking at me, her skin olive brown and fragrant with jasmine oil. For a second she didn't recognise me, but then it must have dawned on her who I was and the welcoming smile suddenly disappeared. Cha-Cha, as she had called herself when we last met, was stood in a silk dressing gown, ready to de-robe after negotiating her fee. We stared at each other in silence. I anticipated her running out of the door and screaming for help, but she did not. She did not move. She did nothing. I stood up, unsure whether I should be the one running or whether I should try and convince her to stay with me and have a conversation about what happened some time ago in Crouch End.

"Do you remember me?" I asked her.

She didn't say anything, just nodded her head and continued to stare at me with those deep brown eyes.

"Please tell me what you remember."

She edged towards the door, her fingers gripping the handle. "You were a man who came to sauna that night. I saw you and I thought nice boy, we have nice time ... but then you do bad thing to me. You bad man," she said pointing at me.

I nodded. "Yes, I was a very bad man, back then. I'm very sorry for what I did ... but you're still alive." I tried my best to sound sincere and soothing, and even as I spoke those words I realised that I was somehow on the cusp of closure to the pain that had stayed with me for over a year. "I need to know – *you* need to tell me. What happened afterwards?"

"Cannot," she said shaking her head. "They say must never tell."

I found myself in a silent stand-off with Cha-Cha, plotting my next move and set of words carefully. I couldn't help but recount my time with her, recalling how proud I had been to have chosen her, and then I remembered the horror of what I did, how I casually left her for dead. She had every right to be angry with me, petrified even. I thought back to my last conversation with Ed, how he had goaded me, mentioning her name to me; I knew that she was somehow connected to them and therefore connected to my father's death. But I had to remain objective and not focus solely on her for my own personal redemption. My dad had died there only the previous week and I needed answers.

My only advantage over her, if you can call it that, was that she believed I was still bad at heart, and that I had the capacity to bring more misery upon her life. I slipped back into character.

I pulled out some cash, threw it on the bed and ordered her to sit down. "I want the truth."

"I don't want your money," she said.

"A man came here last week and died. I want to know how he died."

She started laughing. I couldn't tell whether it was nerves or if she was genuinely trying to provoke a reaction; it worked, the sight of her tittering at my loss sent me into a wild rage. I strode purposefully towards her. She cowered in the corner as I stood over her. I hissed at her to sit down and speak to me properly. I resisted from touching her, despite my hand hovering around her neck. Seconds later she did as I asked.

"I am very sorry for what I did to you," I explained. "But the same thing happened to me, by bad people, and now the same people are manipulating you. If you tell me the truth I can give you a way out of this life."

I wasn't sure how I would do that, but I was confident that Minx and Karl might be able to think of ways to help her if she was indeed still infected.

"You are a bad man, John," she said calmly. "They tell me you are a vampire, that you hunt girls."

I found myself laughing nervously. "That's a lie."

"They say your father was the original type, that he had a taste for girls – all types."

"What do you mean original type?"

"Man like vampire, they said he was before you, they said he worse than you."

I struggled to make sense of her Pidgin English, having to reorganise every word in my mind as she stop-started between words, utterances and phrases. I couldn't tell whether she was recounting a script or being genuine.

"They said he was coming for me and that I needed to be ready."

"Go on."

"They say to me 'be prepared', that if I not . . . he would kill me."

"He would not have put a finger on you!" I snapped. "He was an old man – they lured him here so you could kill him so that I could suffer and then come and kill you." I thought to myself as I said it how much of a genius plan it was.

Then she said, "I did not kill him."

I turned and punched the wardrobe in frustration, leaving a dent in the thin veneer. My body shook with anger, at being toyed with, led from place to place, and pulled along some lonely twisted narrative that had no logical end.

"And now what?" I asked. "When they told you I would come here, what did they say for you to do?"

She was silent for a while, looking down at the floor. "They said you are not brave enough to come back here, but if you did that I should thank you . . . for my gift."

I tried not to react further. It was an excellent script and it was obvious that they wanted her dead, killed by my hands. I realised then that I had touched too many things, left too many trails in my years to just continually leave a path or destruction without repercussion. I had toiled in my head for weeks, even months, about what I had done to Cha-Cha. In the end I had convinced myself that it was just a bad dream, a hallucination induced by a combination of factors: depression, parasites, medication, alcohol, stress, food poisoning – an unlucky combination of the all of them resulting in a drug induced visit to a brothel. And then I confronted Ed and he mocked me. He said I had changed her, but I refused to believe it until now.

I sat down beside her, gently reached across and touched her hair, pulling it up away from her neck. And then I saw it, clear as day, a mottled scar from where I had broken the skin and passed on the infection back in that darkened room of misery. Ed suggested that she had been used to strengthen their organisation. He said she was grateful for her gift, and now here I was, finally face to face with her again, listening to a set of rehearsed lines.

"When will they stop?"

She stared at me. Her deep brown eyes were so alluring; I could have spent the afternoon just looking into them and apologising for my actions, but I realised it would make no difference. Stripped of her dignity, she was just a pawn in the wider scheme of things and I needed to toughen my heart and use her to my advantage.

"They will stop when you can be taken alone, and they can kill you without re . . ."

She struggled to find the word, or remember it, but I had a good enough idea. "And what about you? What do they plan to do with you if you succeed?"

She shook her head. "They say that if I deliver

message to you that they will let me go."

"Just like that? No repercussions."

She nodded.

"You best give me the message then."

She thought for a moment and then continued speaking. "You must leave London and never return."

"That's it?"

She nodded again, bowing her head to the floor. "Please do it so that they can release me. I don't want to die."

I felt incredible guilt. I had given her no gift, nothing but an extended death sentence. I wished I had bitten a bit deeper, perhaps twisted her neck a bit harder or held her under the water for longer, maybe even checked her pulse more thoroughly before running off like a coward. She was at the sauna by circumstance because of men like me. I realised that I had no vial to take a sample of her blood to be tested and I knew nothing more of her to help in my investigation: her background, ethnicity, age; all I knew was that she was a commodity in the sex industry, sponsored by vampirism. What saddened me the most was that I knew - and she must have known also - that she would eventually die at their hands whether she delivered the message or not. She would serve her purpose and be done with. She would never be set free. And I had come to another dead end in my investigation.

"Where did they take you after I bit you?"

She was shaking, pulling her arms against her chest, visibly uncomfortable with my probing. "I wake up in room – have no window – and I call for help. Room is dark but very warm. I follow light and see them."

"See whom?"

"People naked, they are waiting for something and then they see me." Cha Cha held out her wrist and showed me the scars on each one, like they had been chewed and mangled by something quite hideous. "I bleed a lot and I am screaming, then after they leave me, and nice man come to put bandage on. This happening for long time - many days. Then one day, man sit with me, he speaking to me and say I am like them now and bring girl." She started shivering. "I'm told to be like them or I never see my friends and family again. So I become like them, and drink blood of girl until she is not moving."

I was revolted by what she told me and I thought of Alissa. My guilt was now intoxicating. I tried to convince myself that I did not feed from her or bring the girl to them, but also I could not help but consider that this shadowy group was perhaps known to me already and that I had crossed their path before.

Suddenly I assessed my own situation, like I had been given a shot of adrenaline. I was trapped. It was a perfect ploy – kill my dad in a brothel, send the police round and give me motivation to visit the address and exact revenge; perfectly stupid of me to come along alone. I had considered what the implications would be if I were to beat Cha-Cha to death with my bare hands in reprisal for my dad's demise, but I felt no anger towards her, only remorse and pity, for this trafficked woman had been abused by men at all levels and in all parts of society, months before me, riding on a conveyor belt of misery which would lead only to an early grave.

"You should go and seek help," I told her. "Come with me now and that'll be the end of it. I'll take you straight to a police station. We'll find you help and we'll get you out of this mess. Tell them what you know and I'll do the same, we can both wipe the slate clean and make a fresh start."

I was serious, prepared to put my life on the line to try and break the vicious cycle, I wanted forgiveness and a new beginning, but she simply shook her head.

"Cannot," she said. "Make very bad thing happen. Have family."

At that moment in time I knew that whatever choice I made I would have to live with the decision for the rest of my life. It meant going with my heart. So I left. I simply walked away. I got up and I left the room without saying anything else. I exited the flat, walked down the stairs and didn't look back. I felt like I was always one step behind the Ants and I knew that I needed to find a way to level the playing field. Killing Cha-Cha or even turning myself in, or waiting for an attack to occur in the flat, was not going to yield any guaranteed justice or resolve the physical or social problem we were both in – it would merely prolong my misery and that of many others like her.

As long as the Ants still operated in London, there was good chance that I could work tirelessly to bring them down with the help of people like the Donor and Minx if they still wanted to work with me. I had to hold onto that idea and I prayed that I had not ruined everything.

I ordered a cab from the main street and sat in silence all the way home. We hit every type of traffic jam, diversion and red light imaginable, but it didn't' bother me. I was over it. I was done with the city.

I wouldn't find my answers here.

FUNERAL FRIENDS

On the morning of my father's cremation, I didn't quite know what to do with myself. I had no other family to grieve with; I had never had experience of grieving, for when my mum died I was too young. I was born in to grief. I had no extended family that I knew of. My dad was a private man with his own private agenda, and any work friends he had entertained over the years had either moved on since his retirement or passed away. Only now, in death, did I begin to question this normality I had lived in for over thirty years.

An estate agent was due to arrive at my home later that day as I had made the conscious decision to begin marketing the property for sale and start a new life. The Donor and Karl had not gotten back to me since the incident at Michael's flat and I felt strongly like I didn't want to be a part of the life I had been living anymore – the cons far outweighed any pros there may have been. Besides, I had no need for such space and luxuriances, much preferring the practicality and safety of a flat in a secure estate somewhere else.

I wanted to be totally anonymous and have a fresh start – no trails. That was my intention.

The agent, a very posh sounding man called David, had called me that morning, saying he was very excited to be coming to value my home. I explained that I was on my way to a funeral and he apologised profusely, but I could still detect genuine excitement in his voice; the house would probably sell in a matter of days for the full asking price.

I left the house and walked to the main road where I caught a bus to East Finchley, to the cemetery where there would be a service followed by the cremation.

It had rained intermittently for most of that day but there was a very apt break in the clouds as I stood over the spot where dad could be remembered, now represented by a small plaque with his name and dates of his birth and death. I spent minutes simply staring at it.

I thought of nothing. Perhaps it was the cold wind that made me numb, or it was the realisation that I had no feelings, no emotions - no real sense of purpose any more. I was a man so absorbed in my own self-pity that I didn't stop to notice others around me, including the men who approached me.

"John?" a voice called.

I turned round to see three men. One was notably older than the other two: a short, stocky man dressed in a very expensive looking Valentino suit, vintage I thought, with a heavy, black woollen jacket draped over his shoulders like a cape; I watched it skim across the gravestones as he walked towards me. His face had patches of dark brown across it, not tanned but mottled, like it were the result of skin damage or some type of chemical reaction; his hair was grey with streaks of black and he wore thick-rimmed designer spectacles. The other two men were clones of each other: short haired brutes dressed in blue nylon suits and caked in heavy silver jewellery.

"Do I know you?" I replied.

"Not at all, I was a friend of your father." The man extended his hand. I took it and he gripped my arm firmly. His hands were warm and as he spoke I could almost feel his breath coat me in a glaze of mistrust. "He was also one of my best employees, back in the day."

I suddenly recognised the voice. It sounded more natural, less disguised than before. "So, you're an accountant?"

"Was," he said, letting go of my hands. That's when I noticed the thick gold ring with an eagle emblem on a sun. "Your father and I kept in touch, and he was a member at the old accountants club down in the Strand."

I nodded. "Yes, I got your letter. Thank you. He never mentioned any of his friends to me," I said. "You didn't give me your name."

"Gabriel," he said. "My friends call me Gabe."

I just looked at them all, trying to piece together how they would have known about the day of my dad's cremation. I had to ask.

"Word got back to me," he said. "I made some enquiries and thought I would come here directly to pay my respects. I didn't know that you would be here. He didn't . . ." his voice trailed off.

"He didn't what, talk about me much?"

He smiled. "Of course he did, he just didn't mention that you were living back home with him."

"When was the last time you saw him?" I asked.

Gabriel casually replied, "About two months ago. Why do you ask?"

"Did you learn about how he died?"

He shook his head. "I imagine it was from natural causes or some kind of stroke perhaps." I stared coldly at his grey-blue eyes and knew that he was hiding something. "I also lost someone very dear to me recently," he continued. "She was a dear friend, her life unexpectedly extinguished."

At that moment I knew who I was talking to:

Rameses, the man from the party who had led the ritualistic killing of Alissa. Him being there at the cemetery with me was no coincidence.

"What if I told you differently," I said. "What if I told you that my dad's time on earth came to an unnatural end, what would you say to that?"

"Well, I imagine the police would have been involved," he said. "Have they suggested foul play?"

I love the term foul play; it's so very English in its roots and villainy. The whole situation was indeed becoming foul. "For some reason the police weren't interested. I think it's because they don't fully understand what they're dealing with. And in the case of my father, they didn't really need to go beyond what they saw. You see, I knew my father and I knew the type of lifestyle that he secretly led, despite what he thought I knew. His taste in young, foreign women eventually got the better of him. And as for the people orchestrating it all, they're going to be in for a shock, because they probably think that's the end of it."

Gabriel paused, almost unsure. For a moment I questioned whether I had misjudged him. Perhaps he wasn't Rameses and I had just slandered my father, his old friend, over a sacred place. "But it's not, is it?" Gabriel said eventually, almost at a whisper. "It's far from over, John. And I must tell you this: you've got your father all wrong, you really have. You could have learnt so much from him if you'd just followed in his footsteps."

The din of traffic noise seemed to die away and the wind dropped as he spoke again, this time with a bit more malice in his voice for dramatic effect. "Your father was a member of our club, and that's a lifetime membership, not something you can just stop being a part of. We came today to honour him, not to look unkindly at his life, John. You need to show your elders some respect."

I felt like I was back at school about to get a good beating from the headmaster for speaking my mind and challenging authority. "Let's honour him then," I said. "Let's remember him as a kind, generous man, and I'll do my best to follow in his footsteps."

Gabriel smiled at me. "That's more like it, John. Be generous and receive your gift willingly, even though you may have strayed far from the path." Gabriel looked at his two henchmen. "It would be nice to catch up properly at some point, John. We'd love to invite you for a drink at our club, or maybe we can pop round one evening to lend a hand?"

"I'd like to visit the club you mention. I'd love to see some of my father's old haunts."

"I'll make sure you get the full VIP treatment, no expense spared." He pulled out a card and gave it to me. His job title was written in silver stencilling across the bone coloured card: consultant; and not much else, just a number that didn't look like a standard mobile – six digits, just like Veronica's. "I'll wait for your call, John." He smiled and then walked away.

I watched him descend the mount, down towards a silver Bentley parked on the verge some 100 yards away. I didn't get a number plate, but it was hardly a conspicuous model of car, and I had a new card with a new number. It was a start, but a start to what?

I quietly prayed to myself as I said my final farewell, hoping that my father would offer me some useful guidance for the rest of this life and not keep it all a secret, withholding it for the next. Gabriel's visit to the cemetery, as sacred as it may sound, had me spooked. I had already identified several flaws in his story; there was no way of knowing about my father's death other than him actually being there or being connected to it in some way, of that I was definite.

I travelled back to my house by cab and asked the driver to take the longer route, accessing my road from the end I didn't normally drive past. There were a few cars parked on the road which I didn't recognise and in one of the vehicles I saw a man, one of the henchmen who had been flanking Gabriel at the cemetery – I was sure. Things were progressing much quicker than expected. I started to panic, wanting to turn the cab around. Gabriel hadn't come to pay respects but identify a target.

After paying the cab driver, I found myself running up the path to the front door of my house when a voice called out behind me. I froze and turned round to see a smartly dressed man bounding up the steps behind me. It was the estate agent, David. I caught my breath and shook his hand, apologising for running so wildly, before leading him to my door, only to find it had already been unlocked. I pretended not to notice, I was just glad I had someone with me.

There was something definitely not right about the house. The back door had also been left ajar and windows and drawers had been left opened in the study. I hung about each doorway nervously whilst I pondered what to do. The estate agent, paying me a dozen compliments using all the superlatives from his property sales repertoire, stood there hoping for a tour of the house.

"It's a little messy," I explained.

My bedroom had been visited and I could see that journals had been removed; scraps of paper had been torn out and crumpled on the floor. A silver dagger had also been forcefully driven into my bedside table with my name etched on the note beneath it. I subtly took the knife and the card and placed it in my jacket pocket. My laptop was still in the room but it had moved from the floor to the desk, and it was left on; several files had been accessed and my internet history had been left open. My dad's room had also been visited, and pictures had been taken away and added; in particular there was one of a woman I did not recognise, and one of Karl. I started to shake – it was fucking nuts! At that point I wanted the man to leave so that I could get my head around what was happening but I also realised that I needed him there with me: my life depended on it. More importantly, I needed to make a decision within the hour on whether I stayed in the house or left for good.

Before joining him in the living room, I checked the kitchen and looked in the fridge, half expecting another hand or a limb to be cut up and served on a platter, or to find the freezer full of body parts like there had been at Michael's flat – thankfully there was none but I decided I couldn't eat a thing; in the study my dad's book shelves had also been reorganised: books had been swapped about on shelves, Sharpie markers and pens were used to write symbols and crescent moons on the spines, and several post-it notes saying 'finish the job' were written in red ink and plastered across the computer monitor. I felt cold and numb and I nearly keeled over with a terrible stabbing pain in my chest from all the stress. I must have stumbled because the agent called out and asked me if I was okay. I laughed after a few painful seconds of controlling my breathing, explaining that I had been suffering from trapped wind. He mentioned that he was ready to talk valuations.

We sat in the living room and he gave me some comparable data of previous sold prices in the area. I looked at the sheet he had printed out for me and then stared out of the window, and that's when I noticed the other man from the cemetery patrolling the street like a lion. Fuck. Nothing the agent was telling me was going in – his voice was a muffled sequence of words strung together between small air pops.

"Can you give me ten minutes just to check on a few things before we continue?" I asked. "Perhaps you can get all the paperwork together. Something urgent has come up and I don't want to take up too much of your time."

He stammered for a bit before checking through his folder, then nodded to confirm that he could put together the terms and conditions I would need to sign.

I ran back up to my bedroom to check my

belongings. In a compartment only I knew about I retrieved my passport and a roll of cash, approximately £5000. I also took several pre-paid bank cards and the pins. My own diary was also in there and I quickly bundled them all into some hand luggage.

My laptop was next, although I wasn't sure what had been done to it. I was thankful that Minx had explained file encryption, PGP messaging and Tor browsing, but I had to assume that my laptop had been compromised so I plugged it in and set it up on the floor out of site in the hope that I could remotely access it and delete the rest of the files when I got a chance. Next I grabbed a suitcase and chucked in essentials: trousers, pants, socks, t-shirts, a few toiletries to use, the knife I had placed in my pocket. I would have to buy the rest of the essentials when I got to my destination, wherever that was going to be.

Within ten minutes I had returned to the ground floor with a small piece of hand luggage and a medium sized suitcase. I now realised that the timing of the estate agent's arrival was a blessing in disguise and I saw an opportunity to make the situation work in my favour, in both our favours, even if it meant not being able to negotiate half a percent off the sales fee.

I played it cool. David had prepared everything neatly and we chatted about the house and my situation regarding deeds, etc. I assured him it would be fine and then mentioned that I was considering getting a few agents to come and visit the house. We discussed valuation figures and I got the sole agency commission I wanted. I was satisfied that he would find a buyer for the house whilst I was out of the country. I went to get him a set of keys and everything seemed good to go. He thanked me and went to leave but I asked him for a favour: a lift into town so that I could catch a train. I worded it so that he couldn't decline my offer, especially when I mentioned that I had a sick relative to visit urgently.

I locked up, followed him out of the door and

towards his car. Sure enough, one of the henchmen was standing beside a tree some fifty yards away watching us. I cockily waved at him before getting in the car.

The chase was back on.

David drove me to his offices in Archway. I told him I would ring him for an update and explained that email was the best method to contact me on over the next couple of weeks. I quickly gathered my bags out of his car, thanked him and then entered the tube at Archway.

From looking at the underground map I concluded that I would be at Heathrow within 90 minutes. It felt like one of the longest journeys of my life. I was being set loose into the world, hunted by the Ants that had suddenly come out of hibernation to tie up loose ends, namely me. I had Gabriel's face in my mind, or should I refer to him as Rameses? I recall his words, telling me that I would get the full VIP treatment if I ever met him again, and I remember the look of his brutish henchmen, doing their best to intimidate me as they paraded outside of my house. I thought of Minx and Karl, what we had experienced at Michael's old flat days before. I also thought about Jo and The Donor, how they wouldn't be able to help me follow the incident up - because I was running. For the first time in months I was running scared again.

London had suddenly become the smallest place on earth and I felt like I had nowhere to hide.

On arriving at the airport I scouted the ticket desks and thought about where I would like to go. TAP airways to Brazil perhaps? BA to LA? Sodomy in the UAE courtesy of Emirates? Then I saw the desk for Royal Thai Airways and didn't think twice about it. I managed to negotiate a ticket to Bangkok and after parting with close to £400 found myself transitioning through security and sitting in a bar waiting for my flight to board.

On reflection, what I was doing was the type of thing I had always wanted to do – to be spontaneous, to be carefree, to go on an adventure and do some much needed island hopping, stuff I had chosen to miss out on after graduating because I had followed the expectations of society, choosing to enter the corporate world of work and explore the monotony of routine instead of developing character and experiencing new cultures.

When my flight number was called to start boarding at the gate I breathed a tiny sigh of relief, for I genuinely believed that the Ants would have no way of finding me.

The threat of death had all but disappeared and I was genuinely excited about what I might find.

Courage.

SHORE LEAVE

Dad was dead, the house was up for sale, and I had a passport with less than a year left on it.

I could not remember the last time I took a holiday. The closest thing I could remember was a weekend away in Barcelona with Claudia some years ago. I only remember it clearly because I found Barcelona to be a hive of misery much like London. When I had been there it was full of stag parties and whorists trailing the many girly bars, looking to line the pimp's pockets with Euros; con artists and street criminals would stand about and target ex-pats who looked like they had money; and taxi drivers had meters that could double or treble your fare based on what mood they were in or if you spoke any Spanish. I didn't like Spain – just to be clear.

Yet here I was, on my way to somewhere cheerier: the land of smiles, where I could perhaps start afresh. I told no-one about my intention to leave, despite having a meeting lined up with the Donor and Minx days after my dad's funeral. Things had got too risky in my opinion and the visit from Gabriel and his men had riled me somewhat. It just felt like the right thing to do and I wanted to be selfish and indulgent because I knew that there might not be another opportunity to do so.

For most of the flight I drank alcohol and continuously grazed; my mind in a hyperactive state. In between short naps I would look up at the TV screen to see the plane's pixelated emblem on a satellite map; it took forever to cross the Middle-East, the melting pot for much of the world's anger.

Before landing I slipped into another dream. It was not pleasant: my vision included several people in my life, all of them dead. I was sat at a large mahogany, oval table in a grand dining room and people's heads were set on plates, each one turned towards me and each with hollow eyes. The heads included my dad, Alissa, Cha-Cha and Michael, the man who I thought had saved me. Karl appeared in my dream dressed as a waiter and he was sorry to announce that there were problems with my blood test and the chef had not been honest with me about what I had been eating, and then Gabriel entered the room wearing his Egyptian gold mask and ordered the banquet to begin. As I sat, thinking about ways to kill Gabriel, various fayre would be brought to us: steaks, salads, and carafes of red wine; and then stranger dishes, large pickles, snakes heads, beetle shells, and then the body parts arrived, each one branded with different tattoos. I woke from the dream in a startled state after someone forced me to chew on some sinewy elbow. Standing above me was a flight attendant, politely informing me that we were about to begin our descent and that my chair needed to be moved forward.

I had read across online forums that people's experiences of Bangkok was a bit like Marmite: you either loved it or loathed it. The airport was large and surprisingly calm and I had no problems going through immigration and collecting my luggage, but when I entered the arrivals lounge I found myself greeted by dozens of smiling faces, goading me to take a taxi with them. I headed straight for a taxi kiosk away from the crowd (that's what I had read to do) and ordered a ride straight to the Sheraton hotel; my dad had once boasted that they provided one of the best breakfasts he'd ever had and amazing views of the Chao Phraya River.

A quiet and friendly man led me to a Mercedez parked outside the terminal and handed a ticket to the driver. It was customary for those giving service to put their hands together and say 'Kup khun Krap'. I tipped him after he did so and got into the car.

I was driven into a sprawling metropolis, much bigger than the one I had left behind. There were stark contrasts between the decadent luxury apartments and the confined, makeshift homes with corrugated roofs that stole their electricity from the wild nests of black wires, spun back and forth across the roads like a web. The driver spoke very little English so I was spared the painful small talk that often occurs back in England and I was grateful he didn't mention anything to do with football. I did my best to enjoy the ride, giving thanks to God that I had managed to escape London in one piece.

The hotel was amazing, and shamefully decadent; after three nights of sleeping, eating, swimming and massage I felt totally revitalised. I was sat in the bar one evening drinking cocktails when I decided to check my emails for any updates. The estate agent had confirmed that a photographer had taken pictures and that the listing was now live, and that there had been considerable interest already. I saw the images online and the house looked like how I had left it, albeit slightly tidier for the purpose of pictures. I knew that things moved quickly in the capital and that the house would sell relatively quickly. I was on an automatic six week visa and I would have to return at some point to complete all the legal work involved in wills, etc. I just didn't want to face it – not yet.

Minx had also sent me a message asking me how I was. I replied securely so that my IP origination would remain hidden and explained to her that things had gotten too dangerous for me to stay in London. I detailed what had happened, and then hinted that I was abroad until I could work out a solution. I trusted Minx to look out for me, but I didn't tell her where I was. I felt safer if no-one knew.

It was whilst traipsing through one of Bangkok's many hectic shopping centres that I came across a small tourist agency advertising trips towards the South of Thailand. Images of pristine islands were appealing to me and the girl running the stall greeted me courteously and spoke good English. I asked her about destinations that were worth a visit and she explained that Krabi and Koh Samui were very popular with English tourists, but I asked for somewhere even quieter, a real low-key destination where I could totally get away from western society. She nodded and pulled out a map, pointing out a sprinkling of islands on the Thai/Malaysia border, saying they had largely been untouched by the tsunami of 2004 and home to a thriving fishing community populated largely by sea gypsies. I liked the idea instantly and asked about getting there. Within twenty minutes she had arranged a private car to collect me from the hotel (no passport details needed, we agreed a cash price) and she mentioned that she would put together an itinerary of things that I could do on the trip down. Effectively the driver would become my guide for the next few days.

I returned to the hotel in a somewhat jubilant mood, optimistic at the thought of finally being a free-spirited nomad. Michael's money was going to be put to better use, for relaxation rather than plotting an underground war against rich and powerful groups in London.

After packing my belongings, I had one final meal by the river before retiring to a computer screen in the hotel lobby and checking my emails for the last time. I was surprised to read that I had received three offers on the house already; some had even gone into bidding wars. The agent had given me the breakdown of each buyer and advised me which one seemed the best bet. I imagined that he would get a cash bonus from the winning buyer. But I knew the sale couldn't happen without sorting out deeds and transfer of ownership forms, and I didn't want the pressure so I explained that the buyer would have to be prepared to wait.

There was also a reply from Minx. She was glad I had left the country and was feeling safe; she also mentioned that she had informed the Donor on my behalf about the increase in activity. She also wished me well in Thailand (how she knew I knew not) and said I should completely drop off the grid because she was able to somehow link me to a computer in Bangkok. That freaked me out a little and I wished I had brought my own laptop after all.

The next morning I checked out of the hotel and found my driver waiting for me in the lobby. My driver/guide was the young lady from the shopping mall. We had a short stand-off before I found myself smiling at her. It turns out that many of the small shops in the MBK centre are independently run. Daisy, the English sounding name she gave to herself, was to be my driver and guide for the next few days. I loaded my bags into the back of a rented 4x4 and got in. The car had leather seats, aircon and plenty of leg room, so I was happy to be in her company. Her English was good and I was confident that she would be able to suggest good places for me to go and help me avoid any problems we might encounter.

The journey was long and it took over an hour just to leave Bangkok because of the heavy traffic. For most of the journey we drove past some wonderful scenery and intermittent rural snapshots of Thailand: padi fields, plantations, small villages, all packed full of moped riding inhabitants, and the occasional signpost to a resort or industrial powerhouse. We would stop every now and then so that I could stretch my legs and drink young coconut juice, and Daisy would use this as an opportunity to make phone calls and coordinate business back in

Bangkok. I asked her who was running the show in her absence and she explained that she had several cousins and uncles that helped her out. We hit the road again.

Just before nightfall we had arrived at Krabi. The journey had taken longer than expected after running into some treacherous monsoon-type rain and bypassing several nasty looking road accidents. Daisy had booked me into a reasonable four star hotel off the main tourist trail and I enjoyed a comfortable room with a dual aspect view of the hills and sea. Daisy said she would meet me at breakfast and presented me some brochures to read through. They were home-made brochures, professionally printed but with several glaring typos. Nonetheless, the best option looked to be to a visit to the Hat Yai National Park area near the Malaysian border.

After enjoying some amazing seafood from the street stalls that lined one of the main beaches, I sat in a bar and read up on the small archipelago of islands, identifying Koh Lipe as my chosen destination. At three points during the evening, however, I was approached by young Thai women asking if I wanted company. I declined on all occasions but couldn't help but watch them latch on to other single, older British and Dutch men who seemed to frequent the bar in numbers as the evening progressed. I realised by that point that I had chosen a poor venue to drink in as there were no other couples or locals drinking there. Indirectly, I was getting a taste of what many farangs came to Thailand for, and I felt sad that I couldn't seem to escape the darker elements of my past, even in paradise. I returned to the hotel and sat in the lobby bar thinking about my life back in England and how I wanted it to change.

The next morning I shared my plans with Daisy. She thanked me and made some calls on my behalf, and then we agreed a price in Thai Baht for the whole trip. I paid her there and then; in return it bought me my ferry ticket, connecting boats, a week's rent in a seaside bungalow and squared us up for the petrol and toll charges I owed her from the previous day.

As we drove from Krabi down towards the port, I asked her about her thoughts on foreign men who travel to her country to pay for sex. She was quiet for a while, embarrassed most likely; I had obviously offended her culture and social etiquette by even broaching the subject. To assure her, I did stress that I saw my own kind (white men) as the perpetrator of all ill-doing. After a minute or two she said it was common, that prostitution was a way of life for many Thai women who have no education; sleeping with foreign men was a way of paying for food and bills, or clearing debts from illegal loan sharks or people who had abducted relatives and demanded a ransom. I asked her what she meant by kidnapping and she cited corruption as a big problem in some parts of Thailand, especially boroughs where tourism was high. I explained that I was sad to hear that, but hoped that where I was going would be void of any impurities. She gave a sigh and said that fishermen were often part of smuggling rings. I raised an eyebrow but didn't give it much more thought. I had discomforted her enough by asking about the darker side of a culture whose reputation is built on smiles and fun, muddied by sex and western hedonism.

Daisy drove me to the port where the ferry would leave from and explained that I would then have to collect a water taxi from the main island to Koh Lipe. Had I not timed it well I would have had to explore a very run down looking town which had a noticeably different feel; the south was an area that had a high Muslim population and where tensions between radical groups and the police where high – little of what went on was reported on a larger scale, especially to western press given the fact that it would damage the reputation of being a tourist friendly destination.

I thanked Daisy for her time and gave her a generous tip. She asked me to call or email her if I wanted to be picked up and taken back to Bangkok when my holiday was over. Truth be told, I didn't want the experience to end and dreaded my trip even coming to an end. I had been enjoying good weather, good food and friendly vibes ever since I arrived in Thailand, and most importantly I had completely forgotten about my woes back in London.

The boat ride took two hours. I arrived at a small island where, sure enough, a row of water taxis were waiting at the port to take us to our smaller island of choice. Street hawkers offered a wealth of snacks and pointless memorabilia to choose from and there were rows of men and women selling trips to Bangkok, Langkawi or Kuala Lumpur. It was nice to know that I could still make choices. I boarded a packed water taxi, filled with persons from Europe much younger than myself, obviously attracted to Koh Lipe's remoteness and history of being run by a small sea gypsy community. I figured, from eavesdropping conversations, that many just wanted to get stoned on a beach away from any form of law enforcement and that others had simply planned to find peace – I was one of them.

When I arrived at the island I was in awe at the beauty of the place. The island could not have been more than a couple of kilometres long and the long sandy white beaches were peppered with attractive looking bungalows and small restaurants. On disembarking from the water taxi I saw my name written on a card and was greeted by a very friendly and beautiful woman called Pensri. She took my bags and placed them on a trolley cart for a young boy to pull along the beach. We walked through a small clearing into the woods and I saw many of the bungalows had been built with, or incorporated, recycled items such as glass bottles and tin. This was what eco-tourism looked like and I could tell that this community upcycled what they had or put it to good use. Pensri explained that there was no Wi-Fi and that phone service was limited; if I needed something I would have to get a water taxi back to the main island or use their satellite phone in an emergency. I explained to her that isolation from the outside world was my intention.

She walked me over to the main bungalow and processed my stay and I gave her my valuables to lock away in a safe. We then walked back along the beach towards a modest looking wooden hut. It was basic to say the least; there were noticeable gaps in the wood and a small mosquito net hung over the bed; two small windows - one facing the sea, the other vegetation to the rear – and she told me there was no power on in the day, but generators came on at night, and so the room felt more like a garden shed slowly baking in the heat of the sun. Toilets were separate. The bed was firm and there was a small table for me to keep a book and a drink to hand. Pensri recommended a place to eat and drink when I was settled, and said that she hoped to catch up with me at some point during my stay. She gave me a warm smile as she left.

I lay down and took an unplanned nap.

When I woke the sun was setting over tranquil waters. The bars were starting to open for business and local villagers were packing their restaurant display cases with ice ready to lay out the local catch from fisherman. I grabbed myself a seat with a great view of the sunset and enjoyed several Singha beers. Sure enough, Pensri made a welcome appearance and started to talk to me about simple things: my likes, my interests, how I was finding Thailand so far, what I did for a living – the usual small talk. I made similar simple conversation with her and she took great pleasure in telling me about her life, her family and her business on Koh Lipe. She was very proud of the bungalows that she ran with her brother and talked passionately about her plans for her niece and nephew, who would often stay on the island when her sister had to work. She drank with me and I dropped my guard for the first time in months. I felt truly at home.

A week turned into two, then three, until finally four blissful weeks had passed and I had become well acquainted with many of the villagers that worked the island; Pensri had introduced me to most of them and I had met her brother, Jart, and young niece on several occasions, forming a positive relationship with them both. Occasionally I leant a hand by helping Jart lift supplies from his long-tail boat and also helped Pensri translate some letters and memos from holiday companies that wanted to advertise her accommodation through them; I even helped her design what her website should look like on paper with some grammatically correct paragraphs so that her cousin could code it properly back on the mainland. In return Jart had offered to take me to Langkawi so that I could renew my visa for another six weeks when the time came.

After nearly a month being in hiding and withholding secrets, I finally felt like I could open up and make a difference to a small community, and I was seriously considering ways to use the proceeds from the sale of my father's home in London to invest in Pensri's passions and support the community further.

But as always, plans change.

TRAFFICKED

Pensri came running into my bungalow at about 3am one morning. She had not come this time to show affection; she was teary eyed and screaming at me hysterically for help. Without thinking, I lunged at her, holding her by the arms and pinning her against the wall until she managed to explain to me what all the commotion was about.

"My niece," she said tearfully. "They take her."

"Who has taken her?"

"Hathai, have bad dream and so I say play outside, but then fisherman - they come."

I shook my head, trying to make sense of her broken English. "Fishermen took her?"

"Fishermen take Hathai. Put in boat. Hathai gone. John help us, please."

She led me from the bungalow and we ran down the beach together. The moon was out in full and the sea, the sands and her skin had a steely blue hue to them all. But it made the experience more terrifying; her wide, fearful eyes became nothing more than blue orbs looking hopelessly around, out into the distance. A few other member of the gypsy community were also on the beach by this point, looking out for trails across a very calm and still sea.

In the distance I could see the lights of large fishing boats trawling for squid. I asked Pensri if she thought she might be on one of the boats, and whether travelling out to them on a speedy long-tail might be the best way to try and rescue Hathai. But she couldn't answer me, she continued wailing at the sea hysterically, calling to her friends in Thai. I felt a tap on my shoulder and turned to see Jart, Pensri's brother, who said he would take me. He explained that it was risky to even approach the fishing vessels and make such enquiries, but because I was a farang, he suggested it might give us some advantage; not even the Thai authorities could bury the death of a British tourist under the sand. I found little reassurance in what he said but I had to help – a child was missing.

We pushed his boat into the sea together. I was barefoot and barely dressed, running purely on adrenaline. The water was warm and we had enough light from the moon to navigate past the rocky shoreline. Jart leaped aboard and started the engine. We sliced through the calm sea and within a few minutes we approached the first of the fishing boats which had a dozen or so bright lights cast out either side of it.

I thought there were about two boats but when we arrived I saw that there were several moored closely together. I didn't know which one to approach, so I directed Jart to steer towards the middle trawler. We pulled up alongside it and were welcomed by vacant and unemotional faces of Thai fisherman, their skin dark brown and thick from years of being at sea. I relayed instructions to Jart in simple English to ask them if they had seen a boat go past. The men stared back at me in bewilderment; Jart then conversed with two members of the crew and the fisherman pointed starboard and then began having a heated conversation.

"He says," Jart began, "that a speedboat went north about fifteen minutes ago." I nodded to show them that I understood. "But the other man," Jart continued, "says it went south."

I shook my head. I suspected that perhaps the men were in on the abduction and I grew fearful for Jart's safety as the men continued to bicker loudly in Thai; there were no cameras or unbiased witnesses out in the middle of the ocean. Beyond the second fishing boat were a collection of very small uninhabited islands, many of which could have easily masked a trail if a boat were to head that way.

"Did they give you a good description of the boat?" I asked Jart.

"They say very fast ... black ..." Jart looked deflated. I looked over at the other fishing boat, at fisherman watching us silently from the deck, bright floodlights turning the water ghostly green as it mixed with the icy reflection of a full moon. I started to feel the cold as the effect of adrenaline eased off and I realised the full extent of what had just happened to Pensri. I suggested to Jart that we do one small loop of all the trawlers, just to see if anything could be spotted in the waters around them. There was nothing more we could do.

Jart shouted out Hathai's name and we waited and listened for a reply. Hathai may well have been hidden below deck on any of the boats, stored somewhere out of sight, but there was no reply, only a cold silence and the gentle murmurings of fishermen. Feeling at a total loss, waving half-heartedly at the fisherman as we left, my heart was filled with a great sadness for Pensri who had been tasked with looking after her niece, Hathai. Circling the boats yielded nothing; there was no distant object in the sea. We decided it best to return to the island and get the authorities on the case straight away.

Pensri was inconsolable when we told her of the news. She wept briefly on my shoulders but poured most of her grief into her brother, Jart, and some of her close girlfriends before collapsing in the sand and punching the ground.

A message had been sent to the Thai coastguard asking for them to look out for a black speedboat. Jart had hinted to me on the journey back to shore that Hathai had most likely been taken to Kho Lanta or maybe across the border into Malaysia already. She was lost, a small part in a complicated smuggling chain.

It was soon daylight. By this point Pensri had broken the news to her sister about Hathai's abduction using the satellite phone. The police has been notified and a boat was heading over from the mainland. Jart and I took time out to eat some fresh fruit on the beach. Both of us sat in disbelief as the rest of the island slowly stirred and reacted to the news that a girl had been abducted.

"What will happen?"

"The police come," he replied. "They take statement from us, get picture of Hathai, and then they go." He waved his arm angrily, as though the police would offer no solution to the matter.

"How likely are they to find her?"

Jart shook his head. "This happen big thing in Thailand," he replied. "Girl, women, they go missing with bad men. Police and army, they try but much corruption."

I couldn't believe that he was describing the process in such simplistic terms. Back in England, I knew that a whole team of officers and members of the public would be lining up to help; groups of men and women would be out scouring the land looking for someone like Hathai, a missing child, in a race against time, but here Jart seemed resigned to the fact that she was gone and unlikely to return.

"Who do you think took her?"

"Bad men," he said, starting to cry. "Hathai probably scared, with bad men . . . made to do bad thing."

I understood then: Hathai had been trafficked. The very idea that someone so young could just be taken and used in such a fashion, a whole childhood ended abruptly as she is forced to perform god-awful acts to strangers, probably to groups of paying, foreign men who touted Thailand's seedy bars in order to relieve their sick fantasies; at best she would be sold as a domestic slave, but it was the lesser of two evils. I extended my sympathy to Jart and explained that I would do what I could to help in any way, not realising that this was the beginning of my mantra for a much more prolonged fight back home.

By late morning a group of Thai police offers had arrived on the island. They had spent most of the time with Pensri but also made enquiries with other islanders about the events of that morning, including my role. I had been sat outside of my beach hut, trying to read a book to take my mind off the events, when an officer approached me. At first he was very jolly, asking me how I was, if I was enjoying the island, and then he asked if I was Pensri's English friend who had helped look for Hathai. I nodded and he came and sat beside me.

"Sad sad thing," he said in broken English. "Young girl, pretty huh? Now she gone to sea."

I nodded. "Awful."

"You in Koh Lipe how long?"

Until that morning I had wanted to spend months, or much longer even, there in the comfort of a peaceful, friendly community, and in the company of Pensri; but now I felt empty and afraid. I could not escape the wickedness I had vowed to leave behind. Even in the remotest of islands - evil found a way in.

"You show me your passport please," he said assertively.

I stalled for a moment. "May I ask what for?"

"You witness to crime, and you farang - we need details for our investigation."

I left him in the seat and went into my small bungalow to search for the passport then remembered that it was in Pensri's safe. I looked over at the door to see that he had followed me in and was standing ominously, looking over at me. There was something not right about the way he lingered, like a gun slinger expecting me to draw. I explained the situation about the passport and he shrugged his shoulders.

"You travel on your own? What your job back in England?"

"I'm a gardener," I said, trying to throw him off track but it didn't work.

"What does gardener do coming to Thailand, to small, beautiful island in sea?" I saw him scribble down notes. "Farangs like you bring trouble to these islands, bring trouble to Thailand, my home. How long you stay here?"

"Until I'm ready to return home - another day, maybe a week, or a month. . ."

He looked at me coldly. There were no smiles. "Make sure you around to answer more questions. Girl is missing, Mr John."

I watched him leave the hut, and through the gaps in the walls I saw him march back across the shoreline to where his colleagues were waiting. They seemed to silently exchange notes and I saw the officer direct his arms back towards my hut in an agitated fashion. I suddenly felt bad about the whole situation and my heart grew heavy; even in a tropical paradise you could still come into contact with the very people who made you want to leave your life back home in the first place. At that point I couldn't help but think that I would, somehow, be implicated in Hathai's disappearance just for being a single white man abroad. He would surely take my details and run them through a database, and who knew what that would lead to – what did the UK authorities have on file about me? Who else would see that information?

I spoke with Jart again after the police left the island. "What did they ask you?"

Jart's head hung low. He explained that the police had asked him lots of questions about where he was on the night of her disappearance and why he took me out on a boat to look for Hathai with him.

"Did they not understand that we were trying to help?"

"We have to be careful," he replied. "One or more of them [officers] might be involved. Some police in these areas are paid by the local mafia: drug smuggling, stolen goods, women and children. Boats come and go all the time. Hathai may have seen one of them and they decide to take her."

"Then we need to tell someone else – we need to go higher."

"Cannot," Jart said, saddened. "Too dangerous."

His response angered me even more, but at the same time he made me conscious that I was running out of options quickly. I explained that I could get things done better at home, and that he would need to take me back to Ko Phak later that same day.

He looked disappointed. "You're leaving us?"

"Yes and no. I've a habit of running away from things, but I also find it hard to forget. With policemen like him as my only official ally, I am not sure there's much I can do for Hathai here. He didn't seem to like farangs that much."

Jart nodded. "Will you tell Pensri?"

I said that I would and then returned to my bungalow to begin packing my items. As I did so I reflected on weeks of bliss – paradise - now completely lost. The memories that I had anticipated savouring were now totally obscured: the fishing trips, fun laughs on the beach, the quiet intimacy, the amazing food; memories tainted by grey flashbacks of us calling out Hathai's name on a boat in the ocean; the policeman's mistrusting face. Even thousands of miles away from home, there was still an oppressive system of control by ruling groups.

As I packed my bags together, Pensri appeared at the doorway. She remained tearful when I explained what had happened and how I didn't feel safe being on the island anymore. She was angry with the authorities for offering her little hope, and for the way that they had made me feel responsible in some way for her niece's disappearance. I promised I would do what I could from my end, and vowed to stay in touch and revisit them in the future. There was an emotional farewell as she embraced me for one last time, but even the relationship we had built up over a month had lost its spark because of the dreadful turn of events.

Jart had the boat ready and we pushed off shore together. The journey was expected to take a couple of hours by longtail and he had to ensure he had enough fuel for the journey. The sea remained calm and the sun beat down on us both as we meandered between a small scattering of islands; perhaps we were both still hopeful that we might see Hathai playing on a beach somewhere. The breeze picked up as we headed to the mainland .

When we arrived at Kho Phek I thanked Jart and paid him generously for his time, instructing him to use the money to make his own investigations locally, even if it meant paying crooks for information. He thanked me and declared that I was a good man with a strong heart. I didn't have the time to explain otherwise and caught a tuk-tuk to the local train station. From there I decided to travel south through Malaysia and catch the first plane back to London out of Kuala-Lumpur.

Being back in a large, sprawling metropolis like Kuala Lumpur reminded me that London would never fully heal. As I was driven out of the city towards the airport by taxi I saw large storm drains and tunnels buried deep below street level; rats the size of large kittens and hungry monitor lizards peered out of aqueducts, watchful and eager to ambush the unsuspecting, ravaging the remains of the poor and the wealthy. It saddened me that countries like Malaysia should hold western values of wealth and materialism in such high regard.

At the airport I checked through customs having bought a last minute BA flight at one of the ticket desks. As I waited in the lounge I logged on to my email account for the first time in a month and, apart from several concerned messages from the estate agents and my solicitors, there was little else to be fretful about.

I was heading home back to London.

THE DARK CITY

On our descent, the pilot informed us all that the weather in the UK was wet with heavy winds and a temperature of eight degrees Celsius; that was a massive drop of over 20 degrees in the space of half a day.

We touched down late afternoon. London remained grey, how I remembered it, and was getting darker by the minute. I collected my bags and hailed a taxi.

I tried to read the paper in the back of the cab to catch up on everything that had happened in my weeks away, and there had been quite a bit. The cabbie remained chirpy and lively for most of the journey and I would occasionally entertain his comments with a 'oh really' or an 'uh-huh' or a cheek blowing 'pffff, that's crazy' sort of expression to show surprise. Of course, he talked about the weather like most Brits do, but he also mentioned his disdain for the Tories, about the effect of austerity cuts and how it was affecting everyone who had a job; bloody foreigners, he cited on several occasions, were – in his opinion - the root cause of all evil it seemed, and if a new government got in then they would need to cleanse the country of all the bloody immigrants taking British jobs. I grew tired of his cynicism and tried to remember what my life had been like on a small tropical island in Thailand – my memories were already black and white.

I paid the driver, got out of the cab and looked over at my house. All seemed normal, just like I had left it, except for the sold sign that was hammered into the front lawn. But as I approached the front door there was one little problem, one minute detail that bothered me - the hall light was on. I silently approached the house and propped my case in the porch. Using my key I entered as quietly as I could, taking care not to create any sudden movements or noises. I closed the door behind me and locked it shut, and then I stood and listened. I heard nothing and convinced myself that the estate agent must have let someone in, perhaps a surveyor, and they had left the lights on. It was logical but sadly not accurate, because as I approached the living room I could see a fire burning slowly. The embers were gentle on the eye, a soothing red. They drew me forward. This is it, I thought. This is how it ends.

I walked into the living room, half expecting to see Gabriel and two of his men sat with an assortment of knives on a table, but instead I was greeted by the Donor, sat with a glass of whisky, or port, or something dark and rich in one of my dad's crystal glasses; opposite him sat Jo, reading through a bundle of paperwork. They both looked up as I walked in.

"You do know this is breaking and entering, right?" I said.

Jo produced a set of keys and held them out on her hand. "Michael left them for us, just in case."

"In case you needed to finish the job."

Neither of them reacted to that comment. "We're glad you're back," the Donor said. "But if you want us to leave we will. I appreciate you've had a long flight."

There was a silent stare off between us, and then I shook my head and took the keys from Jo's hands. "No more stalling. I left this country looking for answers, but all I found was more misery and despair. I need answers from you both."

They looked at one another and nodded. "Okay, tell us what you want to know."

"You can start by explaining how you knew I'd be coming back today. I told no-one, not a soul of my intention to return, not even Minx."

"Your passport," said Jo. "There's a watch on your passport."

It was plausible. "That's not easy information to get hold of, if that were to be true, which would make you some kind of spook to have those privileges."

"I think you and Minx have some catching up to do, she can tell you more about the who, the what, and the where," the Donor explained.

"Okay, but there's a few other things I need you to clarify, they've been bugging me for months. The day before I met you I received a package, a man's severed hand. Was that you?" He shook his head. Jo remained straight-faced; I could tell from her eyes that she was concerned at my disclosure. "My dad died soon after - mysteriously. You know what happened to him, don't you?"

The Donor didn't deny it, but he inferred that he had a good idea about what might have happened. There were no clear answers.

"The ants, the whole parasite thing . . . it's some kind of logical placebo, right? But they're real aren't they? There really is something like a real vampire."

"Someone," Jo said coolly. "Someone so evil he personifies everything a vampire is. Yes, he's real alright but he's not immortal."

I sat down and confessed. "I can't run anymore. I travelled halfway around the world to avoid danger and I was still looking over my shoulder. This feeling just won't go away. I want to end it. I want a life." I stopped myself. I suddenly grew uneasy that the Donor and Jo might have looked through my house in my absence and found incriminating evidence, like Michael's last letter to me. What if this was all part of the game Michael had set up? Despite having trust issues, I felt they were the only people who could help me find answers at that moment in time.

"Karl's dead," Jo said coldly. I remember looking at her in total disbelief. "It happened shortly after you left."

"How did he die? Was it his condition?"

The Donor got out of his seat. "Far from it. Karl was pushed under a train at Warren Street Station. There was little that could be done to save him. I'd like to think that he didn't suffer."

"Did they catch the person responsible?"

"A drunk," Jo began, "who just happened to be a jobless illegal immigrant from Albania."

"An immigrant linked to the organised crime organisation we think is protecting this 'master vampire' you described to us," the Donor added. "The same criminal organisation owns the flat your father died at, and who also runs a maintenance contract at the hotel you met Ed at, and who also run an illegitimate courier company smuggling drugs and guns . . ."

I nodded. I understood what he was saying. "So it's one vertical crime syndicate doing all the dirty work, cleaning a path for whoever or whatever they might be, so that they can feel . . . untouchable?"

Jo was direct. "We need to infiltrate this group, mess up their supply chains, cause a bit of chaos and watch for any movement. We nearly had him once – we can get to him again."

The Donor interjected. "You're wrong to doubt the parasite theory – Karl was definitely on to something, and we think that's why he was killed. That honey you took from Michael's flat – it had some interesting stuff in it."

"So, here we are," I began, "back to the start, linking everything we know to some kind of source, an archetypal vampire antagonist. And you call that reassurance?

Because to me this feel like things have gone bad to worse. I feel like I've gone full circle, that I'm now back at the start following another pointless hypothesis."

The Donor handed me a drink. I didn't know what it was but it tasted good and I held my head for several seconds as I felt it reach the pit of my stomach and burn slowly. "Where's Minx? She can help root them out also, maybe expose their operations online."

"Minx took some time out after Karl's death, but now that you're back on the scene we hope she'll want back in – so be nice to her on those emails you send her; no more sarcasm, John. I know it's hard."

"Everyone needs a vice. But I'll try." I looked at the pile of mail that had been neatly stacked on my coffee table; a small mountain of legal documents, invoices, final reminders, insurance premiums – stuff that I wanted to deal with but didn't have the will, time or patience to do so.

"We can help you sort through this," the Donor said. "And I've got some friends to keep an eye on the house so you won't have any more visitors looking for stuff. Until you're ready to move on, that is."

I would normally have protested, remained proud about handling my own affairs, but I was so incensed by what they had told me, about Karl, that I was eager to join back in the hunt to find answers, to meet with Minx, to contact NGOs regarding what happened in Thailand, that I might be able to help Pensri find Hathai … the list seemed endless; the thought of me having to get bogged down in legalities seemed fruitless and so I naively accepted their help and instructed the Donor to get me another glass of whatever he had found in the drinks cabinet.

Jo had sorted the post into categories relating to the will and house. She mentioned she had contacts whom would help me get everything done carefully and quickly so that I could help the Donor instigate his plan of action.

In summary, he revealed a strategy about how I should set about infiltrating the gangs who protected the Ants and get the right kind of attention; we also talked about transportation issues and he suggested that I should take my motorcycle license to allow for greater and faster access across the whole of London rather than travel everywhere by public transport. At the time I didn't really see how this was a major hindrance to the operation but, he assured me, it would all become clear soon enough.

In return for agreeing to help him he would give me a list of NGOs that dealt with victim support for those who have family members trafficked abroad. I described the full incident to them both, about what had occurred in Thailand, and they both said they would directly make inquiries with some contacts of their own. That was all I needed to hear.

Several Whisky-Macs later I felt like I was done; jet lag was kicking in and I could barely keep my eyes open. Jo left me several business cards of people I should call in the morning. The Donor said he would contact Minx and agree a time for us to collectively share his master plan and divvy out roles; he hinted that it would offer a very fitting way to avenge Karl and mess up the biggest Ant network in London.

I felt more at ease as they left. Looking outside the window I saw the security car the Donor talked about. It was a short term fix but the fight was back on and definitely real.

ID

Despite my best efforts, I found myself drawn back to my computer and the anonymous world of the internet to plan my next move. I joined several new forums and Facebook groups, connected with people across Twitter and Instagram and Snapchat; wherever a predator might fish for victims I was there also, posing as one. I also continued to research parts of London that I knew were connected to crimes I had knowledge of. For example, the address where Alissa had been murdered was actually a private house hired out to wealthy clients; I got nowhere trying to get the booking details of a previous guest (I'd leave that to Minx). I also spent time trying to retrace Michael's last steps in the hope that he might still be able to offer me closure. I even created a database of old people's homes and care facilities for the mentally ill and infirm across London with the intention of visiting them, but I needed Michael's full name (if that were even his real first name).

Minx came round to the house one evening to rebuke me. She said that I needed to shift away from scrutinising fantasists online and focus my efforts instead on the traffickers who were supplying Ants with a food source, as she crudely put it. That was the Donor's grand plan and we needed to start some dress rehearsals.

I agreed to her plans but mentioned that there was one role-player drifting across the dark web who had caught my eye on a number of occasions. I said to Minx that before I got back into hunting and messing with dangerous groups that I needed closure in the world of online vampire forums, and it would perhaps be less dangerous if we started focusing on one person than a whole army of Albanians and Turks.

She asked me to give her the details of this particular group member and then she set about putting together a search. It turns out her group of friends had also been made aware of this character who had a habit of grooming young girls and bullying vulnerable men.

He worked in London as a sales manager for a high street bank, so getting close to him during working hours was near impossible, but he liked to go out for lunch, and in the evenings before going home to his two bedroom apartment in Shoreditch, he liked to ring around brothels and escorts and try to negotiate cut rate deals for 15 minute quickies. Minx had retrieved a phone log thanks to a friend who worked in official places, and we had identified a pattern of behaviour that pointed towards a series of calls made on a Friday (end of the week treat) to a number and address in North London.

"What do you want to do to this guy?" I remember Minx asking me as we sat drinking hot chocolate round the kitchen table one evening.

"I want to hurt him."

"Why him? There are so many creeps that fund the misery of these women, surely if you punish him you need to punish all of them."

"Maybe it's because I see a bit of me in him. The guy has it all: a house, a good job, a respectable social life and a bank balance that is in the black, but he's not satisfied. He's been shown favour by the people around him, yet he continues to pursue some darkly disturbed fantasy that he's built up online, and he's taken it out on to the streets."

Minx listened like a juror about to cast her verdict.

"For example, I remember posing as a fifteen year old girl," I began.

"Catfish!" she laughed out loud.

"Well, I actually handle myself pretty well as a vulnerable fifteen year old girl against all these older men. After dipping in and out of these circles full of goths and EMOs over a couple of weeks, the attention soon turned on me, and he really shone. He was desperate to meet me after sending me several pictures of his dick in various flaccid and erect forms. I learnt a whole new vocabulary from reading what he was going to do to me when we met, and he said he'd make my life hell if I refused his demands. I was genuinely quite scared."

"So what happened?"

"We arranged to meet. I stalked out the location beforehand and then, on the day, watched him agitatedly pacing about from afar. I'd chosen the first floor of a large book store. I sat in the café and watched him, reading each abusive message he posted to me after I explained that my dad had caught me web camming for another man."

Minx found the whole story hilarious. "I feel pity for the guy, I don't think practising vengeance on him is fully justified – the prank was enough."

"Except it wasn't. I followed him out of the book store, pursued him on the train until he got to Manor House, and stalked him right up to an address down some deprived looking residential road. Fifteen minutes later he came out looking even worse than he went in. I guessed that he had visited a makeshift brothel so I paid a visit to the same flat after he left. When I went in there were two girls, one of them clearly distressed and weeping. Both of them were scared. I paid them money and asked them to tell me what happened. One of the girls showed me where he had struck her across her back with his belt, and then I saw the bite mark. But what upset me more was the fact that they were terrified about telling their pimp that they didn't want to work there anymore. I'll never forget the look on her face. I wanted to kill him that day."

Minx gave a steady breath. "Wow, he really pissed you off. And I guess you felt indirectly responsible for her injuries?"

"I didn't look at it like that at the time, but yeah, in hindsight it made me realise that pursuing these monsters through deception was not the way forward because men like him need a cathartic outlet. But now that I'm associated with an experienced and equally cruel hacker, there really is no need to reel them in because you can give me all his details. If he arranges another one of his sadistic Friday evening sessions, I want to make sure that I'm ready to surprise him."

Sure enough, one Friday did come along and he had been busily ringing up girls to enquire about the best deal. He had contacted a woman based in a flat near Arsenal football club. We found her profile online and concluded that she shared a flat with another girl. She was young looking, claiming to be 25 but she looked more like 15, barely developed and posing for pictures that looked candid rather than posed. Her profile read the same as her friends: anything went as long as you paid up; no girl could like and want to do so many horrible things to strangers, yet the profile claimed she was wild and passionate and for extra money would not use protection. I felt repulsed reading it – she was clearly a victim in all of this.

From his phone records and pattern of leaving work, we concluded that he would arrive between 6 and 7, which meant that I had to get to the apartment before him. I arrived and was greeted by a plain looking girl in jeans, t-shirt and thick rimmed glasses. She was the maid. She took me up the stairs and into a room where the two girls were brought in behind me, wearing lace underwear. Both put on a façade that they were pleased to meet me, and knowing that the target had a penchant for blondes, I opted to stay with the more mature looking brunette; she looked like she could handle herself in a fight. The remaining blonde, however, looked disappointed, perhaps because she knew her client was coming for his weekly session to use and abuse her.

I was taken into a bedroom and asked to sit down. I pulled out my phone to check messages from Minx. She said he had just left Finsbury Park station and would be there within 10 minutes. The woman stood over me, asking how long and how much I wanted to pay. I pulled out some notes and handed them to her.

"This for one hour," she said.

"Yes, that should be enough time to get everything done."

"You lie on bed and change while I get ready."

She disappeared to give the money to her conservatively dressed maid. I did not get undressed and I did not lie down. I got my instruments ready, which included cable ties, pliers, some silver knuckle dusters and a Taser. I hid them on the floor under my jacket and waited. When the woman returned to the room she asked why I was not naked. I explained that I wanted her to lie down naked first, that I liked to watch and be silent before doing anything. She shrugged her shoulders, mechanically undressed and lay on the bed face down. She tried to make small talk but I insisted on silence, that's what I liked.

Ten minutes later I heard the door buzz and the sound of him being let in. He sounded jolly, like he had been having a good day, and there was a familiar exchange of simple dialogue. But as I listened harder I could detect sadness in the girls' voice as she was united with him. She called herself Sammi.

I had to plan my move carefully. The girl lying on the bed grew suspicious, almost annoyed that I was just sitting there. When she spoke to me again and asked if I was nervous I simply told her that she should enjoy being paid to lie there and do nothing and not ask again. Then I asked her where the toilet was. She offered to take me but I insisted that it was part of my ritual and that I would need to see her lying on the bed when I got back.

Hearing that the house had settled down, and detecting that the maid was watching TV in the living room, answering phone calls and responding to text messages across several pay-as-you-go accounts, I slipped into the hallway and prepared for my ambush. First, I opened the bathroom door and started running the tap, then I left and shut the door behind me and because of the lock being on the handle I was able to lock the door from the outside. Then I snuck across the hallway and placed a mask over my head, got my Taser ready and breathed deeply until I felt ready to sort this man out. I could already hear him breathing heavily and cursing her using derogatory language. I didn't knock.

When he looked round at me I saw complete terror and dread in his face. The girl, Sammi, didn't see me at first because his hands were firmly holding her head to his crotch, but when I swung a punch at his face he seemed to let go and Sammi staggered back, whimpering. I removed the Taser next, holding it under his arm pit and releasing a burst of voltage that made his body judder violently before he temporarily passed out.

He was subdued, that was the easy bit. Sammi had lost her voice in the panic and went to run for help but I hissed at her to say, explaining as best I could - dressed as some gothic vigilante - that I had no vendetta against her. I stared at her for minutes, my finger pressed to my lips as I urged her to silently close the door. Amazingly, she did so. I kept her in that room with this man was because he was a bastard to her on a weekly basis and I wanted her to see some degree of justice served.

I bound his wrists behind his back, gaffer taped his

mouth and sat him upright. Then I looked at him, tilting my head like a street artist stands and admires a mural or a piece of urban graffiti, until he started to come to. I had one intention: to scare the shit out of him and promise to ruin him. Why? At that point in time I had forgotten my motive. This was about prevention rather than cure, that's what I'd told myself. But this was unfamiliar territory.

He came round eventually and by the widening of his eyes I knew that he was fully aware of the situation. Surprisingly, Sammi (if that was her name) had remained a silent voyeur in all of this

"You know me," I said to him slowly.

He shook his head wildly from side to side. Blood was starting to trickle from his nose from where I had hit him. I nodded my head again and he made one more defiant shake of his head.

"We met online," I began. "As a girl, as someone who just wanted to connect with people who had similar interests. This girl wasn't normal, of course, she was into vampires and death and black magic and showed a natural curiosity about the darker practices of pagan worship, shit like that. She was misguided, but she was also just a girl freely exploring her interests."

He was listening intently. His eyes trying to gauge mine.

"You befriended me, told me you liked the same things as me, and complimented me that the way I wrote about these things on my page showed that I was special and different to all the other girls on the forum. You made me feel special. But that was just a ploy, wasn't it? You just wanted to control me, to dominate me and hurt me. Well, Peter, haven't the tables turned now?"

I could hear a whimper from behind the taped mouth, one that hung in the lower larynx; he was almost gargling in his own spit. Without thinking, I had removed the blade from my pocket and was switching it between hands.

"And what about poor Sammi, here?" I looked over at her. She looked scared now and I realised that I was at risk of losing control. "Sammi doesn't want to do this job, am I right, Sammi?"

She shook her head. I gazed at her face and her curly blonde hair, realising that she was actually a natural brunette and that he face was heavily laden in foundation to make her seem younger. She was not underage, of that I was sure, but nonetheless, she was aging quicker than she needed to.

"Sammi doesn't like what you do to her, what you do to all of these women. I've been following your movements, Peter, and your actions are very unclean, very different to what you do as a sales manager." His eyes rolled and his body started to twitch. "What would your boss Simon say if he knew about the kind of sick and perverted stuff you go up to in your spare time? What if some pictures of you appeared on Facebook showing all your hundreds of friends what you really got up to? How many likes and reactions would you get? What if we could show your current situation to all the women and young girls you had forced yourself upon during these past years, do you think they would want me to show you pity?"

He shook his head. He was listening intently now. I heard movement in the hallway and I realised that my date for the hour was getting restless, knocking at the bathroom door. I looked at Sammi, testing her loyalty to this whole illegal set up. She didn't make a sound. Peter, on the other hand, did something very silly and started bashing his head against the wall and yelling from within. I lunged at him, punching him in the gut just below the ribs; he gave an uncomfortable grunt and tried to start coughing. I could hear footsteps along the hallway, walking towards Sammi's door. Surely I was rumbled – I didn't have long. I could hear her, either the maid or the other prostitute, listening at the door. They must have been hovering, listening to the sound of a grown man whimper. Then

Sammi started to moan with no eroticism at all, just a semi-satisfied groan a woman might make if she were experiencing a fraction of the pleasure that a man might have. I stared at her, eyebrow raised as she made appropriate background noise. It worked because the footsteps walked away.

Realising I was nearly out of time, I got my camera out and started taking pictures of Peter in his dreadful predicament. Then I took out the pliers and picked up his left foot. "The next time I see you abusing women in places like this," I said bitterly, "I will put a clamp around you balls and keep twisting it until there is nothing left to squeeze, and your will be so fucking high-pitched that everyone will believe that you're a girl, that's if you're ever brave enough to start chatting using broken web cams again."

I took his little toe and crunched the pliers down hard.

Peter gave an angry, guttural growl and started crying. He would have a limp, for sure, and that was the point of the exercise, to carry with him a mental and physical deterrent from ever engaging in this type of stuff again. This was not my finest moment, and by writing about it I am not boasting or showing off how broad my retribution is; I just chose Peter to bear the brunt of all the pain of such lonely, broken men who struggle with their addictions. *He* will suffer for them. It was not my job to show compassion or forgiveness to a man who, on several occasions, has raped, tormented and led children astray, I was merely a catalyst for justice in the form of rage. I did not declare my workings as some type of divine retribution, for I was definitely in the lead when it came to sinning and I knew that I would have to meet my maker on some day.

Lost in my own thoughts, and content that he had tasted a glimpse of hell, I turned to Sammi who had sadly lost her composure from earlier. The crunching of bone and the sight of blood had obviously been too much for her, and the pressure of being a vessel for loathsome men all day finally led her breaking down. As I left the room I told her I would pray for her, and for Peter, that they could both find a way out of this life.

I didn't return to the room where the other prostitute was waiting for me, I simply walked myself out of the apartment and back into Islington where I hoped to disappear amongst the crowds and make my way anonymously back home.

As I sat on the back of a bus travelling up Holloway Road, I uploaded the pictures and emailed them to Minx. She messaged me back later asking if I was okay, and confessed that she was doubtful whether I had it in me to follow through with what I had done. She declared that I had entered a new realm of hunting that would put me back in the front line and in mortal danger.

I'm not sure 'proud' is the word I would use to describe my feelings that day. I was surprised that I had been so brazen and focused in following a plan through, but in hindsight it was the outcome of working in darkness; I had been driven by the blackness of my damaged heart which belonged to an unclean soul. I desperately needed cleansing and I took it out on him.

I'm sorry, Peter.

I spoke with Minx hours later after she had been monitoring his internet activity; he had not posted messages on any forums or pictures of himself seeking sympathy, Peter had merely retreated to his home to lick his wounds. I remember clearly breaking down in tears on the sofa, a glass of wine in hand, a scene reminiscent from a Bridget Jones novel as I tried to see a way out from a very bleak and lonely situation. I had repositioned myself on the periphery of sanity and inadvertently put distance between myself and Minx, who now saw me as some dark villain who was ready to fight monsters, except deep down I didn't want to fight anyone anymore - I wanted out.

I needed help.

I did not want to be the vigilante, travelling across London causing chaos and exacting wrath upon all those who embraced sin.

'Converte gladium tuum in locum suum. Omnes enim, qui acceperint gladium, gladio peribunt.'

a wise saying, too clichéd to print in English

THE ESTONIAN

Five thousand pounds is still quite a lot of money in today's terms. I tried to equate what you can actually get for five grand, or 5K – however you want to look at it - and found myself researching this in a bit too much detail. You can buy a good second-hand car or a new mid-range motorbike, perhaps even a caravan to tour in parks up and down the county (although the ground fees would push things slightly over budget); I could certainly treat myself to a luxury holiday, or a very generous night out, or two, at some of London's best bars and nightclubs; £5000 can even get you a lease on a small fried chicken shop, or a deposit on some merchandise that you could import from China and sell on eBay. I never for one second realised that I could buy myself a human being for this amount of money, but the process was relatively easy.

The Donor had left me a plan, an outline of what was needed to infiltrate one of the many gangs linked to the darker side of London, one we suspected was connected to the Ants. I had quizzed him on the depth of his knowledge, about the seedy world of organised criminals, but he remained cagey and tight-lipped; he reassured me that what he was asking us to do had been done successfully before by others. I wasn't allowed to ask about the others.

To this very day I never suspected the Donor of any foul play in the mess I'd become embroiled in, and I considered him to be a good man with a reliable moral compass. Deep down I believed he was trying to make things right in this world. He gave me the option to back out on several occasions, but when I said I wanted to make a difference he helped me. He started by giving me bundles of twenty pound notes equating to five thousand pounds in a tightly packed rolls, with some loose change which I could use to carry out the trading process and have as a contingency fund.

Minx showed me how to connect with groups of men and women on the dark web who had an interest in buying and selling women, and she highlighted several forums where men discussed regularly paying for sex with prostitutes or 'punts' as they would call it. She had directed me to certain sites in particular, one of which had a catalogue of women whom you could contact in London and read through a menu of their services. We trawled this together, Minx and I, putting together a list of possible names of women who were likely to be trafficked. I felt very awkward, ashamed even, after reading some of the services offered by these women whilst Minx sat by my side. The women we identified through the site were, we suspected, paying off a bond to their pimp; we looked for patterns in the phone numbers to see if they had been bought as a bundle of SIMS from the same phone company, and if the profiles read the same - this included things like having generic typos, derogatory name handles, crudely written descriptions, and very cheap rates for not very nice services; typically, if the depiction of services offered showed a degree of malice and a lack of physical care for the worker, such as unprotected sex (bareback), ejaculating in any orifice possible, rough role play, humiliation, spanking, then it was most likely that we were dealing with a group of organised men who had a surplus of female stock ready to bring to a thriving London market of deprived Johns.

Sadly, to take the investigation further, this required visits and I had arranged several appointments around Manor House, Green Lanes and Finsbury Park to ascertain the condition of the women working at these addresses, and to scout out the premises. I would visit at various times during the day and night and I would pay the women for their time, but they were often unwilling to talk and got angry with me if I asked who their boss was or whether I could meet their pimp. On one occasion the maid came into the room and started shouting at me because I was not 'fucking' but 'talking' to the girl, so she called for back-up. I made my excuses and went. Minx and I soon noted a pattern of activity at each property and we could determine whether the same gang controlled each brothel.

We would often talk, Minx and I, during our stake outs and she'd chat candidly about Karl and share anecdotes about some of their work together before I became part of their cell. But Minx was smart, and she would never let on too much about her real life and I had to learn to respect her for that; everyone has boundaries and she stressed that identities - at all costs - must be kept secret in our line of work.

The car that made the most appearances across the addresses was a silver Vauxhall Astra. Each time, two men would arrive at the property and make a collection that lasted only a few minutes. We noted the registration and Minx was able to trace it to an Estonian living at an address in Hornsey. Using that information we were then able to trace other group members who used the same address as their registered home, and slowly we built up a profile of the gang and key members. They may well have been involved in other wrong-doings, such as dealing in drugs and supplying guns to gangs across Hackney and Haringey, but we were limited on resources and man—

power, and so we figured it would be much better to arrange the purchase of a woman from the group online before delving deeper into their wayward operations. And anyway, the NCA did a pretty good job of all the other stuff – we were after vampires.

The Donor had been very specific about whom he was looking for and when we presented our findings to him he said that the gang matched all the criteria. Minx had successfully linked them to a group that operated on the dark web, arranging encrypted auctions on apps like Telegram or across comment boxes transversely through a sequence of social media platforms; if you followed the hyperlinks wrongly you didn't make it to the bidding page. These guys were pros. There was talk of fresh merchandise coming in from Moldovia and Albania; and on another page there were some small .jpeg pictures of the girls scanned from a passport confirming their nationality and age, seventeen and nineteen; hosted on another page were some very awkward pictures of each girl showing off their assets in what looked like a small hotel room or caravan, perhaps taken before they were smuggled across the border.

A bidding process had already begun and all interested parties who had not bought from the gang before had to attend a pre-meeting, where a non-refundable bond of £500 had to be made to arrange an inspection of the goods and be 'validated' by a gang member. Through Minx, I had agreed to pay this bond using Bitcoins online and through cash in person. We were given a time and place in Wood Green to pass the money onto a man name Igor. I understood that this process was about gaining trust, a bit like playing poker where you have to pay the big blind to enter the race; it was a clever way to judge whether the buyer was genuine and whether they could happily trade bigger payloads with that same client. Also, it was a good way to rip people off.

I arrived at Wood Green on a bus and alighted near the cinema. There was a busy café on the corner and that was my designated rendezvous point: a location to meet with a man and make payment. In theory, assuming the deposit was made successfully, the next process would be to meet at another location and sample the goods, a very crude way of saying 'have sex with the girl' to make sure that she met our expectations.

I sat at a table and put down a newspaper and an empty brown envelope with three numbers written in black capitals. It was the sign used to identify myself to the group. As my mocha arrived, so did Igor. Normally I would have stood up and shaken his hand, but he seemed in a rush and I took an instant dislike to the man. He wore an old, grey knitted beanie hat, his face was unshaven, he had filthy hands like that of a labourer, and he was smoking a very strong roll-up cigarette as he hovered over me.

"Igor?" I enquired.

"You're British, that makes me nervous."

"This *is* England," I explained bluntly. "I'm simply a business man looking to invest."

"You look like a policeman," he said, refusing to make eye contact with me. "Everything about you says I should just walk away now. What do you want with girl?"

"I have very important clients," I responded, recounting practically word for word the script that the Donor and Minx had given me. "My clients don't want English girls; they talk too much and complain when things get rough. They want good European girls who do what they're told and keep their mouths shut, unless they're being paid to put something in them." I leaned forward and looked up at him. "If you don't want my business, then fuck off and walk away. You're not the only guys selling whores on the internet, and you standing over me is attracting unwanted attention."

I picked up my paper and started to read, holding it

high enough to cover my face so that he couldn't see me catch my breath. He didn't reply, instead he was busy tapping away on his smart-phone. Minx had deduced that they would have done their own background checks on the user account we created to make contact; they would have their own team of hackers, if they were as big as we thought they were. For that reason we had made several purchases of drugs and other paraphernalia using Bitcoins on a Silk Road inspired site, an underground website where trading in illegal vices was the norm. Minx was good at her job.

When Igor had received the texts he was hoping for he sat down opposite me and began to speak again. "If you have the rest of the bond I will take this from you now. You will have half an hour with girl, and if you like it then you tell us and we do the exchange in public place. We'll tell you one hour before deal where to meet us."

"And what if she runs away?"

"She cannot, you get her papers - you control her."

"What about the bidding process you talked about. Why do I have to bid? Five thousand is a fair price."

"That's not my decision," he said, sliding across the empty envelope.

"Write the address down."

He shook his head: "Money first."

I looked around the café and across the road to see if there was anyone studying us. The streets were busy, and there were men stood on the street using phones, sat in other cafes, leaning against bus stops, even sat inside the café we were at. Any one of them could have been in contact with Igor sending him instructions about what to do.

I put the envelope away in my jacket and pulled out another envelope. "There's fifty cash in there, you get the rest when I arrive at the address."

"No deal."

I shrugged my shoulders and pulled the envelope

back towards me. "No deal then," I said. "I haven't used your services before, and all my other clients usually bring the girl on the first visit. I'm being very accommodating."

The man said nothing; instead he tapped away on his phone, then he waited. I watched him whilst maintaining my best poker face until he received a message. He swiftly took my money off me and then brought out a small slip of lined paper ripped from a cheap notepad; it had a badly written address scrawled out in smudged black ink.

"Be there within half an hour, with the rest of the money, and enjoy your sample.," He left the café.

That was the easy bit, getting the information. But I knew there were two possible outcomes. One, that I had just been duped and was now another £50 lighter, or two, a woman was now being told to look her best and be compliant, waiting for me to arrive at an address somewhere in Haringey, North London.

I finished my coffee and slowly walked to the bus stop, checking the destination on Google maps. I sent Minx a brief message to let her know that I had made contact and began psyching myself up for the meeting. Half an hour wasn't very long to convince organised criminals that I was also into organised crime. I needed a regular day job again.

The address led me to a non-descript flat above shops on the road between Alexander Palace and Wood Green. I stood at street level looking at the slip of paper and pressed the buzzer. Seconds later the door clicked open without anyone asking who it was. The hallway smelt of damp. There were only two flats. The one I wanted was on the top floor.

I knocked on the door and waited. I could hear at least two sets of footsteps move about before a chain and two locks were undone. The door eventually opened and a woman greeted me, not the one in the passport picture but a more casually dressed lady, late twenties with black hair tied in a pony-tail and deep brown eyes with heavy makeup. I showed her the slip of paper and she ushered me inside, locking the door behind us. The kitchen door was closed and that was where I suspected at least one male member of the group was waiting, should anything not go to plan. The woman led me to a bedroom and ushered me inside. I sat on a sorry looking single bed in the corner of the room. Pale blue sheets had been used as makeshift curtains for the smallest of windows; I checked them and saw it had been nailed shut. On the bedside table some talc, oil and tissues were my only company, and in the shelf below was a Serbian to English dictionary. The rest of the room had been stripped of all character and warmth; if someone lived here it was clearly a temporary home.

The door opened and the girl from the photo came in. She smelt of overly-sweet perfume and her eye makeup was impeccable. "Hello," she whispered. Her clothes were made of thin cotton and I could see her underwear clearly beneath it; the bra was ill fitting. She came and sat beside me and looked at the floor, her small bobbed haircut shielding her eyes. I stood up and paraded around the room, checking that the door was closed and listening for people on the other side. I had half an hour to try and communicate with her my intention but I was doubtful if she would understand anything I said. I knew the men controlling her would ask about me and what I did her, so I kept the sales pitch running.

"What's your name?"

"Ana," she said, nodding.

"And where are you from, Ana?"

"From Poland."

"How old?"

"Nineteen years."

Minx informed me that girls were often prompted to speak little, obey a lot. "How long have you been in London?"

She took time to process. "How long? I think . . . not long."

Anticipating her English to be bad, Minx and I set about producing a simple slip of paper containing the same phrase written in different languages. Simply put, the message read: *We can help you. Stay calm and nod if you want us to take you out of slavery.* It was plain, direct and almost rhetorical, but before doing so we also suspected that the sellers would be watching, or even listening.

I told her to take off her clothes. She nodded obediently and began removing her garments. She was thin, not starved, but her body was in proportion; she had little colour to her skin, more of a milky white complexion, probably from always being kept indoors; her hips still seemed adolescent and she had been crudely shaved around the pubic area; she had a couple of small tattoos around her ankle, and one on her right shoulder. I was neither aroused nor interested in her physically; I pitied her. I figured that if she had been coerced that there would be evidence of bruising or burning. I sat back on the bed, raised my arm and rotated my hand in a circular motion. "Turn around."

She obeyed me again, slowly enough for me to notice a small cigarette burn on the back of her arm, and some bruising at the top of her back just below the neck where she had been grabbed forcefully. I asked her to come and sit beside me. She was shaking at this point. I held her arm gently and pushed the notice on the bed for her to read.

I watched her study the note, her eyes scouring down the list of languages until I saw her eyes lock and focus on the words. Her breaths grew shorter. Then a tear appeared in the corner of her eye and she nodded her head gently. I reassured her it would be okay and held her a bit tighter. I was ashamed. I was ashamed that in England this could happen with such ease. I didn't have to ask for her story, not that she would have told me there and then; Britain's borders were so permeable that the trafficking of women like her was increasing and fast becoming a profitable business.

I honestly didn't know what to do next. I had hoped she might speak more, or ask questions, but Minx had predicted correctly that she might just appreciate having time to reflect, and so I lay her down next to me and held her, gently stroking her hair, so that if someone were to walk in they would not think otherwise. The saddest thing about the experience, however, was the uncertainty; final bidding was not until that evening and I might not be the only man willing to pay a high cash bond to buy her out of slavery; I tried to block out the idea that she might be abused and raped later that same day, or had already been subject to such violations earlier that morning.

The sellers didn't care; she would make them money.

After fifteen minutes or so there was a knock at the door. By that point I had ripped open a condom, spat in it and cast it aside on the floor with some crumpled tissues beside it. A man came in and saw us lying there together. "Time's up," he said. Ana sat up and started to put on her clothes. I looked over and saw that it was Igor, the scruffy messenger from the café. "I hope you enjoyed the sample," he continued. "I will fuck her myself later."

I wanted to punch him in the face there and then. "She has great potential; it would be a shame to spoil the goods in such a way. I'm still interested - what's the next step?"

"First, the rest of the bond, then tonight we agree price, and if you are the highest bidder then we can arrange delivery tomorrow: cash only."

I nodded to show him that I understood and left the flat without looking back at Ana. In my heart I hoped she would be safe.

When I met with Minx later that day, she sounded pleased that I had made progress, if you can call it that. Infiltrating the gang was the hardest step, she said, and if I could gain their trust and secure a purchase then we knew that I could possibly go deeper; so long as the money kept coming in and the questions were kept to a minimum, they could continue to feed off me like a cancer until we had what we needed to close them down.

Later that evening we received a message from one of the members. They said they were happy to exchange the next day, but that the bidding price was starting at £5000. I asked why the reserve had gone up and they said it was to match the offer of another pimp who had sampled the goods that same day, and because there was a lack of 'fresh meat' on the market. We had an hour to put in our best offer.

£4000 was cheap for such an item as a living, breathing human being, and getting hold of more cash was not a problem since the Donor had given us over £5000 to buy ourselves in. I suggested to Minx that we might be able to get away by offering £5500 but she was adamant that we follow the Donor's orders. The men we were dealing with didn't seem to care about loyalty at this stage, just a good price for goods sold.

We put our offer in and about fifteen minutes later we got a message saying our bid was successful. The Donor had mentioned that the price would keep going up right up until the day we bargained, so I had to expect this type of greed from such animals, which meant taking the contingency money with me just in case they refused to part with the goods for the price agreed online. We would get a message an hour before payment and collection was due.

I dreamt that night. I imagined that I was somewhere else, another country surrounded by pine forests which spilled out into rolling moors; everything was covered in moss of all different colours. I felt at peace. I was clothed but bare-footed and walking across this strange land when I heard a fanfare, and so I began to sprint. I never turned round to see who was chasing me: I just kept running. I negotiated boulders, scrambled through scrubland and dipped in and out of streams until I came to a cliff.

Beyond the cliff was a town, a picturesque scene typical of the Scottish Highlands, and there was a light house and calm green waters rolling into the distance. Dead below me was a rocky ravine, full of bones and red cloaks, books and bicycle wheels, and gold – lots of gold. As the fanfare grew louder, a cacophony of angry voices and wild beasts snarling, I stepped off the edge and fell vertically. I focused on the small white house near the shore in the distance, hoping I would make it there, until I hit the valley of bones and the dream ended with a jolt.

I sat up in a sweat. It was around 4am and the moon was shining brightly through my window. I got up and looked out into the garden, and then checked the front of the house. It was quiet and empty like I had expected, but there was one car which seemed to have a small glow from inside the cabin. As I stood focusing on the one vehicle, my veins still pumping furiously, I noticed that the glow was the end of a cigarette, and seconds later a trail of smoke came from the window. I went downstairs and got dressed.

When I left the house and walked towards the car it was quick to start up and drive away. I couldn't see the driver, or the person in the back of the car as it drove off, but I knew that they were there for me and that's when I understood that I was treading on dangerous ground again. Gangs lived by their own codes and rules, and despite our acting and best intentions we were neither a gang nor a formidable organisation.

As I went to go back inside, wide awake and now freezing, I saw a fox staring at me on the opposite side of the road. The moon reflected in its eyes and we shared a moment, two nocturnal beings dwelling in a savage world; it leapt over a fence and out of sight. Smart move.

I was tense for the rest of the morning, high on caffeine and regularly refreshing my inbox and checking forums across the dark net for any hint of an address or rendezvous point for the deal. Minx messaged me to check I was still happy to go ahead. I reassured her that I could keep it together and make the deal.

At just after midday I received a message from one of the gang telling me to meet at Finsbury Park station. On the corner of the high road and the station was a coffee shop, a popular chain that was to be our meeting point. I sent a confirmation message and then left the house with two envelopes of cash, wanting to arrive there in good time. It was going to be tight.

Finsbury Park is a busy interchange where people change trains and buses for most of the day. Coupled with ongoing building work, there is a constant movement and energy about the place, yet there are also pockets of calm when the traffic lights turn red and everything seems to stop and reset itself. I arrived and approached the Costa coffee shop which afforded a great location on the corner of the road, drawing punters in through the two sets of doors and churning each one out with red cups of warm brown liquid. As I approached I saw the man from the day before, Igor, sat with two other men at a table with three empty espresso cups, like they had been waiting there for a while. The men were on their phone but Igor clocked me and nodded at the other men to regard me coolly. I saw no girl with them and suddenly thought that I was about to find myself a few thousand pounds lighter.

"More drinks?" I asked jovially. They all pointed to their empty cups and so I went in and primed myself, bluntly ordering a round of espresso shots from a moody looking barista.

When I returned outside, a space had been made for me to sit down. In their attempt to show some degree of warmth and personality, one of the men cracked a joke that I had women's hands as I set down their drinks. The others laughed. I gave a pained smile before explaining to the man that his mother didn't mind them. Thankfully my sarcasm was somewhat lost in translation and I found myself trying to remain disciplined, the Donor's voice in my head pleading with me to keep cool and not blow the operation with a careless joke or a slip of the tongue.

I avoided eye contact with the men and looked directly at Igor. "I don't see any merchandise."

"Boss coming. You're a little early. You have the money?"

I nodded. He gestured that I should hand it over but I firmly shook my head.

"You don't trust us?" he said, a cigarette in the corner of his mouth and his arms open wide in a display of hyper-masculinity.

"I've been ripped off before by Turks," I said, probing them for any animosity against rival gangs.

"That's what happens when you deal with those filthy animals" he said. "Their girls are usually hooked on heroin and carrying all sorts of diseases. With us you get a nice girl, a simple village girl from a big family; not much experience and most importantly, a nice tight pussy."

"I learnt from my mistakes," I said. "They left me out of pocket and feeling very angry."

"So what you do about it?"

"I organised a hit," I said boastfully. Realising that sounded a bit American, I went into more detail. "Or rather, I paid one of the Hackney Turks to tattoo one of the Bombardier boys at a local snooker club. I didn't get my money back, but I got a nice photo."

Igor sat up, nodding in approval at my lies. "You will like the boss. He will be straight with you."

I sipped my espresso and studied the surroundings. It was so brazen to deal publically, but it also made perfect sense; a clever strategy was being used by them. There were no cameras in the vicinity and we were almost in a blind spot, away from prying eyes and covered by a steady stream of moving traffic and a public phone box. The men were all wearing caps and the café had two exits; any of the roads leading away from the station branched off into more roads which led to small ethnic shops which were like rabbit warrens, the perfect place to afford some cover should things go wrong.

After several minutes, a well-built man, about five-foot nine and wearing a black hooded Adidas sweater, sat down with us. Ana accompanied him. I smiled at her but she looked away. I had never seen a girl look so scared before and her skin looked blotchy and her eyes were puffy, like she had been crying for most of the night. I stood and greeted him formally, extending my hand. He waved at me to sit, not wanting to make a fuss of the scenario.

"Igor tells me you liked the goods."

"Very nice," I said. "My clients will approve."

"Your clients, do they get through many girls?"

"They have a good appetite," I said, not really gauging where the conversation was going at this point. "If you're asking about repeat business then, providing everything checks out, I am happy to work with you again."

He pointed at Igor to show me what I wanted to see: Ana's official documents. I flicked through them, at her passport, a copy of her birth certificate, and some fake travel documents that had obviously got her across a border of some sort. She wasn't Polish at all but from Moldova. Without the documents she was an illegal, someone who would be arrested and deported back home should everything not work out under the pimp's control.

"If you still want her the price is now £6000," the boss said brazenly.

"Why does it keep going up?"

"Because I like her, I might want to keep her for myself. I set the price. That is what she's worth to me."

Ana refused to look at any of us. I noticed that she was carrying a small bag, perhaps this was all her belongings. I knew she spoke little English and had limited understanding of what we were discussing, but that didn't make my conscience feel any better. The Donor had correctly predicted that these groups used such methods, to try and renegotiate prices after allowing clients to sample the goods – I was wrong to doubt him after a price of £3000 had initially been set online – it was about hooking people in, letting them all sample her. All of the men sat before me were motivated by greed, in particular by the cash in my pocket. It is what had brought them over to London originally, either legally or illegally, to exploit the weak. Even if they trafficked one woman a week at three or four thousand pounds a turn, this equated to around £200,000 of untraceable money each year entering the black market. Each woman was a bond, something to sell and trade up; saturate the market and the price went down, but if the police and border force agencies do their job properly, the price for trafficked girls went up. As for Ana, if I successfully purchased her I would become her pimp and control her, force her to see up to ten or more clients a day at £30 or £40 a time, earning perhaps £1500-2000 a week just from immoral earnings. She would pay for herself by the end of the first month if I worked her hard enough and then start becoming profitable, and then if after a year or so she started to look tired, or lost her looks, I could just sell her on to someone else where she would have to repay that same bond again.

Not much of a life.

The papers that I held were her original bond, the original debt for travel tickets and a false promise of a new life, perhaps working as a cleaner or a nanny for a nice Western family in England, or perhaps a job as a care worker in a home for the elderly, definitely not servicing strangers in a damp London apartment with locked windows.

"All looks good," I said.

The man studied me intensely. "You remind me of another client."

I studied the faces around me and grew concerned

that I was about to become a victim of my own sting operation. I played it cool. "Is he an older man? Tall with grey hair?"

"No, she is red-haired woman – skin white like snow. Cold-hearted bitch. She wanted girls for client, she never say what for. But she paid well, price six thousand each girl, sometimes seven, even ten if the girl could go high end."

"What are my guarantees?"

"She does what you ask – you have her documents. I give no guarantees. We have no contract. There are no refunds. She run away, it's your problem. If police arrest you, you tell them you buy whores off Turks. If anything comes back to me – I give you headache. Today you pay me cash. I'm happy to give you discount on next purchase."

I loathed everything about him; his arrogance, his whining voice, his grotesque size – bulked out by baggy clothing. I imagined where he might be from, and what he might have been in his country before turning to organised crime. "You're from Serbia, aren't you?"

The other men laughed. "Nice guess, my friend," he said, smiling at me. "But I am man of many countries."

The men around him were hired hands, henchman from the eastern block – manual labourers turned freeloaders, or ex-convicts who came over on an alias or a fake ID; I imagined all of them had criminal records as long as their tattooed arms and they had now anchored themselves across London, building their own crime network. Minx had run background checks on the group, and if her research was right then the man opposite me was called Zladic, an Estonian trafficker with convictions for drug offences, trafficking, arms dealings, aggravated assault, rape and manslaughter, many of them committed back in his own country. Though this information would not show up on whatever fake ID he could produce for me, my inkling was to call his bluff.

"Well, get me a nice Estonian girl next time please – a blonde," I said.

He nodded, laughing out loud. "Blonde Estonians are very good girls," he said "And they make great wives. I should know, I've had two!" The men laughed like robots at his comment.

I looked over at Ana who had remained subdued throughout. Then I removed all of the money, including the extra the Donor had predicted I would need, and packed it in to a paper food bag like they had asked.

One of the men took the bag and went inside the café, presumably to go to the toilet and look inside. I was left in the company of thugs, finishing my espresso and planning my quickest route home. I looked up at the cameras facing the station, not once had they moved round to take a snap shot of our deal, not that they would be able to; the phone box blocked the view.

The man returned, minus the bag. His hands were buried deep inside his pockets. He looked over at Zladic and nodded.

"It seems we have a deal."

I didn't shake hands, and I didn't look over the moon about it either. I tucked Ana's travel documents into my jacket and stood up. I hoped that the Donor had not paid for this deal with honest money, that he had reused Ant money somehow. Regardless, she was now mine.

"Let's go!" I said assertively to her. She snapped out of her trance and followed me to the nearest black cab. I opened the door, let her in and gave the driver the name of my road. As I looked back out of the window and over at the tables, Zladic had already disappeared, leaving the original three men and their empty espresso cups. They gave me a dismissive hand gesture and carried on talking like nothing had happened.

The journey back to my home was completed in silence. Ana seemed cold and her arms were crossed tightly over her body as she stared out of the window. I sent an email on my phone to Minx telling her of my success. She was quick to reply and tell me that Jo would organise things her end and meet us back at my house.

I called over to Ana, telling her she would be okay. She looked at me dubiously, then down at my pack of documents – her identity. "I'm going to help you," I assured her. "I'm going to make things right."

She remained silent .

When we arrived at my home I took her bag and led her to my front door. She seemed surprised, almost relieved when she saw that my residence was not another basement flat or 3rd floor loft room. I led Ana inside, sat her in the living room and lit a fire, just to give her something to focus on and perhaps allow her to reflect on the situation whilst I made a cup of tea for us both.

I did what I could to offer her some warmth, something she had probably not felt in weeks or months even. But by this point I was at a loss. I had just bought myself a human being with someone else's money; a counterfeit mail order bride found through the dark net with the help of a punk-loving hacker who held a grudge against human traffickers, traffickers who might just be linked to Ants, the group who killed Karl. My situation just got a hell of a lot more complicated.

A couple of hours passed and Ana had not moved; she had managed to drink two half cups of tea and eaten some toast and jam; She did not try and speak to me or signal for help, she just remained enclosed in herself, locked and bound by morose thoughts.

I was relieved when Minx finally turned up at the house. She had kept true to her word and brought with her a translator. When I heard the female translator speak I saw a transformation in Ana's behaviour. At first she looked at them both in disbelief, then with such joy, and then the tears came. Minx and I watched as she wept and cried and wailed for minutes on end. I suggested that the translator take Ana upstairs, to a room where she could lie down and perhaps freshen up. The translator did so and I was left alone with Minx to decide on the next steps.

"I don't feel like we've really achieved anything," I said. "We just paid £6000 to a group of wicked men so that they can repeat the whole process and recruit more vulnerable women. What have we actually accomplished?"

"We know that the ants like to dine on young women, and that one of the victims we discovered came through this gang. If we can infiltrate them, gain their trust, then we can get introduced to one of the leader's contacts – and that might lead us closer to the top of the chain."

"The top of what fucking chain exactly?" I blurted. "This is all just hypothetical. These mobsters live by their own honour codes. Even if we got to the top, there are probably several other gangs trafficking women to them – they'll just swap sources and keep dragging us along, using up all our money until they realise we're trying to entrap them."

"You need to be more positive, John," Minx replied. "When we get what we need we'll give everything else we have to the police. Nothing more – no one is asking you to fight this group on your own anymore. We just need a way in."

"I'm not sure this is going to yield much. If anything I think my mind has just been diverted away from the Ants, from vampirism. My attention is now focused on this new world of crime and misery. This guy I met today, the ringleader of the gang, I just know that he's pure evil. I'd like nothing more than to remove him from society completely."

"Then you're no better than them," scalded Minx. "I can see why Michael used to bitch about you – you don't think things through. You make rash decisions."

I didn't respond because I knew she was right. I felt cheated that Michael had been sharing his little anecdotes about me with others whilst I felt so alone. I reminded

Minx that Michael may have stitched us all up before focusing back on the task in hand. Minx apologised. We focused on the positive outcome of the operation: we had taken Ana out of slavery.

I paced about the room for a few moments before changing the subject. I asked about the encryption software she had downloaded onto my computers and enquired whether there was any news on the Ant front in London. She talked about a 'party' that was scheduled to take place in Paddington a few days later and we spent time discussing ways we could try and catch wind of the address.

The translator came down about half an hour later and asked to speak with us. Ana's story checked out and was typical of a girl in her situation: she had been coerced to seek work as a cleaner in Italy but didn't have the funds to pay for her ticket, so she effectively took out a loan with the recruitment agency (a bogus outfit) in Moldova; they took her across the border into Romania and through to Hungary; a second group of men collected her and drove her near the border to work at some bars in a holding house near the border of Slovenia where she was forced to work in bars and nightclubs as a dancer. She was beaten and raped and forced to have sex with several clients whilst a price was agreed on her head, then another gang trafficked her the rest of the way to the UK where she'd been kept in London ever since. She mentioned that Ana was grateful for my arrival at the flat and for the kindness I had shown her. It didn't, however, prevent her from being violently gang-raped that very night by the men I had all sat with only hours before. It explained everything. None of it was justified.

I wanted to kill them all.

"They're fucking animals," Minx declared.

"Did you tell her that she is going to go home?" I asked. "That we'll pay for her to get back to her family."

"Yes," she replied calmly. "But I don't think she

believes me. She is very shocked and extremely anxious about telling her family what happened to her. She thinks they will disown her and that she will fall into the same trap, trying to take up work in another country."

"Surely there are organisations," I commented. "local NGOs that can take her statement, rehabilitate and then reintegrate her back into work if she wants to."

"There are, but a lot has happened and it will take time for her to heal. I don't think she can trust anyone right now."

I agreed, especially trusting men. "We need to ask her about other women she may have met, and other clients she came into contact with. We need to know if her sellers drove a car, if she can remember a house number, a phone number, how many different voices were in the group – anything that can help us close this operation down."

"In time, John," cautioned Minx. "These things take time."

The translator nodded. "She is sleeping for short time. I will speak to her when she wakes."

Only Ana wasn't sleeping. She was in the process of trying to take her own life.

It was during our conversation that I head a crashing sound from upstairs. We all looked at one another and made a dash for the top floor. The door to the bathroom was locked and we could hear the tap running. The translator called through the door, asking if everything was okay. There was no reply. I went to smash the door down and then remembered that, as a child, I had learned to unlock the door from outside. I did so subtly, twisting the lock with a coin and then pushing the door too. What greeted us was a bloody mess: Ana lying in a bath of her own blood as cold water streamed over her.

"Fuck!" I remember shouting loudly. Blood was everywhere, spurting from two cuts on her wrists. Minx grabbed a load of towels, I turned the taps off, and we both hauled her out of the bath and onto the floor.

"We need to call an ambulance," the translator cautioned.

"No ambulances!" Minx and I replied in unison. Minx told me to apply pressure to the wrists whilst she went to ring the Donor for help. Ana was drifting out of consciousness. The translator told me she was at risk of going into shock and that we needed to get Ana to a hospital urgently. I tried my best to explain that we were in a difficult situation, but then Minx came back in and made the decision easier.

"The Donor is sending a cab – we're going to have to drop her at A & E ourselves."

I was frustrated but at the same time relieved. I did not have the resources or medical knowledge to deal with so much blood, and neither did Minx. My hands were now covered in the stuff and I noticed how quickly it seemed to coagulate in my hands. My heart thumped wildly and I found myself strangely pondering whether there was any of that killer instinct left in me; a desire to feed, to make use of this delicate life-force draining away from her. I felt none.

"We need to stem the bleeding if we're to get her downstairs and out of the door," advised Minx. We made makeshift tourniquets around her arms and put her in the recovery position. I left Minx with the translator and went to grab some duct tape. When I returned, with thinner towels, I began taping them around her wrists tightly to apply pressure.

We put a dressing gown around her and carried her downstairs, and between the three of us we made it look as civil as possible when we walked her to the cab, which had arrived as promised.

I didn't get a good look at the driver but I was adamant I had seen him before, like he was one of the Donor's special workers who helped during a clean-up operation, perhaps he'd even driven me home after a bloody encounter of my own.

The translator went in the cab with Ana to the hospital. We knew that the driver would have prepared his own back story to tell officers that he'd picked Ana up from a different part of London. It didn't disguise the fact, however, that our plan had gone drastically wrong. Minx and I turned and walked back to the house as they drove off.

Minx sat down in the living room and poured herself a drink. Her hands were still shaking and she was swearing under her breath. I joined her, noticing that I still had dried blood on the back of my hands and spatter marks across my trousers.

"What's the plan now?" I asked, having run out of ideas.

Minx just sat there and shrugged. "We need to pay them back, on Ana's behalf more than anything."

I nodded in silent reflection. I wanted justice and I hated that we had paid criminals with so much cash. Minx received a text ten minutes later stating that they had arrived at the hospital safely and Ana was being treated by a team of doctors and nurses. Then Minx caught me off guard and asked me to pray with her.

"I don't know how," I said.

"Just rest your hand on my shoulder and open your heart."

We prayed together that Ana would pull through, but as we did so I couldn't help but feel that she might have been better off dead. I still had all of Ana's paperwork and if she did survive she would have a very different experience with the Home Office to what we had planned for her. But as I waited and prayed with her I found peace. A warm feeling passed over me; Minx must have felt it too because she squeezed my hand, thanked me and gave me a hug. She seemed a lot calmer and happier once we'd sat in silent reflection for a moment. In many ways it made me admire her more, for Minx was slowly letting down her guard each time we met and I got to see a little bit more of the real her.

Perhaps Minx noticed this and she put her mask back on as we talked about next steps. "John, deep down in my heart I know that you're a good man."

I disagreed. "Good men don't want to kill people in revenge, and good men don't bring fear and misery to the people around them. Wherever I go there's a shadow hanging over me." I recounted to her what had happened in Thailand, and what had happened at various other stages in my life, including Alissa's death, during the past two years. "I have tried to protect people but I always end up having to run away when I should have stayed to fight."

She assured me that I could seek forgiveness and redemption, that with the mouth one confesses and is saved, but I didn't like where the conversation was going. I needed punishment, not redemption – ultimately I had gone too far and what had just happened was about to push me over the edge.

"You might not seek redemption, John, but I'm going to bring down this group of men who traffik, rape and abuse women with or without you, so you might as well man up and get involved."

"Do you think the Donor will give us one more shot?"

"If we bend the truth somewhat, we can probably find another way back in. But we will have to put finding Michael on hold for a bit longer."

I looked at her and nodded. Finding Michael and Rameses seemed a bit like a lost cause; both men were ghosts lost in the murky depths of London, I was focused now on hunting ghouls.

We had a tangible opportunity to do some good and see our talents put to the test. Vampires, traffickers – they were both parasites and it was hard to distinguish between the two in my eyes.

Parasites are of no use to anyone.

Rather than go to sleep and start a fresh in the morning, we started planning our next move that same evening.

ORGANISED CRIME CROSSOVER

What happened to Ana was unforgiveable. I felt incredible guilt and anger; to this day, I struggle to forget the moment I burst into my bathroom to find her dying. I made comparisons to my own experience, when I had nearly been bled dry by Ed and was nurtured by Michael, only to discover that he attempted to drown me in some bizarre baptismal process. Perhaps there was something in my house, or someone watching over us to ensure that all hope was not lost. I like to think so.

I was sleeping a lot more on the sofa, an electronic device not far away from my hand. My head remained fuzzy and my eyes stung from all the researching. Whilst Ana had survived, we did not see her again as she went into care and declared asylum on the grounds that she had been trafficked illegally into the country and exploited by a gang who had left her to die. That was the story. We don't know how far her story was pursued by relevant authorities.

It took almost two weeks before the gang we had bought Ana from replied to our message requesting to purchase another girl. When they did reply they recommended some new merchandise for me to inspect.

The procedure was roughly the same: I would pay a deposit, meet them at a location and inspect the goods. All being well, the price would be agreed and a location chosen for the exchange to take place. I didn't suspect for one minute that they might have an ulterior motive for meeting with me, which is probably why I bear the scars to this very day.

The signs were there from the start of my own personal crusade. Sadly I chose to ignore them because I was hell bent on revenge. The meet-up was at a car garage on a brownfield site around Hackney Wick, just a stone's throw from the Olympic village. I was to meet with Igor again and collect information about where to meet the new girl. Minx had done some research by this point but could find no link between the address of the garage and the gang, either financially or through known family connections. But realistically, who meets a bunch of criminals at 6pm in the middle of an industrial estate when the garage has closed?

Me.

I had checked my route beforehand and planned to adopt the same persona as before, perfected from years of working in estate agency and business administration for big banks and insurance companies. I looked the part and so my veil of arrogance was perfected. It was going to be a simple deal, I had told myself.

The main reception to the garage was closed but there was a badly written sign that said 'enquiries this way' and a black arrow. I followed the path and gained access to the main workshop through a small gap in the shutters.

Igor was waiting inside, exactly like I had imagined him to be: scruffy, scrawny and smoking roll-ups. He acknowledged me with a nod. "The Englishman returns," he said softly. "I hope your clients enjoyed Ana as much as we did."

I didn't say anything, still believing I was in a position to bargain. As I approached him he continued to tap frantically into his smartphone. I stood opposite him and waited for the demands of more cash to see the goods. As I did so, two men came in to the workshop from where I had entered. And then another man followed shortly after, the driver I assumed, and he closed the shutters completely.

"And how is Ana really getting on?" another voice called.

I turned to see Zladic emerge from the back of the workshop, his misshapen bulk falling out of a black tracksuit with sparkling white trainers. Thick gold chains were around his wrist and neck as he approached me.

"She's in a much better place," I said, realising the game was probably up.

"Yes, you see Ana was a very loyal girl," he continued, "so when she got out of hospital she rang her friend, who also happens to be our friend, and we heard the sad news."

He stopped opposite me and there was an awkward silence. Five men now surrounded me, several paces away. I didn't quite know what I should do, I simply held my ground. "Then you'll know why I'm here. You said no refunds, but I thought perhaps next time if I buy from you I can have someone who is not so damaged."

"I told you she was your problem, not mine," Zladic began, pointing his stubby fingers in my direction. "But when a nice Moldovan girl gets spoken to by the police, people start sniffing round my business. That becomes problem, you understand?"

"It was unfortunate."

"Yes, unfortunate for her, and for you."

"Are you trying to tell me the deal is off, because my clients are expecting girls."

As I finished my sentence I felt my legs give way after they were hit with metal jack. As I collapsed backwards, two men grabbed my arms and began dragging me to the side of the workshop. I protested, stating that they were making a big mistake – that I wasn't to blame. But I knew at that moment that this wasn't about retribution for what happened to Ana – they didn't care about her; this was about asserting their authority, living by their codes.

"There's something about you that I don't like, that doesn't quite check out," Zladic continued. "We have so many girls, yet you took Ana. You were so quick to buy from us. Ana was a filthy whore who was past her best and yet you paid for her when we could have given you many kind of girls, which made me think that you were policeman. Except we can't prove that, which makes me think you are other type of man."

I was sat in a chair, a man either side of me, my arms still gripped tightly. Zladic picked up some heavy looking wrench and loomed over me. Igor peered over his shoulder and the other man seemed to be keeping watch of the building, almost anticipating an ally of mine to arrive. I half hoped someone might intervene before things got messy. Where was Michael when I really needed him?

One of the men held my left arm out on a bench. I tried to resist but the other man then held his arm around my neck and twisted my other arm behind my back.

"You know, British man, if you mess with things you have no understanding about, then you will get hurt. What the hell are you doing messing around with cars?"

I looked at him confusedly, just before he slammed the wrench down on my left hand. I can't fully describe the pain, it was like placing your hand in boiling water and then having it dipped in ice. My whole body shuddered and I lost my breath. All I could hear was the echo of men laughing at me. I knew straight away that my hand was broken, and as the blood pounded around my fist I felt light headed. My mind came to the snap conclusion that I was going to die for achieving nothing. Even when I felt like I had bought Ana out of slavery, in reality I knew that these men would probably have a dozen more like her passing through their filthy hands in the months to come. I had a chance to stop them and I was about to lose it.

Zladic pulled out a large bunch of keys. One of them had a plastic handle which he removed to reveal a very large spike. He held it in front of my face. I contemplated whether I was about to lose my sight when he quickly stuck it into the top of my hand to leave a puncture wound. At this point I managed to find my voice, but I didn't scream. I wouldn't give them the satisfaction.

"You're making a mistake," I said. "You've clearly got me all wrong."

"We shall see," Zladic continued, reaching for a bucket of used motor oil. He splashed it at me, on my clothes, soiling a perfectly good jacket, shirt and pair of trousers; then he poured the rest on my hand, and then for good measure hit it again with the wrench.

I gave in. I screamed and I begged and I yelled. I wanted to curl into a ball and die at this point than give them any more pleasure. They continued to laugh and cast me to the floor.

"I see we clearly have got you all right," Zladic said. "If you were really one of us you would not make a sound, but take everything we give. You really shouldn't mess with fast cars. Look at your hand! Look at what has happened. Next time, get a mechanic to do your dirty work."

He cast a dirty rag in my face as I lay on the floor. One of the men rooted through my pockets and pulled out my wallet. There was only cash and pre-paid credit cards inside. He took them all and threw the wallet to the ground. Then he took my old smartphone; despite having a simply key lock on it, there was nothing that would give away my details or that of the cell. Minx always called on a withheld number, and we took a new phone and number each time we went out. It was a good rule, one that would save us – I managed a half smile to myself.

"I have dealt with charity workers, priests, do-gooders, grieving relatives and even police men," Zladic assured. "If you mess with expensive cars again, you may lose more than a hand. Don't ever contact us again." He waved his hand and his entourage suddenly just left me lying on the floor in agony.

Assaulted. Robbed. Humiliated. Those were the three things that I took away from my meeting with Zladic that day. I had no way of contacting Minx without her call, or sending a message to her.

I waited for about five minutes before getting up. I used the rag to clean my hand and searched for a first aid kit to stop the bleeding. When I left the garage I realised that I looked like a man who had had an accident whilst trying to fix his car. I had underestimated how smart and calculating Zladic had been. I also felt cheated. How did it go so wrong?

When I made it to the main road a passer-by saw me looking distressed. She asked what had happened and I explained the incident I'd had with my 'car' and then I asked her where the nearest hospital was. God was looking out for me that day, because she didn't just tell me: she took me.

I caught a glimpse of my reflection in the mirror as she drove me to A and E. I was shivering and in shock. I found it hard to believe that she had bought my story, a stranger staggering about Hackney Wick covered in motor oil. I explained that I had no money on me, that I had left my cards at home but she was dismissive – she didn't want payment for her good deed. She even offered to call her brother-in-law round so that he could help fix my car. I explained that I was covered and it was my own fault for being impatient, for trying to fix the car myself when I should have left it to the experts. It gave me a chance to fix the story myself, practice it a few times before entering A & E. I asked if she would at least write down her name and address so that I could write to her, which thankfully she did.

I'm forever grateful to Taneisha for her compassion and kindness, her grace and her mercy. I'm thankful people like her exist in this day and age, and I strive to be more like her – perhaps I can one day when all of this darkness is behind me.

I spent the rest of the afternoon and most of the evening in hospital. I had a breakage in my left hand and several fractures. My hand was heavily swollen and I not only had to take a series of strong pain killers, but also anti-biotics to stop the risk of infection from an open wound. I found more grace and love from complete strangers, from immigrant nurses and doctors that treated me without prejudice, without judgement. When I explained my situation, regarding the car and lack of money, they let me use a computer in the hospital where I was able to get a message to Minx.

Afterwards I waited in the hospital café, high on painkillers and feeling sick with nerves. When Minx found me she was angry, anxious and upset. I remember apologising to her, affirming that all her early assumptions about me had been true, that I was a liability, a risk to their organisation and that she should just leave me out of the cell – that I could effectively contribute no more.

She dismissed my comments and put me in a taxi home where she cared for me whilst I got myself ready for bed. My whole arm ached and the small suture on my hand felt itchy already and I had a desire to tear off the dressing and inspect the wounds.

Minx came to my door before she left. "I'll come and see you tomorrow."

"Don't worry about me anymore," I told her. "I'm done with this – I'm the most hopeless investigator you'll ever meet. In fact, I'm not sure I want this life anymore. I want to change but for better not for worse."

"You're just saying that because you're tired and feeling low. This is just a phase, John. You're capable of so much more. This is all my fault – I should have read the signs."

"But you didn't because I didn't want you to. I was so thirsty for revenge that I didn't think things through: I never do. This isn't the first time that I've been like this, it's why my ex-partner left me, why my dad turned his back on me, why Michael abandoned me. I'm selfish," I declared. "And I've become too proud. Working with this cell, with a sponsor who is prepared to pay for my adventures, has given me the wrong type of confidence. I deserved what I got."

"That's bullshit," she declared. "No-one deserves what happened to you. It's humiliating - barbaric even. You can't just roll over and let them win, John. Where's your famous stiff fucking upper lip?"

I shrugged. "Gone. Fucked."

"Well then, get some sleep and figure out where the fuck you left it, because I am not giving up on you and damned if I'm going to let you back out of this investigation now. You're a force for good, John."

I didn't have the energy to debate much longer. I simply help up my mangled hand and waved it dismissively. I shouldn't have, I realised this at the time, but I was in no state of mind to debate my future high on painkillers.

She closed the door as she left and I heard her weeping. I felt angry with myself that I let her down. What I didn't realise was that Minx actually cared for me. It was hard to believe given our first encounter where she was so blunt, but it was true - and I hadn't seen it until now because I had been so selfish and inward looking.

Over the next two weeks I remained a prisoner in my home. The curtains remained drawn for most of it, I ordered all my shopping online and spent the day hooked up to the internet. Those were the worst two weeks of my life. It felt so wrong to be living my life online, a second life that I struggled to control. The social media profiles we created had not yielded the desired impact; the groups and forums I had joined had lost all of their zing; everything was negative, it was all the fault of the rich and the elite; everything was someone else's fault. There was no accountability for anything anymore. Society seemed to have given up and declared itself a sore loser.

I spoke to Minx on the phone one evening and I asked about Ana, if there had been any contact with her, and if she was safe. Minx explained that she had been given refuge and, thanks to our intervention and provision of her documents, she was in a safe place. I still worried about her, though; I worried that she might be found by Zladic and his men and stressed that something needed to be done about them, recounting to her what they had said to me. When Minx asked if I had a plan I flatly declared that I could do nothing. I was just an ideas guy, someone who made suggestions…no use to anyone. She remained my sycophant.

I had made two visits to the hospital during this time and the specialist mentioned that I was likely to have permanent nerve damage because of my loss of sensation and numbness in the hand. The swelling had reduced but I found it hard to bend my hand and I suffered from a severe lack of strength and power. Perhaps it was for the best that I was retired in this fashion. I declared it was God's intervention, that he had somehow protected me from something much darker had I not been humbled.

I contemplated God a lot during my time recuperating. The compassion I had been shown by Taneisha and the hospital staff left me somewhat recognising my own emptiness. For years I had tried to make it on my own in life, clearly denying my need of God. But now, badly wounded, no longer brimming with the confidence I had felt having defeated Ed and Ants alike, my ego massaged by Michael's manipulative words – now I was rightly humbled. I was reluctant to lead the fight, a fight I no longer believed in.

I began to realise that I could no longer carry on alone in life, that I needed to start building relationships with people I could trust, not destroying them, and the first person would be God, my spiritual father who wanted to restore me to his kingdom.

A number of online 'friends' had asked why I had been so quiet. I explained that I was investigating, contemplating my next move. But truth be told, I was waiting for a sign. I was lost and needed saving and I began to take comfort through prayer as I sought to make sense of my past mistakes and transgressions.

Another week passed. Minx paid me a visit one evening and brought with her one of the finest selection of Turkish foods I have ever eaten. We talked about our interests, things we used to enjoy. That was also the first time when I mentioned my love of writing and she coaxed me into channelling my experiences into some type of cathartic output. She explained to me that I had talents, embers inside of me, and that all I needed was for someone to fan into flames my gift so that they could burn and shine through. But when she attempted to lift my spirits with such rhetoric I just diverted attention to another subject, or another cause. I wasn't ready to write about my experiences just yet, I was still resting, reflecting, and unsure about everything that had happened.

I was waiting for a sign.

I asked her about previous boyfriends, or whether she fitted the stereotype of a heavily pierced and tattooed lesbian hacker. She told me to fuck off in a nice way. She said the right man was out there somewhere for her, but she was in no hurry to find him. Truth be told, I wanted to be that man, but she would never know until I finally got round to publishing this book. Love you Minx.

Minx stayed over that night – separate rooms – and I went to bed feeling content that I had a good friend who would watch over me. That night I also had a vision. I only remember it because my sleep had been so poor and I rarely dreamt. In the dream there were two islands. On one island there lived an old man. He lived in a simple house, owned plenty of lush land, and had a rod to catch fish. The waves regularly crashed against the shore and the elements were fierce but he never complained, and he always caught one fish, and he never hungered for more. I would watch him from my island opposite his; the weather was better on my island, I had a big house and food was plentiful, yet when I went to fish I caught nothing. So one day I hired a boat and travelled to his island, but as we approached the shore the boat hit choppy water and ran aground. We started drowning, the crew and I, and sadly they perished, except for me - I did not drown, for the man on the other island lifted me out of the sea. When I complained to him that I did not have my belongings, he got up and left me his home and everything in it except his fishing rod, and so I grew hungry until the point of death because I did not know how to fish.

I still don't understand the dream, but I'm sure there's something in it. I pray that wisdom will come and I will meet others who are gracious enough to share their love and wisdom with me.

When I woke it was morning and Minx was making strong coffee for us both. I told her about my dream and she laughed at first, saying she had no answers, but as we sat and drank she told me that an interpretation would come. That's also when she told me news about the Donor.

"He wants to meet you," she said.

"All of us together?"

She shook her head. She seemed concerned. "He has something for you, but he won't say what it is."

I felt sick at this point. "Is it because of what I've been saying – who I've been talking to about my experiences?"

"He hasn't said. But he was very insistent that you go to see him. Alone."

We finished our coffee in silence. I thought about the dream, the two islands, and the man who caught the fish. If the man on the island was the Donor then I would have to journey there on my own or risk losing others. Or maybe it was just another one of my messed up dreams that I would never gain clarity about. Either way, I felt like I was leaving what I held dear to me – my past life in search of something new.

I thanked Minx for the company and her affection in looking after me. In return she kissed me on the cheek and left me with an address and time to meet the Donor. She didn't say anything else. She looked sad.

I returned to my room and looked up where the Donor wanted to meet. It was at Alexandra Palace, of all places, and so I figured that the journey might not be so perilous after all.

A bus ride later I found myself enjoying the walk to the top. There were no events on that day. My only other company were dog walkers, joggers and passer-by's, meandering through the paths and stopping to enjoy the view. As I approached the car park I saw the Donor emerge from an expensive silver saloon. He was unaccompanied but when I scouted the rest of the car park I could see two men sitting in a red Volvo, looking in my direction. Pure coincidence, I told myself, but no doubt this was potentially looking like a situation I wanted to avoid. I stopped about two car lengths away from the Donor and looked around.

"Are they with you?" I asked him directly.

"Yes," he replied, "but they're not here for you. They're here to protect me."

I looked at him quizzically. "You think I'm a bad man still, a danger to you?" I waived my bandaged hand in the air.

"Come closer, John. I want to show you something."

I walked over and realised that this was the first time I had met the Donor in daylight. I found it difficult to age him, but judging by the lines around his eyes I made the assumption that he was in his early fifties, so definitely still old enough to work an honest job if there was still such a thing. His hair was greying but had a lustrous sheen and physically he was leaner than I remembered.

"Are you ever going to tell me what you really do, or tell me your real name?"

"When our job is done I might just do that." He looked me in the eye. "Minx says you want out."

I took a deep breath, and then when I was ready I let it all out. "I'm not who you thought I was. I'm just going to keep messing things up."

He nodded towards my hand. "How bad is it?"

"Pretty bad, I'm going to lose some functionality for sure."

"I guess the joke about being a pianist would come across as being insensitive right now, huh?"

"You didn't invite me here to practice your stand-up routine. You said you wanted to show me something."

"Getting more direct, John. I like that – that's a sign of leadership!" He walked round to the rear of his car and beckoned me to have a look. I looked at the boot and then back up at him. He stared at me expectantly.

"Is this where you bundle me in, or pull out a secret weapon . . ."

"This is a gift to say thank you for your loyalty, and to show you how sorry we are for your loss."

The Donor popped the boot open and it levered up electronically in slow motion. I had half hoped a gun would be inside so I could shoot myself in the head and be done with it all, but instead it was something much worse. At first a wave of nausea came over me when I realised what I was looking at. I stood in complete shock, then I refocused and looked carefully at the body. I remember my words clearly: "Are you fucking serious?"

He looked at me confusedly, almost anticipating a different response. "Now's not the time to be rhetorical."

I stared inside the boot and looked around in a panic, then I glanced at the Donor, and then back down at Zladic, his cold, stiff body wrapped in clear plastic sheeting. "You killed him."

The Donor didn't say anything, measuring a response in his head. "Well, technically it wasn't me that killed him."

Zladic's face was poking out of the plastic like he had been carefully unwrapped to check he was still fresh. His face was bruised and there was dried blood across his temples and around his ears, suggesting trauma and perhaps torture. I didn't see much of the rest of his body, only that the logo of his branded track-suit was identifiable, and his trainers had been removed and were resting neatly below his thigh.

"I'm speechless."

"How about saying thank you?"

"I didn't ask you to kill him. I didn't ask anyone to kill him for me."

"But did you not stress on several occasions that you wanted him dead?"

I thought back to conversations I had had about him with Minx, with the interpreter, and with Ana. I had made statements that had now been delivered, but not by my hands. "This changes everything – again. Just who the hell are you? At first I thought perhaps police - some relic of SOCA - or a covert branch of the NCA or perhaps, in my wildest dreams, something moral, even spiritual, like Crusaders 2.0 or some other extinct group hunting down vampires."

The men in the red Volvo got out of the car and I suddenly panicked. I had said too much. I felt like running but my legs were jelly from the walk up the hill after weeks of being stuck indoors. Surely the Donor knew that, surely he had anticipated my response - it was all planned.

"Relax, John. They're not here for you. Zladic was

an unpopular man, and very corrupt, and a great liar, not to mention a rapist, murderer, and a sexual predator with an unhealthy interest in young men. He was going to die sooner or later, we just moved him to the front of the queue."

The men arrived and looked at me, assessing whether I was a threat or not. The Donor watched them inspect the body, take Zladic's trainers and then shut the boot. He exchanged car keys with them and then beckoned me to walk with him over to the red Volvo.

"That's Zladic's car by the way, not mine. An extra pay-off to the gang that gave us key information before having him killed. Oh, and he raped that man's younger cousin – a big taboo from his culture."

"Is this just some game to you?" I remember saying to him. I heard the car engine start and rev frantically before the two men pulled away swiftly. "How long has he been dead, a couple of hours, a day even?"

"Oh, he's fresh – fresh as they get. In his line of work, John, he was always destined for one thing. Those who live by the sword die by the sword. Which leads me to ask you this: how do you want to live your life?"

"What are you, my psychotherapist? My conscience personified? Are we talking about a job promotion? I never wanted any of this, remember?"

"Actually, I remember meeting a very angry man who had a score to settle," he said bluntly. "You've done nothing but carry out your little crusade fuelled by rage and shielded by mistrust. You think we didn't know about the things you were secretly pursuing? Personally I never wanted to take you in, to show you any of this, but when I discovered that Michael had been playing with you, exercising a little too much control . . . well, I felt pity for you."

"I don't want your fucking pity."

"You have none, don't worry. Despite what you've been through you were still free to make a choice, you just chose wrongly. You've brought much of this upon yourself – God will judge you fairly, of that I am sure, but you've been living in sin, John, and you've denied it and continue to do so, or at least you did." He paused momentarily, almost like he was noting some new evidence that had come to light before his judgement continued to spill out. "But it was always someone else's fault, wasn't it? Or if you crossed one finish line you were prepared to enter another race, just to try and undo the mess you made getting to the end of the previous event. What changed you, truly, was your little journey abroad to a tropical paradise. When you returned you seemed to have found compassion, and rediscovered kindness. Hell, even Minx warmed to you, especially when you wanted to put others before you. And you took the bait each time we dangled it, always wanting to eradicate a more logical evil and put others above your own agenda; when you boldly decided to fight traffickers on your doorstop rather than chasing elite shadows - vampires - across London, that's when I realised that this was someone I could maybe work with."

I took a moment to recover from being rebuked so heavily. "But I thought the traffickers were linked to vampires."

He nodded. "Oh yes, no doubt about it, but you can't do this kind of work half-heartedly, John. People are going to continue to get hurt, whether you want them to or not, which is why I asked you what you wanted to do with your life. So far, you're making a pig's ear of it all."

I thought back to my conversation with Julian years before, my ex-boss asking me if I was happy at work. Look how far I had come since that day. Did I really want to go back to a normal job knowing what was out there? "Well, I'd quite like a normal life, if I'm perfectly honest. I'd quite like to go back to being human."

He scoffed. "Which is a good thing, I guess. To do that, however, you must embark upon some type of redemption; repent for your sins in a crude sense – don't just cover it over and hope no-one will notice."

"So are you a priest?"

The Donor laughed out loud. "I may be a follower of Jesus, but that doesn't make me better than you or perfect in any way, and I'm definitely no saint – not in this line of work. However, I recognise my failures, my weakness, and the fact that I am a broken man – we are all broken - but rather than dwelling in self-pity I seek forgiveness for the things that I do and I build relationships with people that show love and compassion to other human beings. I can't force you to do the same, to choose Jesus as your rock, because that's not how it works, John - but I do see a bit of the old me in you. I need you to recognise that the world is bad, but I also need you to find hope again in darkness when we face our greatest challenges, because in our world, John, there is a lot of good that goes unnoticed and when we restore people into good relationships with their father, that's when life gets a whole lot better. And there are a lot of good people who work tirelessly to make it happen but they don't seek praise or recognition for their efforts, they're just living the values. I don't think you recognise that yet. Learn to speak life."

We got to the car and he asked me to ride with him in the front passenger seat. "Please don't tell me you're taking me for an ice cream now or I swear, I'll run us both off the road."

He laughed. "I'm not going to force you to do anything. If you don't want to ride with me, you can just walk away. Walk away from this life and seek a quieter life that doesn't involve sacrifice or surrendering yourself to a greater good. Go and be a vampire hunter, doing things your own way, but don't expect our support."

I opened the door and got in.

He was silent as we drove back through Crouch End, perhaps giving me time to reflect. I asked him if he wanted me to be part of his team, in some sort of official role, and whether he could offer me a path to redeem myself and perhaps save others. He didn't answer, instead he deliberately pulled up outside the Sauna, the residence where my darkest moment had taken place years ago, the trigger which had effectively led to my downfall.

"What do you feel when you see this place?" he asked.

I shook my head. My stomach turned. "Fear? A deep regret, for sure. Shame. A tremendous sense of guilt."

"Yet you wrote about your experience and you shared it with the world."

"It was significant - a real low point. What's the point in writing about all the good stuff if you can't acknowledge all the shit that happened along on the way? That's why people love reading autobiographies about celebs who were hooked on cocaine and alcohol, right? If I didn't tell the truth I would be deceiving people, making out that my life was somehow mysterious and magnificent. It really isn't."

"I want you to tell people the real story, John. But this time, don't hold back. I want you to tell them about what we do. I don't want you to give up on your original motive for writing about your experiences, to change perceptions about the vampires of today. I think people will listen to you eventually."

I nodded in agreement. "Will I not just be filling people with dread? Creating a moral panic?"

"Look at the news, John. Children are stabbing other children, dads are raping and murdering their daughters, Muslims are killing Muslims in a country no-one really gives a shit about, and wave after wave or war torn refugees are spilling out across Europe in the biggest mass migration since the holocaust. Is that not more horrific than a loner telling people about a few sick individuals who sport a deadly fetish for human blood, and exercise an ancient ritual to hunt and murder? Because that's all it is, a very small bloodline of nasty fucks doing a whole lot of evil shit to good people like yourself."

I didn't speak. Here I was, sat in a car with the man I thought was quiet and reserved, giving me an impassioned and colourful speech about my whole life.

"I'd still like a normal life one day," I answered.

"As would I, John, as would I. Have you not seen any good come about as a result of your actions?"

I shook my head. "I didn't know people were going to get badly hurt or routinely murdered who crossed my path, or emotionally damaged in the process."

"But do you not think that because of the places you've been to, the people you've reached, that the world is any better because of your intervention? Whole areas in London have since been redeveloped, people in authority have been studying your trails, John, looking at the mess you've made and tidying up after you. I would like you to see through what you started – then you will have new life."

I looked at the sauna standing like some cold afterthought on the corner of the road. Places like that brought misery to areas, attracted vermin, infected countless bodies. "What's the plan, then? Are you going to give me an honest job and put me on the payroll?"

He smiled, started up the car again and drove away. When he got to Archway I expected him to take me home, but instead he drove north towards Cricklewood. I asked him where we were going and he reminded me that I needed to buy packaging boxes, and lots of them; contracts were ready to be exchanged and I had a two week window to get my stuff packed and put in storage before I moved house. I hadn't even thought about where I would live. By signing over all the admin to Jo, whom I had not seen in weeks, I had not had to deal with a single thing apart from validating a legal document heavily decorated in sticky tab notes telling me what to initial and what to sign. I was going to be a nomad at last.

"I'm lost," I said.

"You'll be fine, and financially in a good place for a few years. Pack your own basics, chuck out what you don't need, and store the rest. I'll make sure your first few weeks of accommodation are in a safe place."

We loaded the car with flat-packed cardboard boxes bought from a storage warehouse before the Donor drove me back towards the A1, but he turned off again and dropped me at Hendon. I looked at him, totally bewildered, angry almost (at myself) that I was letting him take so much control over my day – I might have made plans! But when he mentioned that Minx was waiting for me in a Turkish restaurant, I didn't mind so much.

"What next?" I asked, my head peering through the window at him as I stood on the kerb.

"Same as before, John. If you're in, I'll be in contact."

"And if I'm not?"

He didn't answer. He didn't need to. I was a terrible poker player.

Before he drove away he mentioned that he would arrange for packers to help me with the moving process. My possessions and that of my father would be kept in storage somewhere in Luton - paid for - until I was ready to return to a normal life. It was a nice incentive to get things done.

Minx was sat in the restaurant - she was the only one there - busy texting, or coding, or hacking, or messaging using some type of new app, whatever she did in her own time. I greeted her and sat down. She began ordering lunch for us both.

"So, how was it?" she asked.

I remember watching her face as I described the moment I saw Zladic's cold body lying in stasis, wrapped up like a piece of meat. She was fascinated, pulling childish facial expressions of wonder and surprise as I explained to her the events that followed. She enquired about what the Donor had asked me regarding my future, and I told her that I was prepared to see things through. That's when I realised, seeing her face light up, that I would have really missed her company; she afforded me a glimpse of a life I could still have as a young man – she gave me hope. *She* had been my rock in recent months and I had not known it until now.

Minx pledged that she would spend more time with me trying to wrap things up, but said that she had also reached a point where she wanted to take her life back also. Tracking these people – the Ants - had been an obsession for Minx, especially after the death of Karl, and seeing the abuse suffered from women like Ana only motivated her further. I agreed that acting on and being motivated by such evil acts takes its toll on the human body, and slowly erodes the mind of logical thought. She described it to me as a real test of faith.

"Are we nearly there yet?" I asked.

"I'll be honest - there have been moments where I've felt like I've been here before. The last time was just before you were born."

I looked at her quizzically. "You're definitely younger than me."

"Michael came to us during a meeting, just when we thought we had cleansed London of some pretty evil shit, proclaiming that October's Son had been born."

"That sounds pretty pagan to me."

"And anything paganist is definitely not from God. Michael practically proclaimed you as the Anti-Christ. When we looked into your case a little deeper we realised that we had missed one final part of the puzzle, a remaining network of Ants who were gathering in strength and numbers in a last ditch attempt to repopulate."

"I'd really like to see Michael again so that I can punch him in the face. The man has done nothing but slander me publically whilst he groomed me into a mistrusting, cruel man with a guilty conscience about everything I've done."

"Maybe that side of you was always there. Maybe he just made you see it clearer?"

"Thanks. I'm really getting it from all sides today. You know what, I hope that one day we find out what happened to him, because I don't like the idea of men posing as bishops or occultist leaders taking the city's most vulnerable people and turning them into killers."

"We know that none of that is true anymore," she assured me, holding my hand. "And soon, when it's over, none of this will seem like it really happened. People will eventually discover the truth. Sometimes the most stubborn, stiff-necked people have to walk the same path as us or experience it first hand; they can't just be told in a book or on a blog, not in this age anyway."

Up until then I had never treated Minx with suspicion but I couldn't help think that I was being thrown off the scent of bigger fish. Michael had a lot to answer for yet finding him never seemed to be a priority for anyone except me.

I wouldn't need to worry about it much longer.

THE PREACHER

Minx had arranged to meet me at Piccadilly. She did not say what she wanted to meet me about but when I saw her waiting for me outside of the station she seemed excited.

"We've got time to grab some sushi," she said, ushering me into a quiet store off the main high street. We sat together and she explained why she had invited me there as she munched on avocado maki drenched in soy and wasabi. "There's a big talk, today, one I think you need to see."

I raised an eyebrow. "Not another crypto party with all your techy mates – I really didn't fit in to that last event."

"No, even better. Some of the biggest names in human trafficking are going to be speaking at St James' Church. It'll be good for you to go there and network."

I found it odd to describe charity workers and campaigners as 'big names' like they were sports stars. "How many people will be there?"

"Hard to tell, I'm hoping loads will be there, hundreds perhaps. I've already booked us tickets." Minx held up two printed paper tickets under some pseudonyms we sometimes used online.

"It sounds very charming, but what use is it all?"

Minx frowned at me. "Considering you've seen the effects of trafficking first-hand, I was hoping for a bit more enthusiasm and optimism."

I apologised, reassuring her that I was naturally pessimistic: how could being part of a talk really benefit me or her or them (the trafficked). She explained that we needed to revisit our actions on social media, that we had been wrong to write it off as a medium to share our message. I disagreed. The last thing I wanted to do was spend my time using Twitter and Facebook to spread the word – about a thousand other false hacktivists were happily adding all of my online personas to online groups and 'freedom' movements, but it was just an excuse to share narcissistic messages or falsely promote a lost cause.

I will get them all back one day when my mission is complete.

"Do you have any idea how tiring it is to post stuff – it's just one big social distraction. I must have set up hundreds of accounts at one point to try and make contact and track people who I thought were involved in Ant colonies; I ended up being ratty and rat-faced half the time trying to filter out all the nonsense. I don't think we should be tweeting about what we do."

"Not about what *we* do, more about the problem we face. Why do you think it's so hard to get people to believe you?"

"I thought this was our fight?"

"It is, but you effectively put yourself out there as a poster boy years ago," she explained. "To many it looks like some type of vanity project, so don't lecture me about motives for what we should do, we're being different to raise awareness for all the bad shit that goes on out there."

I was silent. "I didn't say I wouldn't go with you, I just don't want us to take our eye off the main prize."

"You won't," she assured me. "I've got something lined up for you at the end of the month."

The church was beautiful and very welcoming. Two

people greeted us at the door, not asking to see our tickets, they simply directed us into the church. I enjoyed the feeling and felt slightly nostalgic, like I did in the few times that my dad had taken me to church for a remembrance service or the occasional Christmas event during my pubescent years. There was a slight buzz about the clientele, but I mentioned to Minx that there were far from hundreds of people there.

We sat ourselves near the front, behind the cameras and out of sight of the main crowd, watching the speakers flitter through their notes at a table that had been prepared for them above the aisles. The speakers were Amy Jasper, Steve Chalke, Rev Marcus Walker and Andrew Wallis. All of them were involved heavily in trying to bring about an end to human trafficking and end modern slavery.

The event began shortly after we arrived and each guest was introduced. Amy was the first to speak and outlined the problem by definition and then by giving out facts. Aside from being the fastest growing black economy, there was a clear contradiction in figures; Amy suggested that the number of people being trafficked and kept as slaves in UK was close to 20,000. The reason why it had grown so much as an industry was because the practice was high value and low risk; if cases weren't being properly investigated and followed up with heavy prosecutions, what was stopping organised gangs from profiting from the vulnerable? I sat there and considered how many men and women had been preyed upon by the Ants and categorised the same way as traffickers. Whilst the group we pursued did not actively run nail bars, cafes and fruit farms, the same groups were likely to be involved in running brothels; much of the depravity quickly escalated from there into darker practices.

Before she finished talking she gave a particularly vivid description of how trafficking can also be internal (within the UK) and how, for example, members of the homeless had been groomed at soup kitchens and forced into macabre practices, including organ harvesting: people simply went missing. I was distracted by my thoughts, retweeting excerpts from her speech as my mind frantically linked traffickers and Ants together. Minx sat there beside me, totally absorbed.

Reverend Marcus Walker spoke next, representing the Global Freedom Network; he was adorned in typical ministerial clothing and during his introduction spoke about his work with other Christians and Muslims globally to try and address 'a worldwide problem'. He discussed the wider picture of slavery, how it had become an industry more profitable than oil! Then he explained that if you want to end the practice of slavery worldwide then you have to bankrupt the industry to effectively 'draw out the poison'.

This linked to an idea discussed later by Andrew Wallis, another speaker, who suggested industries around the world needed to proof their supply chains to ensure all workers were there by their own free will. There was also lots of talk about reform, increased transparency and the need for organisations to share knowledge and awareness at all levels to try and fight an industry worth $150 billion.

The talks continued along the same bleak line, that the most vulnerable were being exploited and international law was failing most of them. I was gobsmacked for most of it, purely by the size and scale of the problem. There were breakthroughs and changes to policy, especially in the UK with the Modern Slavery Bill which they anticipated would encourage other countries to adopt a similar practice.

But despite all of the tough talk, the mood of the venue still felt like this was an awareness talk and nothing more, that most people at that place that evening did not really know how to combat trafficking on their own doorstep.

Steve Chalke, a confident evangelist with the persona and looks of actor Steve Martin, gave practical advice and talked about how to spot the signs of trafficking. I found myself, alongside Minx, thinking about how many people were oblivious to the signs of trafficking on their very own doorstep. He mentioned plans for an app to help raise awareness and directed people to their website. I looked at Minx and she whispered to me that she had already taken quite an interest in their work and come up with some ideas. I smiled, realising that Minx was more compassionate and caring than I had initially thought.

After several questions from the audience, including a string of tweets about the subject, there was a chance to have a drink and chat with the guests. I didn't want to – I had seen enough and was conscious that I was tweeting from our most obvious account, but nonetheless Minx wanted to speak some more. We grabbed a glass of wine each and stood and waited for an opportunity to talk, but we did not end up speaking to the main guests; not by choice - they were very pleasant and engaging - but because we were approached by a man who revealed to us that he was a preacher from another church. His opening line was something along the lines of 'so, what did you make of all of that?'.

He was not what I expected a preacher to look like outside of church, or sound like even. The man was smart, savvy, handsome and sometimes muttered at the end of his sentences as he drank red wine, holding the glass in such a way that made me feel like he was a professional socialite and not a man of the cloth.

"Where do you preach and what's your interest in human trafficking?" I remember asking him formally, like Minx and I had suddenly become an authority in the subject.

"I preach up and down the country, working with a range of churches on the issues affecting members of their congregation who may be involved in modern slavery." He looked at me in particular as he spoke. "I have a very generous sponsor who allows me to do a lot of the work with the needy."

I paused for a moment and sipped my wine. Minx

remained straight faced, talking to the man candidly about the topic, but I couldn't' help feel that I had met him before or that we were connected somehow, that the evening now had its own hidden agenda. I excused myself and headed to the men's lavatory but took some time outside instead. I stood on the roadside, taking deep breaths and looking back at the church and the banner that had advertised the event. I would hardly have called the event low key and run exclusively for church members. However, as droves of people went past the busy street without so much as batting an eyelid, it reaffirmed my belief that society didn't really want to know about this problem, that it had somehow been eradicated years earlier by William Wilberforce. That's what I believed.

As I turned to go back into the event a man approached me from out of the shadows, slim and tall with a brown trilby hat, as though he had been waiting for a moment to strike. He grabbed me by the arm and pulled his face close to my ear. I reacted as best I could, gripping him by the arms, and if he had any real malice I would have been dead for sure (my reflexes were piss poor), but as he spoke I slowly began to relinquish control.

"The man your girlfriend is talking to right now is a convicted criminal," he whispered.

I looked at him in total bewilderment. I remember my response clearly, like it would somehow nullify his claim. "But he's a priest."

"Was," the man hushed back to me, "years ago, he was a good man. But men change, as you know, John. Men are not like gods and they should not refer to themselves as such. Don't let his past persuade you otherwise. Keep your eye on him - he is connected in ways that you won't fully understand yet."

I asked the man who he was and he replied that he was simply a friend of the Donor. That's when I surrendered my grip. He took my hand and placed a key in my palm.

"Is this some kind of fucking joke?" I asked, not in the

mood for another round of treasure hunts across London from a new Michael character lurking in the shadows, jumping out and surprising me every time I took a stroll through London.

The man began walking away towards the road. "Keep hold of it – on you at all times. You'll know when to use it." Then he was gone, another person beating a path across the concrete. I stood for a minute, shaking my head and muttering ungodly words out loud

When I went back inside, Minx was still talking to the preacher. I tried to play it cool, the best one can after being presented with such damning allegations, and stood and listened to their conversation.

"Robert used to be involved in the church," Minx began. "Then he left to focus on helping victims of human trafficking."

"Really?" I asked in an attempt to sound genuinely impressed. "I didn't think you could just leave the clergy when you wanted. What do you do exactly?"

"Rehabilitate," he said proudly. "We help the victims find a new life, give them hope, a second chance. I was just telling your friend here how I'm holding a fundraiser next month in Chelsea. Perhaps you'd like to come along, get to hear a bit more about our work?"

Minx looked over at me, expecting one type of response.

I nodded. "That sounds like a great idea. I've been moved by what I've heard this evening. I want to do all that I can to help victims of this terrible crime."

Robert smiled. "Great." He handed over his business card to Minx. "I look forward to seeing you both there!"

We didn't hang around to chat to the main speakers; they were heavily engaged in discussion with a group of people that had amassed around them. I had the web addresses of their organisations and their twitter handles. That would be enough for me for now. I was still troubled by my encounter with the man outside of the church.

As Minx walked me back to the station I told her about what had happened. She freaked out a little bit and begged me to tell her that I was kidding, that it was another of my sick jokes. I asked to see the business card and we scrutinized it further, half expecting to see just a list of numbers like I had seen with Rameses and Veronica. I suggested to her that she run some background checks on him, just to be sure, and send a message to the Donor asking whether or not the message was genuinely delivered by him.

I forgot to tell her the bit about the key, which was probably a good thing because like the man predicted, I would need to use it in the near future, and if I'd told her she might have taken it away from me. But that's another story.

Most worryingly, however, when the Donor heard about my encounter he vehemently denied that he had sent anyone to give me a message about the preacher. I met this with the same level of cynicism I did most things; that I was somehow having my loyalties tested by him, or them, or whoever the Donor actually worked for.

I realised two things that day: firstly, that the scale of human trafficking is bigger than I could ever imagine; secondly, that myself, as one man, could not make the massive difference that I wanted to just by running around London in a mask chasing a few bad guys. Like others before me, I will no doubt leave an unfinished legacy behind in the hope that a brave soul shall put on his or her armour and sharpen their sword.

Time will tell.

POSTMODERN MICHAELSON

Before I bring my story to a close, I feel that it is important to share with you and reflect on life as The London Vampire and my relationship with the media.

When I initially began using social media, often without a clue about what I was doing, I registered accounts simply to try and find people of a similar 'type'. That was a very long time ago, and as proof I can tell you that I first started with Myspace. Yup, I know. Vampires and vampire hunters, that's who I was initially interested in finding out about and connecting with. Without going into too many details, it was a definite lost cause. The only type of people I found on Myspace were gothic atheists, women who dressed as goths and sold used panties and other lacy paraphernalia, oh, and men, lots of guys posing as vampire hunters and vampire overlords.

If anything, the only thing of use from the social media platform was the inspiration I took from the imagery and the darkness of many of the profiles; ironically, I was looking to create an online identity that could be taken seriously without looking too fake. I decided that the best way to do this was to manipulate an image from someone's social media profile to create a silhouette, to look obscure but also fit the idea of being a regular guy who one day turned a bit dark and mysterious. The image perfectly represented me, a man who didn't really understand his own identity, but hid behind a screen hoping to make progress, waiting for Michael to return with answers.

It took me years to realise that answers could not be found on the internet but only through real activism. My early years online were more about encouraging slacktivism than instilling a grassroots movement of netizens.

It was Minx who showed me the errors of my ways. She picked apart my identities, found my real identity through various internet server pages, warned me about using GPS on my phone and even ran my writing and web pages through editing software to identify patterns that could be used to trace me. I was a little freaked out by how careless I had been. With her help I managed to change a lot of this by sleight of hand, point pages to similar pages and point them back again, create a web of lies and deceit to alter the trail which would lead to obvious but mistaken conclusions.

Building up a less obvious fan base with so-called Anonymous and friends of Minx, several alias accounts were used to make contact with foreign hunters on Facebook and Twitter – real people who seemed like me and matched our vision. We were building up our own network. I am glad to say I no longer have to manage much of this because I found the whole process daunting, exhausting and confusing. She knew all the shortcuts, how to code, tag, embed, plus any other technical jargon you can think of, so I leave all of that to her now.

Oh, and we went back to using simple phones, too. That saved a lot of time, although I do like to tweet stories of interest now and then.

The Interviews

At time of writing this there have been several real interviews and opportunities for interviews that I have declined. In fairness, I did not always respond to these requests as graciously as I could have because I do not regularly check my messages (I get an awful lot of spam). But in hindsight, I do not feel that I have missed out on any opportunities since the messages were all self-indulgent; such as: a woman working for a PR company wanted me to share content about a new vampire film, Abraham Lincoln: Vampire hunter; a generic press release instructing me how to promote the West End debut of Let the Right One In (stage version); a 'researcher' from This Morning looking to speak to a real vampire; a university undergraduate looking to take pictures for their final project ... Notice how all of these requests were about getting something for nothing, in fact, there was a general tone or assumption that I would be grateful for the attention, that I was perhaps desperate to become something bigger or a part of an exciting product, to happily reinforce the stereotypes I was trying to destroy. In truth, what did they want? Firstly, they wanted me to reaffirm the simulacrum of vampires from another era living in a modern world, purely for entertainment purposes. Secondly, they assumed that I was a vampire, or a stereotypical cog in the chain of vampire or Goth culture, and that I needed them more than they needed me. Furthermore, some of the messages and requests just highlighted the lack of social etiquette that exists between people today online.

Email culture has reduced us all to nothing more than superficial beings.

Those who took time to address me by name and develop a rapport were most likely to get a response, albeit a brief and usually cursory one, given the typical nature of the email: 'hey there, so do vampires exist? I really want to meet on – please respond!'

I mean, seriously, many of the people sending these messages were men and women in their twenties, although some confessed at being in their forties or much older. The problem addressing identity, it seems, is more widespread than I imagined. In fact, it explains perfectly how the Ants use Vampire forums and social media groups to groom and target the vulnerable so easily. Simply pay someone enough compliments, offer them a new olive branch of identity and watch how they gush in the attention and totally open up. The real concern, however, is the carefree attitude of today's youth (said from my thirty-something lectern); I worry about how they invite danger upon themselves by being such risk takers. I remember being that age once and engaging with all manner of people whom my father would have disapproved of, purely to get attention and feel wanted. Although back then, I didn't have as much choice as I do now.

The problem is choice.

Interviews I did take part in were few and far between, and in many ways I am unsure as to whether they achieved anything positive for my goal then and my revised goal now, in fact, in hindsight, they were all probably counter-productive, which is why I remain aloof and deliberately difficult about doing any PR because I feel that it obliterates what we're seriously trying to do now and sensationalises my actions of the past.

Let me explain using an example. I recall one of my first ever speaking events, it was for Seriously Staked, an event focusing on all things vampire related. I was in two minds right up until the day on whether I, contributing publicly (albeit via Skype), would do more damage than good, since the line-up included academics talking about mono-myths and vampire culture through the ages, even guys who collected artefacts and antiquities relating to vampirism across several cultures.

This was really the birth of the vampire image you see today – the use of a mask. Up until that point I had relied upon the enigma of not having a physical identity or real images of me online. Inevitably, however, as my mission got noticed, my work needed more merit and credibility, something tangible that people could identify with or relate to, which is why I feel this became a significant turning point in showing people that I was real and not an online persona.

My debut was met with laughter. I was wearing an old Halloween mask at the time and when my image was broadcast onto a cinema screen I must have caused quite a stir. The speaker was a gentle man who I know enjoys politics, rambling and eating out, but the mask or his questioning was not the issue (more later). Thankfully the interview was short - tokenistic almost. Despite being billed as a modern day 'Buffy' type hunter; I felt more like the silly cabaret act that somehow made his way onto the billing because of a last minute cancellation by Sarah Michelle-Gellar. Strangely enough, I wasn't asked back by the organisation or followed up by anyone else for other interviews.

My second interview was given over the phone with a young journalist who wanted to pitch a story to a newspaper (The Guardian, I think), although I remember clearly that it was nearly the end of October and he had probably missed his Halloween pitch deadline for editorial content. I certainly wouldn't have taken his angle, but I gave him my time anyway despite agreeing initially to meet at a hotel in London. We talked extensively on the phone, but the questions were the same as other interviews: how many vampires have you killed? When did you first 'get' into vampire hunting, like it was a lifestyle choice, and how do you protect yourself? Again, I struggled to keep it together and my latter answers must have seemed quite blunt as I started clock watching and trying to wind things up. I began to realise that the whole process was pointless. The market was saturated by commercial vampirism.

After that interview, I plainly ignored several other people who approached me online enquiring if I wanted to be on their podcast, or take part in an online radio show, or be the focus of a personal project some students or 'creatives' wanted fulfilling. Inevitably, I grew tired of having to explain myself.

Minx had become one of my best friends by this point and also my fiercest critic. Perhaps it was because she was brutally honest, or it was her wicked sense of humour; she made light out of the darkest of situations with her sarcasm, and her deadpan delivery of jokes were always a welcome distraction during any investigation. What I loved about her the most was the fact that her intelligence and intellect far exceeded mine yet she was very modest about her amazing talents. In another life, and in any other situation, I openly confessed that I would have happily courted her, and that she was perfect girlfriend material. Minx told me the same, near enough, and it was this mutual, professional respect for each other that made us a more of an effective team: feelings often get in the way. Feelings were a weakness in our line of work and something we had to learn to switch off.

I'm deviating slightly. Sorry.

Contact with the Donor was rare and Jo had said that things had gone quiet – that with media coverage of national paedophile rings like Operation Yewtree, secret clubs being exposed by newspapers and online vloggers releasing leaked data, etc. that the Ants had been unexpectedly compromised in certain areas as people's connectivity had improved The rise in grassroots journalism was nearly at its peak; any average Joe could research using the internet which meant that no-one was safe online anymore.

As such, the Ants were doing their own in-house cleaning by sacrificing liabilities and putting to bed any loose ends that could compromise their security. I would have liked to have believed that the police and rival gangs would have taken down many of the Ants during some of the more famous, widely reported investigations, but I knew deep down that the Ants had links to authority and VIPs. I also assumed that being fed this information was another system of control.

The website was in third party hands. My publisher would sometimes forward me contact forms filled out by people browsing the site; many of them had been asking questions or leaving contact details asking for me to tell them more; more often than not people were just telling me about their fascination with vampires, like I gave a shit. I would rarely reply to these emails or through those specific channels. Minx preferred to chat with me on forums, darting from page to page using a Tor browser. She said there was something very retro about visiting chat rooms that had moderators, taking her back to misspent youth at university libraries. She wasn't a fan of big internet multinationals sharing user data and still scalds me for using Facebook now and then to engage in cathartic relaxation as I look at everyone else's problems and their cries for help or attention.

Several requests for interviews or meetings had come in various shapes, forms and guises; some I considered but most Minx told me to stay clear of. She would do a quick search of their background and social media accounts and tell me whether it would have any positive impact on our aim. I felt sorry for the art students and the university graduates looking for their next creative project, but if I crossed the line then I surely made what we were trying to do seem trivial and fun. There were several journalists from newspapers and TV programmes, but when I spoke with many on the phone they seemed disappointed to hear that I did not belong to the traditional representation of a vampire hunter that millions of readers and viewers had bought into. Whenever I steered the conversation towards human trafficking and secret rings protected by organised crime gangs, the phone-call usually went a bit south or I was treated with such scepticism that I found myself winding up the conversation.

People weren't interested in challenging such a widely perceived idea of what a vampire is. Audiences wouldn't get it – no-one would watch or listen to their show. There were, however, a few exceptions.

One day, out of the blue, I got an email from a producer conducting some research into real-life vampires. The programme would have the feel of a documentary as the commentator, Jamie Theakston, would travel up and down the county (and abroad) talking to people about the origins of such a widely accepted mythical being.

Minx looked at it all and did some research into the producer, a man called Bruce Burgess. He had a track record of good quality documentaries and we saw our first opportunity to try and set the record straight and get viewers and the public looking at the real and very seedy underworld of organised crime operating outside their front door.

A few phone conversations later, where I imagine Bruce was sussing me out as much as I was evaluating his intentions, we agreed that I would meet somewhere in London and share my experiences and definitions of what a vampire was. By this point, Burton Mayers Books had already released a fictionalised adaptation of my story, October's Son, and I was unsure as to how much he had engaged with the material since much of it had been edited to appeal to a wider readership as possible. This felt like a chance to get our voice heard.

"There's too many stupid plot holes," I told Minx on the day of the interview. She reminded me that the real story would be told in time; real investigation work took years not months, and good journalists never broke a story until everything had been checked and counter-checked again and again. We agreed that any questions about the book in particular should be deflected back at him unless it was supporting what some of our work was about, like traffickers and the illegal movement of immigrants. She said other interviewers would seek to ask questions about this in more detail when we began publishing our own content, but by then it wouldn't matter.

I felt reassured, then proceeded to ask why she had suggested I wear a black suit and tie. I looked more like a waiter about to start a shift at an Italian restaurant off Wardour Street, not a man involved in covert investigations. She laughed and said it would look good on camera.

Since October's Son had been edited and published, we (Minx and I) discovered that Michael had been using a range of drugs to maintain control over me. Any questions about Michael being the great man I thought he was were going to have to be watered down somewhat – that would be the hardest part of any interview, trying to defend my actions when the trust I had in him had since been shattered.

On the day of interview, a summer's day late in July, I had spent lunch with Minx at a nearby sushi bar talking about ways to project authority on the subject matter. She revealed to me that Bruce and his wife had an interest in all things paranormal and dark histories, especially based around the Catholic church and the Vatican's involvement with organised crime; Minx theorised that the interview had more than likely been set-up to fuel his or her own interests, which is why she was happy for me to go along with the interview. We were both interested in the same things it seemed, just both looking in different areas and from different perspectives.

From my conversations on the phone I had deduced that Bruce was very polite. As I traversed the back streets and arrived at Poland Street car park, I remember seeing him standing by the entrance, waiting patiently. Minx had already completed a recce and assured me that there was no trap, revealing that a TV crew was waiting for me inside the car park.

He looked a little embarrassed as I walked over to him, not surprising given that I was wearing a skull printed balaclava covering my face, a black trilby hat and black suit in the height of the summer. I felt ridiculous myself but only in a city so big and diverse like London could I do such a thing and not look out of place. I introduced myself and he shook my hand before walking me, reluctantly, to his unit/van where I met the rest of his crew. They seemed unfazed by my appearance and I was, in many ways, laughing with them inside about the situation. I stressed the importance that I wanted to remain anonymous for various reasons, mainly due to my undercover investigations with Minx, Jo and The Donor, but also because I planned to have a fresh start in life once investigations had naturally concluded. This wasn't about me becoming a celebrity on television, this was about me telling people the truth about vampires across all mediums.

I thought back to the last time I had given an interview. It was at an event for Seriously Staked in 2013, a Skype interview streamed to an audience of fans of the genre who had paid to hear about the wonders of vampirism with guest speakers from around the world, many of them experts (historians, collectors, authors) who had all written in detail about the existence of vampires. In many ways I was the party pooper, the uninvited, unqualified guest who had turned up at the last minute after nearly ducking out of the event for lack of planning. I was prompted via email beforehand that I would be able to share my experience. But in the end it was very short and I had been asked all manner of clichéd questions about vampires, such as 'are vampires undead like zombies?', and all the other fodder fired at me was batted back quickly as I tried to speak without losing my train of thought. I said my piece about trafficking and organised crime and, despite not being present at the event, I could hear the eerie silence in the auditorium – like I had said something totally outrageous and confused every single one of them. I remember being thanked for my time: 'Okay John, we really appreciate you joining us…' and then the Skype line went dead. My contact had been with an audience interested in the subject matter but we both left none the wiser about what a vampire was exactly. Even I started to have my own doubts about their existence.

Bruce planned to film me on the roof of the car park but there were health and safety issues, so we filmed in a dark corner of the car park beside some large windows with bars across them. It was quite apt really, for I felt a bit like a prisoner inside the sprawling capital. Outside it was warm and muggy and jolly; inside it was much cooler, the scent of exhaust fumes was palpable and I was sat on a window ledge like some modern day poet, being interviewed about my experiences. Bruce was more interested in me as a person, he said. Rather than asking me questions about what a vampire hunter does, how many vampires I had killed, etc. He was more fascinated in my perception of what a vampire is and why it was so different to what history had made it out to be.

We talked candidly, pausing between takes now and then as cars drove up or people exited the lifts, and I felt very comfortable in his presence. He was a perceptive man and noticed that I had a hand injury despite my best efforts to conceal it. I explained that I had been stabbed in the hand by an angry European (pre-Brexit) during one of my investigations and he seemed genuinely troubled that I had chosen this way of life. Surprisingly, he was not the only journalist to feel like this.

We parted company and his crew asked to do some stock footage of me walking around tourist hotspots in my mask to be used during the documentary cutaways/edits. I should have really thought twice about doing this but I was satisfied that my angle would get through, so I gave them what they wanted before politely saying my farewells and heading back to home.

As I travelled back to meet with Minx I kicked myself for going against the plan – Minx said to do the interview only yet I had let them film me walking round Soho with a skull-print balaclava on looking like some day-release lunatic. She said I had been blinded by ambition and cautioned me not to do a TV interview again. I wanted her to be wrong.

When the film was finally broadcast several months later I was less impressed. Minx was annoyingly right. My back story had been changed to that of a city trader who was attacked at a party by vampires who drank my blood – I never said that! It was so frustrating to hear that I had been discredited in a matter of seconds by Jamie Theakston's voice as I walked around China Town wearing a skull mask and trilby hat. The rest of the interview seemed farcical, so I decided never to put myself in that position again. What saddened me more was that I was never told when the interview would be on television – someone else had to tell me.

I felt very different after that interview, like I had somehow become detached from my work. As I sat with Minx in a small Turkish takeaway on Green Lanes one evening, we discussed where we should go from there. Our situation looked pretty bleak. There had been no active investigation on the cards and I was growing restless.

Minx had a job outside what we did, and she made it clear that if she could do what we did full time and get bills paid, then she would do it at a drop of a hat. I offered to give her money to support her but she refused, citing that she was a feminist and that it was no longer the man's role to support the woman. I joked further, citing she had never proclaimed this during previous meals out or drinks where I had footed the bill. On a more serious note, she said she would make contact with her friends who shared Anonymous' ideology and ask them to do what they could in terms of infiltrating online groups, hacking social media profiles, breaking up networks and removing pages that had links with Ants.

We raised a glass in memory of everything that Karl stood for and I hoped that at some point in the future The Donor might introduce a new budding biologist into the mix who could carry on his great work. Without him our credible research into the link between vampirism and parasites would remain strictly theoretical.

Jo, if that was even her real name, remained the real enigma. We figured she might have had some involvement with the NCA and was unofficially outsourcing an investigation to us through the Donor, but that will never be proven. When things got heavy with the Estonian, that's when she dropped off radar and left us to clear up our own mess. We think we did a clean job, but I guess this book kind of blows the lid on that.

Thanks for leaving us out in the cold, Jo. I understand now and I forgive you but it was very hard to deal with the silence.

From then on I would meet with Minx for a monthly update if we felt it was necessary, or fancied some good food. I would carry on my investigations as a lone warrior (of sorts) until she came to me with something to investigate.

At the time of print there have been several interviews and articles featured about the London Vampire, including the aforementioned TV interview for Forbidden History: Bloodlust. I also took part in a podcast interview late one night with an egotistical Irish man called Brian who billed me as someone who tried to rescue illegal immigrants from blood-letting parties (I shouldn't have bothered with that interview either); I did respond to one interview by email which was published in a horror magazine, and in some ways I actually preferred this because I maintained a degree of editorial control and have since contributed to my own page, imaginatively titled 'Confessions of a Vampire Hunter' where I was allowed to be as cynical as I liked about everything wrong with people's perception of vampirism. I found it quite cathartic. But like most things, it fizzled out. The editor left and the people who took over didn't seem remotely interested in giving feedback or asking for new content, just producing hedonistic podcasts.

There were a few more radio interviews of varying success, one for Audible with Mark Dolan which I have yet to hear (I'm told it's good but I doubt it - again I felt used!) and another pointless exercise for Fubar Radio. Who? Exactly!

In my heart I think engaging with the media was more damaging than good. Real heroes don't do their job for the recognition, but for the good of others. That's probably why I'm not a hero.

I can assure you, reader: you'll be hearing a lot less from me after this book is published.

WELCOME TO THE JUNGLE

We continued to mount a thorough investigation into the lives of real vampires across London. Minx called me on the phone one day and asked if I had been following the news. It was a daft question because she knew that I often spent most of my day watching and reading the news, both current and archive. I would also review court hearings, local and national obituaries, scrutinise job adverts, scour through the back pages of free papers ... anything that might hint at or suggest grooming, or any other activity that might attract, or be led by, Ants.

"What are you referring to?"

"It's the refugee crisis, the media have whipped themselves up into a frenzy about it."

I agreed but I wasn't shocked. Forced migration through war and famine had been going on for years; it was only brought to the forefront of headlines as a political issue and the threat it posed to the nation's services. But I wasn't cynical about it in a way that meant I didn't care, I was generally angry with the images of people being exploited by gangs and having their money, sometimes life savings, traded for a few inches on an unsafe dinghy or to be shoved in the back of an arctic lorry, moved about like cattle from field to field.

"If I could do something about it, I would," I explained calmly to her.

"It's linked," affirmed Minx. "There's no doubt about it, the supply of women and children to feed gangs in the UK is coming from across the border."

We already knew this and had talked about this several times before. "So what are you suggesting?"

"I think that you should go over there and see if you can find a lead - approach things from a new angle."

I paused. The thought of me leaving London hadn't crossed my mind since my journey to Thailand, and that had not been a success. I grew anxious at the thought. "You know, not all immigrants come through from Calais," I said. "If you're suggesting I go abroad to look for smugglers, I might as well do a European tour. Heck, why not send me straight into Syria? If I can kill a few vampires I can probably execute a few members of so-called Islamic State."

"I can help arrange that," she said confidently.

At this point I considered that she was being serious but I couldn't help but think that this was the Donor's idea, that Minx was merely acting as the messenger.

"Okay," I said, "but only If you can find someone who's prepared to be my guide, because I don't speak a word of French; I'd stick out like a sore thumb trekking across Europe, some ageing backpacker trying to recapture his youth. If you can promise me that I won't trawl the continent's seediest spots as a cynical white guy – then I'll do it."

Minx chortled to herself. "I'll send you the details." She hung up.

Minx emailed me an itinerary of what I would be doing. She explained my mission: I was going to volunteer in the Jungle camp at Grande-Synthe, Dunkirk, to see for myself the lengths migrants were prepared to go to in the hope of crossing the border; once there I would liaise with a group who would walk me through how the smugglers worked as a criminal network.

I would discover much more, however, and like all of my previous investigations, plans would unexpectedly change.

I met Minx at a café in Westfields in Stratford a couple of days after her call. I had a backpack full of essential items, a roll of cash in my pocket, my passport and some prepaid bank cards. No weapons, that was the deal, I would have to use my wits and nothing else. She introduced me to the man who would be my guide.

Djemal was a Belgian national of Algerian descent. He had a round but friendly face with dark patches of stubble across acne-scarred skin. When he stood to greet me I noticed how tall he was, even though he seemed hunched over. We shook hands, I ordered a coffee and we sat down together. Djemal spoke candidly about his upbringing and the work he had done with NGOs across Europe who had all worked with refugees and migrants displaced by war and famine.

"Did Minx tell you why she wants me to go?" I asked.

"She mentioned to me that you are some kind of journalist wanting to write an article about the smuggling routes used traffickers. I don't fully believe her but we'll go with that story."

I smiled and nodded at her; that was the backstory I would stick to. "Will we be safe?"

Djemal assured me that he would do a good job looking after me, he also mentioned that he spoke several languages and had connections all across Europe who could help us if we needed support or ran in to any type of difficulty.

We finished our coffees and headed to the train station. Minx wished me luck and said she would check in with me and Djemal once we got across to Calais, but after that we'd be on our own.

Our route from Stratford consisted of us catching

trains to Dover where we would collect a car. From there we were to cross the Channel by ferry into Calais. I asked how long he thought he was going away for.

"I am told that you will let me know when we are done," he said. "You have a very generous sponsor who is paying me a daily rate and also donating money to the charity that I work for. A couple of days is okay, but if you want to stay longer - that is also good for me and my charity." His smile told me everything I needed to know.

It seemed the Donor was able to buy himself any favour he wanted. I secretly wished I had that kind of influence; however, I was just grateful that the Donor still believed in me.

Within a couple of hours of leaving Stratford we were sailing across the English Channel. I got to know Djemal a bit more: he had a good spirit and I could tell that he was passionate about the work he was doing. I asked him if he thought trafficking was a big problem and he started laughing at me.

"You're the journalist, right? I thought that's why you were coming over – to see for yourself."

"I want to investigate first-hand," I said, annoyed that I had already blown my cover with stupid questions. "I want to see it for myself."

"You will be saddened by it all. My friend, your heart will remain heavy for the rest of your life after you've seen what these people are going through."

We didn't speak much after that. The weather changed halfway through our crossing and the rain began. The cliffs of Dover had long disappeared, replaced by a grey fog. After drinking coffee and enjoying a long period of silence, the fog eventually cleared and ahead I saw the beaches of France in the distance. There were notices and cautionary leaflets on the ferry, warning people about the severity and penalty of trying to bring someone back from Calais.

We got in the car as the ferry docked and followed a

trail of vehicles away from the main ferry port. Either side of the road were fences, 20ft or so high and with sharp wire on the top, and behind them more fences. Patrol vehicles and sniffer dogs were lined along the fence at several points and signs and notices made it very clear that border security was going to be tight. Jungle camp at Calais looked more like a festival site from a distance, if I'm being perfectly honest. I had predicted it to be a raucous rampage of men trying to scale the fence, but it was not. The people had been contained and it seemed calm; they would not threaten the tourists and goods vehicles arriving to and from France every day. Not on that day.

As we drove north along the A16, Djemal turned to me and asked if I had any type of camera or recording device on my possession. I said I had none and he explained why that was good, because where we were going didn't allow filming of any sort. 20 minutes or so north of Calais we turned through the maze of Dunkirque's industrial quarter, snaking into a concrete wilderness.

"The people who manage these camps are the same people who organise events like Glastonbury," he said. "The main differences being that the music is better but the living conditions are much worse - it makes the muddy wash out look like a Dead Sea spa experience."

He pulled up to the camp as close as he could. There were a number of other cars that belonged to volunteers given the variety of number plate nationalities. We got out of the vehicle and I noticed groups of men, obviously refugees by their faded clothing and the way they operated with a pack mentality.

"Ignore them," Djemal said. "They're looking out for the lorries."

My belongings were held tightly inside my pockets and I kept my hands out of view.

"My friend is expecting us," he said. "He'll have some

passes ready for us. Just show him your driving license and you'll be fine."

As I approached I started analysing what the litter was made up of: muck, food packaging, tins, more muck, empty cleaning bottles, dirty rags, bottle tops and old batteries were just among some of the lovely finds that had been stamped into damp earth. The smell hit me first, not putrid or rotting, just the scent of moral decay; I could sense nothing positive about the place we were approaching and I felt more vulnerable than I did being stalked by Ants across London. I knew that whatever I was going to witness would have no mental reference to what I had come across before apart from the grey skies and sadness that sometimes inhabits London.

The entrance to the camp was similar to that of a thriving music festival. Men and women in high-vis jackets stood at certain points checking people walking past, as were French police officers. No materials: blankets, wood, gas - nothing was allowed to be brought in which might allow these people to live and thrive – that had to be smuggled in; this was a temporary settlement not a new permanent residence and the authorities were keen to make that clear to visitors like me. Djemal spoke to one of the officers, a young French man, and was directed to follow a path along a narrow stream of makeshift tents and wooden huts. The row seemed to go on for perhaps a few hundred yards, during which I saw families, whole and incomplete, packed into the tightest of living spaces. Children, almost feral in their appearance and mannerisms, tracked behind me singing songs in their native language whilst small groups of men would be engaged in heated conversation and stop to acknowledge me, to see if I could offer them any salvation. I had none.

Eventually Djemal came to a larger tent on one of the outer rows of living quarters. He went inside and beckoned me to follow him. I was met by an English man and his partner, both of whom were busy working with a small group of children, of various ages. Across other tables in the tent were volunteers who were giving up their time freely to try and educate the jungle's lost children. I watched as Djemal greeted the man and woman warmly and had a chance to listen to what the children were learning: basic maths, simple salutations, the sounding out of vowels, and some essential geography. It all seemed higgledy–piggledy at first but as I listened to the conversations I realised that this was an efficient but small dose of organisation amongst a sea of chaos. Djemal beckoned me forward.

"John, I'd like to introduce you to my good friend, Neil." He paused to allow us to formally shake hands. Neil was tall, athletic and had a certain degree of vigour and optimism for a man slightly older than myself. "I've told him that you're looking to write an article about the human trafficking going on in the refugee camps."

I looked to Djemal, almost to silence him about my intentions. "I'm covering many angles," I said as I let go of his hand. "This looks amazing, what you're doing here with these children."

"It's nice to see people from the UK wanting to share what life is really like over here in this hell hole. Don't use the word amazing in your article, it kind of sends out the wrong message. This is my third time over in as many months. There's a whole army of volunteers coming to try and do the best for the kids who have no control over any of this mess. It's good that the police let you in – they're trying to stop aid getting in. No-one wants this camp to become a permanent thing."

I could only nod. I was embarrassed that Minx had convinced me to come. I thought I was coming over to hunt and track down traffickers linked to the Ants, instead I was sat amongst orphaned, half-wild children displaced by war and famine, about to get political with a man I barely knew. Perhaps it was deliberate, I considered, as he led me around the tent and explained what each person was doing, why they were doing it and why he believed that what he was doing was making a difference. My heart was heavy. I was moved to tears by his unfaltering love for these kids whilst I felt nothing but guilt and shame for my own selfish actions. I desperately wanted to be back in London, in the comfort of a hotel room, watching the news reports from a distance, that somehow I could be more effective in front of a computer screen sending tweets whilst I sat in coffee shops and convenience stores and libraries.

We stopped by the entrance to the tent and I looked out across a sea of misery. Not all news reporters were denied access to the heart of such camps to show the true horror of the situation, but it was becoming harder to get in, I was told.

"Where do they all come from, and more importantly where do they all go?" I asked.

"For some of them this is just another stop on their journey. They won't claim asylum here because many of them are either waiting for relatives to join them or they are waiting to cross over into the UK."

"But security is so tight," I said. "It will be a miracle if they even make it over without being detected. The border forces were using so much equipment – stuff I've never seen before."

"There are others who will take them on the final leg. It comes at a cost, sometimes far more than they bargained for."

"The traffickers?"

Neil nodded. I sensed Djemal behind me and he nodded also. "You want to see, don't you, John?"

"Yes."

Neil and Djemal walked me through rows of makeshift tents until we came to a junction point and the area near basic water and power terminals. There were queues of people waiting for what looked like a tiny row of showers. But we were going beyond this point, to an area where the homes looked a little more robust, where materials like wood and UPVC and even basic flooring had been acquired and skilfully applied.

"What is this area?" I asked.

"This is where the traffickers live," Neil said.

I raised an eyebrow. "They live on site?"

"The traffickers are making a fortune from everyone's misery. Look around you, John. How many people want to stay here? Conditions are no better, if not worse, than when they were at home, in Syria, Afghanistan, Libya - they are just a handful of countries ejecting their most vulnerable onto the streets of Europe. Many arrive as families, yet they are prepared to do anything to ensure the safety of their children."

Djemal interrupted. "What would you do if you had a child?"

"I'd keep them with me at all costs."

"But imagine if someone told you they could take them – give them a better life, spare them the misery of all of this." Djemal pointed at the third makeshift house in the row, the one that looked like it had power and maybe even its own homemade water delivery system. "Imagine if a man, a friendly guy who claimed to be a person of good spirit, could take the thing most precious to you and keep it safe. Would you not gamble and risk everything for that?"

I couldn't imagine being put in that situation. Djemal was being rhetorical; he didn't want me to argue, just to accept that people were being trafficked and organised gangs were profiting from the misery of these people, and that they were obviously doing very well from it.

Djemal gave me a gentle prod in the back and told me not to stare at the house.

"They have immigrants working for them. They pay them, give them discounts for tip-offs that lead to good information. If you stare too long, you look like a police man, or worse, a journalist. I don't want to blow your cover on the first day. Come, let's meet some families."

Neil left us at this point and asked us to join him later for some mint tea. I trailed behind Djemal as he walked along a sodden path where not even the water could escape.

"Who are we meeting?"

"Victims." The tracks got narrower and dirtier, like we were entering the poorest part of the camp, if there could be such a thing. "These places have always existed," he said. "We just never had a need to know about it – it wasn't in the national interest to know that people desperately wanted to get to the UK. But if you start linking extremist organisations like so-called Islamic State to them, then you have no choice but to sit up and take notice."

As he walked past one tent he pointed to a series of holes that had ripped into the canvas. "Gun crime is a real problem here. The traffickers have their own way of dealing with problems in-house. The immigrants, they live in a culture of fear. No one wants to have to police the camps – containment is the real priority."

"Why kill each other with guns?" It was, in hindsight, a stupid question. I had already adopted the stance and reasoning that you would create a greater climate of fear if you used knives or pure physical strength to intimidate your victims. Not here it seemed.

Djemal didn't answer. We came to a small clearing that was used for cooking and cleaning. Women were doing their best to wash clothes whilst their children played football or chased each other with sticks and made loud roaring and banging noises; teenagers sat around and laughed together. One of the older boys looked over at Djemal and waved.

"Follow me," Djemal said, leading me over.

The boy stood and shook Djemal's hand and then formally introduced himself to me. "I am Youssef," he said. "Welcome, welcome – you talk with me?"

I looked to Djemal for reassurance and nodded my head. Youssef waved goodbye to his friends and led us down another narrow, muddy strip towards a small tent made from tarpaulin odds and ends.

"Youssef used to do favours for the traffickers," Djemal said. "Now they've recruited his friends and he hears second hand what's going on. I want to speak with him first."

Youssef beckoned us both inside his tent; it was shallow and gave us little head room, but it covered us all and kept us out of sight. He pulled out an old first generation smartphone and let the screen cast a little light on our faces. He spoke frankly and with a good level of English, seemingly unfazed by my presence. "There have been many trips," he began. "The traffickers pay many of us; they make us ask questions with people here. They give us ... what was word you taught me last time, quotas?" Djemal nodded. "We are asked to find families who are desperate and give their names to the traffickers. There is competition though. Rival gangs, they all want to take families who will pay. Many people have life savings with them or a relative in the UK who can pay money. Then they are making offers, setting big debt."

I raised my hand. "Djemal, from what I understand, this sounds like a business model, no different to trading in goods."

"That's exactly how it is, John. The traffickers are trading in people, splitting up family units and promising them a better life. But the reality is much different."

"Once, maybe two times a week," Youssef continued, "they take a group of them to the beaches where a small boat is waiting for them. They go to UK very fast -- better than boats from Turkey and Libya. But they don't take them all."

Djemal looked at me like I should be leading the questions from this point.

"What do you mean?"

"Some people who pay never make it across the border, they are taken elsewhere."

I felt a shiver down my spine. There was something already dark and disturbing about the way he kept pausing, like the worst was still to come. "What happens to them?"

"They sell them again," Youssef said, almost half smiling. "The men increase the bond at the beach just before they board, they tell them the price goes up because of fuel costs, or security, or something else. All a big lie. Those who don't pay extra at the beach are taken to a house and go process."

"Go process?"

Djemal interjected. "The women and children, typically, are graded and then conditioned before being auctioned off again. They take them to safe houses where the good looking ones are forced into prostitution and the children are sold on the dark net for a fate worse than death."

"How the heck is this allowed to happen?!"

"This is a military type operation, John. Many of the gangs involved are well connected to criminal organisations like the mafia, made up of ex-soldiers or resilient ex-convicts with particular skills. Minx said you had some experience of this and wanted to chase these guys which is why I brought you here to listen first-hand. Some of those kids you saw in the tent might not actually have a real life outside of here - ever. The world needs to know."

It sounded fictitious, like some familiar plot from a Liam Neeson film, repeated to me because Youssef and Djemal had probably seen it together, but I believed them both.

"I was under the impression the children made it on to the Lorries themselves, because they're under age - they can't be punished; I thought traffickers used them to break into the lorries for that very same purpose."

"There are some who take that approach, and they

charge less, but we are losing women and children like Youssef, and younger, to these monsters. There's an endless supply of them."

"There is another wave leaving tomorrow night," Youssef said. "I can tell you where they will leave from."

Djemal continued to speak to Youssef whilst I pieced together reasons why Minx had sent me here. I needed to get back to the hotel and make some calls, check out the geography of the area and figure out what they hell I was going to do exactly. Djemal and Minx had put together some kind of witch hunt for me to lead, except I didn't know what the damned hags looked like or what I'd do if I found one.

Happy that Youssef seemed in good health, Djemal thanked him and they gave each other a firm embrace, blessing each other in the name of Allah. I thanked Youssef for his time, paid him some euros and then we left him in the tent and began walking back towards the main entrance.

"This place is lawless," Djemal declared. "You heard him, right? These animals are preying on the children because they have no father or mother, because they are rejected by their country and by Europe, because no one wants to believe that they can be better than any other child."

"How do you know Youssef?"

"Years ago he was a child in a similar situation. His family broke into a truck to try and get into the UK, but the lorry driver was prepared. He opened the back of his lorry and beat Youssef's father to death in front of him, all because the driver's livelihood was at risk. Youssef watched the whole thing. The police said his father must have fallen from lorry and that's how he got injuries – no one believed Youssef which is why he does not trust the police, or any western men. No one listened to their wild claims, so Youssef and his mother went back to the camp. The traffickers caught wind of their story and exploited them. The mum was convinced by them to send Youssef to a better place, but it was costly. To cut a long story short, I don't know what happened to his mother. He likes to think that she made it across the border, or found work, but I am doubtful. She is most likely looking after groups of trafficked girls."

"If he's prepared to give us details of the dropwhat do you suggest we do?"

"You're the journalist, John," he replied. "I say we investigate – what's the worst that can happen?"

I nodded. "Where's God in all of this?"

"Oh, do you think God is not here? He's here okay, John. He's suffering with these people – for some he's all that they've got to make it through the day. You will never know how much God is doing to save his people, John. All the pain and suffering is caused by man, inflicted by Adam. You and I, we have been brought together to show grace and mercy, but who are we to think that we can end this without God's support and his everlasting love? Minx tells me you are a man growing in faith."

"I'm not worthy of his love. And I'm not strong enough to make a difference."

"I tell you this, John. Truly, we are made strong through him. His grace is sufficient for you, for his power is made perfect in weakness."

I didn't say anything. I suddenly felt warmth inside, a type that I had not felt before; I considered that maybe being with Djemal was part of my calling, that I should serve the most vulnerable and rebuild their lives than be remembered as a destroyer.

TRACKING SHADOWS

The place we were staying overnight was a budget, non-descript hotel-hostel hybrid about ten minutes from the camp in Dunkirque. I could hear the hum of traffic from the motorway nearby but it was clean and warm; I had basic amenities: water, power, a semi-soft bed. Compared to what I had just seen, this was luxury. Djemal said he was going to get a nap before we were due to leave, at about 9pm, to 'get into position' he had said. I deduced that Djemal had actually done this many time before and that we were going to meet some more contacts.

I managed to Skype Minx and gave her a breakdown of what had happened. She said I should listen to Djemal and follow his lead, that he was the best person we could wish for in terms of knowledge and skill. I quizzed her more about his backstory, probing her about how and why she had such contacts like him. Her answer was to be expected: it's the Donor's idea, he's very fond of him. I thanked her for nothing and she smiled at me and told me to take care and get lots of rest when I could.

Lying in bed, my mind was restless. I was totally unprepared for what I had seen and I still doubted that I could have any impact on these people's lives. By the time my eyes grew heavy there was a knock at my door. I was still dressed in jeans and a t-shirt and felt lethargic as I opened the door; Djemal was much more prepared: thick trousers, three layers, a scarf, woollen hat, and a smile.

"It's going to be windy on the beach tonight," he said. "Grab some more tops – you'll freeze to death."

I shuffled through my case and did as he said before following him down into the carpark. The car was in a different place to where he had parked it before, which should have given me a warning about what he had been up to, but I simply deduced that he had gone out to get something to eat. He was energetic and every step he took was much bolder and more purposeful than mine.

"What are you hoping to find?" I asked as we got into the car.

"The same as you," he said cryptically.

The roads were quiet and the clouds were low and dense, their outline cast by light pollution from the docks. There was a prevailing wind from the east which animated the trees as we made our way back towards Dunkirque and the camp where we had met Youssef earlier.

Djemal pulled up on a side road not far from one of the main roads leading into town. There were nothing much more than a few empty or closed businesses and warehouses leading off the main strip. Djemal had his eyes fixed on a black Nissan Navara parked about 100 yards away.

"This is where they pick them up," he said.

I sat up and waited patiently, eagerly watching for any sign of movement. I was accustomed to observing and waiting back in the UK, longing for things to happen, but that night in France was different – I felt like I was undergoing proper training from an expert. Being with Djemal made me realise how ill-equipped I had been in my pursuit of organised crime – the hand injury was testament to that.

We must have waited for about twenty minutes

before we saw a man arrive at the car. It transpired that someone was in the driver's seat all along because another man got out and started to pull the cover away from the rear of the car. A few minutes after that we counted eight women and children being ushered into the vehicle; it seemed like they had also been waiting in the darkness all along.

"Just eight?" I asked.

"There's probably more," he replied. Sure enough, a few minutes later, another two women (younger looking, one with a small boy) were ushered into the back. All of them were lying down; some must have been on top of each other.

The two men, dressed in black, also looked ready to brave a windy night at sea. They patrolled the area before getting into the car and driving off. Djemal waited a second and then started the engine. The chase was on.

We drove at a steady speed like others on the main road. They were heading away from Dunkirque, and away from Calais.

"Are we going to Belgium?" I asked as they took the main highway. Djemal shook his head and explained that there were smaller, discrete beaches away from the view of patrols much further along the border. We were actually heading south down to a small bay called Cran aux Ouefs. We didn't pursue directly behind the car, and it was obvious that Djemal had been tipped off about the location beforehand, he just needed to get a head count on numbers.

When we arrived at the coast, Djemal found somewhere to turn off the road and park the car for a little while. He killed the lights but left the engine running and then waited, watching from the lay-by we had pulled into. It was a single track road which explained why he needed to get there first. The black Navara appeared ten minutes or so later, turning off suddenly down a small dirt track. A silver van followed after the car and their headlights turned off as they pulled off the road. Both cars seemed to just disappear. Djemal put the car back into gear and drove after them. His lights remained off.

"I hope you're as handy as Minx says you are," he muttered as we turned onto a small bumpy trail. I didn't say anything; instead I focused on the winding, hazardous road that we navigated in near dark conditions. After about a hundred metres he pulled the car up behind some trees and into what seemed like a small dip which kept the car out of sight. Then he killed the engine and turned to me. I had never seen a man look so serious. "We go by foot. Don't draw any attention to yourself."

I nodded but I was suddenly uneasy about the whole thing. Djemal ran to the road edge and he beckoned me to follow. After fighting our way through some scrubland, we came to a small clearing on a cliff-edge and watched the scene below us. There, on the beach, was a rigid inflatable, black with a cover, being pulled towards the shoreline. Three men were now coordinating a military style operation and the women and children who had been bundled into the van and black Navara were being marched down a steep and narrow path and cajoled onto the boat. The rib was small; perhaps it could take no more than eight, ten adults at a push. The refugees were lined up and some type of inspection was taking place. One of the older teenagers seemed to be protesting and was dragged out of the line and beaten around the head by one of the drivers and left motionless on the floor. I could just about hear the women and children scream before their cries were muted with the threat of force from the same man.

"What are they doing?" I whispered.

"Trading," he said. "Whoever has the most potential to make profit will not make it onto the boat. But the refugees don't know that yet, they all believe they are on their way to England."

"What's the criteria?"

"Virgins, maids, potential to have children – a kind of crude grading system. They will take the low risk to England, and if they get stopped it doesn't matter, they are already rich. Effectively, these bastards are doubling their money."

"What's going to happen to the ones they don't take?"

"That's what we're going to find out."

That's when I noticed that Djemal was using some kind of night-vision camera cupped in the palm of his hand. He was scouring the beach, watching for signs. It started to rain.

"The wind is going the right way for an easy launch, but isn't it risky to cross the channel in such a boat in the dark?" I asked.

"Risky, yes, but it's a quick journey. You don't need a great big boat to make the distance. They'll make it to somewhere on the Kent coast, somewhere quiet like Dungeness. There's a chance they'll get spotted but they have the advantage of speed. This stuff happens all the time but you're country would rather not admit it."

"What do you want me to do?"

"You ask too many questions, John. Just learn the details and enjoy the show."

We watched for about five more minutes as the selection process continued. Fourteen refugees were crammed onto a rigid inflatable made for half that amount and then the boat started up and they left.

"Were we supposed to stop them?" I asked.

"Stay down!" Djemal barked back at me. "They have spotters on the other side of the cliff looking for patrol boats. We don't want to tell them we're here." Djemal slowly slipped back away from the cliff edge and pulled me with him. I watched the boat snake its way out to sea, unsettlingly unstable as it struggled to reach the 'pace' Djemal had hinted at.

"There's a chance they might not make it," I said.

"They know the risks – but there's good money to be made. And there's a waiting list. People are desperate to get to the UK."

We got back into the car. "Thanks for showing me that," I said, thinking our evening's spying was complete.

Djemal looked at me intensely. "You haven't seen it all." We drove back towards the main road and pulled into another layby, lights off, waiting for the black Navara and silver van to drive past. About ten minutes later they did exactly that and Djemal put the car into gear and began following them.

At the main junction, the cars went in different directions. We followed the silver van which was not heading towards the motorway. It was about 1.30 am by this point. When the road was clear, Djemal suddenly threw the car into action and overtook the van on a bend before cutting the vehicle up and forcing it halfway off the road.

The van beeped its horn loudly at us. Before I could figure out what the hell was going on, Djemal had leapt from his seat and was charging towards the van. I panicked at this point. Djemal was a fucking loon, bolder than anyone I had ever met. I scrambled out of the car in an attempt to make myself seem useful, only to see that Djemal had a gun trained on both men, ushering them both to step out of the vehicle. The men complied, speaking in their native tongue with each other.

"John, you'll find some cable ties in the passenger glove compartment. Bring them over here and tie their hands behind their back. Do it now!"

I was compliant. Stepping beside each man, I forced their arms down and behind their back. One of the men was deliberately resisting my efforts, the driver who had knocked a teenage boy unconscious on the beach; he was almost mocking me, perhaps he could sense that I was uneasy about the whole situation. Djemal saw this, too. I didn't like being put in a situation and tested. so I kicked the man's legs apart and pulled one of the cable ties around his neck, pulling it tightly. It caught the man off guard and he brought his hands to his neck, pulling wildly at it so that he couldn't breathe. As he staggered back, Djemal stepped forward – without any warning – and shot him in the head.

"Fuck!" I remember crying, watching the man roll backwards into a ditch. The other man, who had been quietly compliant before now, began to spurt out all types of frenzied soundbites. I quickly grabbed him and told him not to resist, assuring him that he would be okay if he did what we said. I had no guarantees.

After I had caught my breath and the ping of gunfire stopped ringing in my ears, I heard a few screams from the back of the van. Within a matter of seconds I had gone from passive observer to active participant in a gangland style murder. I poured scorn at Djemal. "You need to tell me who the hell you are!"

"I'm like you, John - the humanitarian thing was just a cover to get you on board. The Donor wants you to know that the trail goes far beyond London."

"He could have just fucking explained it to me!" I said. "I know that bad shit like this goes down, but I don't need to get involved in such a way."

"He disagrees. He told me that you think you know enough about this world, that you believe you have truly suffered. He still thinks you're a coward, that you're not bold enough to take matters into your own hand. You've convinced yourself that you still have to live by some kind of righteous code, a moral obligation to not break the law unless only your life is threatened. But the fact is this: you're a hypocrite, John. I've heard about the things that you've done – so please don't judge me. God will make that call."

"God will judge me, too," I rebuked. I thought back to my conversation with the chaplain in the hospital. I made it clear that I wanted to be doing God's work but I was going about it the wrong way. "The Donor might be knowledgeable, but he doesn't know me as well as he thinks he does. We can be philosophical about that matter later; right now we have a slight problem regarding a dead body."

Djemal looked at me sternly. "We need to load it into the back of the van, along with this guy. We drive to Calais and you abandon the car there. Then our friend here is going to tell us where he was heading to, and then we're going to do some more sightseeing. Is that clear enough for you, John?"

I looked away and tried to assess how much time we had. "No, but it doesn't look like I have a choice. Let's open the back of the van and get this over with."

When the door popped open we got our first glimpse of the terrified women and children inside. They spoke no English. They simply hugged one another and prayed in their mother tongue, shouting the name of the country: Syria, Afghanistan and Libya amongst others. Djemal began to speak to them, his voice soft, and his body actions slow; lowering the gun, his arms slowly fell to his side like eagle's wings being folded together. There was one woman the other refugees cowered behind and he spoke to her in a language I did not understand. The exchange was heated at one point, and then Djemal turned to me.

"They still think they are being taken to England, they refuse to get out of the van and leave. I'm trying to tell them they've been duped and we're saving their lives. Help me show them."

I shrugged my shoulders. "I don't speak their language."

"Show them the body – that will make my point clear." He continued to speak to them and I ran to the ditch and started pulling the man along the side of the road. He was heavy, perhaps 80kg, so it was no easy task, but eventually they saw me appear and attempt to lift the cadaver into the van. Djemal was close to shouting now, ordering them off the van. One by one they filed out of the van and cowered by the roadside as I set about laying the body flat.

"Take the car and drive to this address." Djemal gave me a slip of paper. "Use the SatNav in the car. Leave now and don't stop."

"What are you going to do?"

Djemal didn't answer. He bundled the remaining trafficker into the back of the van after he had shamed him in front of the women and children. Then he just stood there, getting the women to line up. I didn't ask again; Djemal had a gun. "Promise me the women will be safe."

"For what it's worth, you have my word."

As I got into the car I noticed that my trousers were stained in blood. I cursed myself. My hands were shaking as I started the engine, programmed the address into the SatNav and swiftly pulled away. As I drove I grew increasingly agitated by the events that had just unfolded. Djemal, not the clean-cut charity worker I thought he was, had just executed a human trafficker and was herding women and children along the roadside; I, on the other hand, had proved to myself that I was nothing more than a coward. And to dent my pride even further, I was now complicit in the events of that evening. I wanted nothing more at that point than to get home, go back to Blighty where I believed I still maintained an element of control over my life.

As I drove I grew paranoid that a police officer might pull me over and ask me out of the car. I spent the rest of the journey fretting about what my reaction would be. Thankfully the roads were quiet and within an hour I was back on the outskirts of Calais at the address Djemal had given me. My heart was still pounding as I pulled into another industrial estate. I saw a man in a silver boiler suit standing outside the building. He looked like a railway engineer, beckoning me towards a dark entrance. I drove the car inside - into a spacious warehouse - parked up and got out. The man stayed some distance away from me. He simply raised his arms and instructed me to stay where I was. I took in my surroundings, a kind of workshop for lorries or buses; heavy sodium lamps were suspended from the grey-metal roof, and there were several rows of steel rails, rubber pumps and hydraulic-machines that lined both sides.

Ten minutes later the silver van arrived and pulled up opposite the car. Djemal got out, accompanied by another man I did not recognise. He didn't look over or say anything to me at this point, he just went to open the rear of the van and pulled out the surviving trafficker, who continued to rant and shout at him. At one point Djemal swung the back of his hand into the man's face and his cursing abruptly stopped.

I didn't have a clue what Djemal's plan was at this point. His newly acquired passenger was a burly, bearded man with straight red hair. He barely acknowledged me as he walked towards the car I had just driven, asked me for the keys and then got in. Djemal handed the trafficker to the man in the boiler suit and briefed him about what to do, and then he came and spoke with his new companion who was ready to drive away. Within minutes the car was gone, just leaving Djemal and myself with the silver van.

"You owe me some answers," I said.

"You need to help me with the body," Djemal replied.

We took the dead man out of the van and placed him on the ground. The women and children were nowhere to be seen. "What did you do with them?"

"They're the problem of the French authorities now."

"That's it? You just going to pass them on? You're no better than the traffickers."

"Listen, John. It's easy to be righteous about the situation but maybe we should reflect on how we just stopped them being raped, abused and murdered at the hands of many evil men. I call that a result."

I reflected on what he said for a moment. "What did the man tell you?"

"Nothing much. He said someone will kill me in retaliation for killing his friend. They live by codes. It's a bit primitive but that's what makes them so ruthless in the business of trafficking human beings. I have, however, been given an address just across the border. Are you still interested in seeing how far this chain goes, John?"

"You don't need to be so rhetorical all the time. You think I'm a coward but I've come this far, before I get arrested I want to see where the trail ends."

The man in the boiler suit came behind us with another man and started carrying the body of the dead trafficker away. I didn't want to ask how they were going to dispose of the body; I left that to the imagination.

Djemal got into the van and beckoned me inside. We drove to the hotel and he parked up, giving me a ten minute window to shower, change my clothes, bag the dirty ones, and then leave the room with the rest of my belongings and cash. When I came outside, Djemal took my used clothes and gave them to someone new who had pulled up in a car beside the van. I wondered how big this chain was. I was almost inspired by their efficiency, but in the back of my mind I couldn't help but think that the level of organisation and discipline shown by him was part of something much bigger and sinister that I had touched upon before; I was more concerned about which side Djemal was actually working for. Michael, for all his flaws, had instilled in me the idea that no-one could be trusted except for oneself.

"You look nervous, John," he said to me.

"I'll be less so when you fill in all the blanks on our little road trip. Take me to a service station, please, I need a strong coffee."

Djemal honoured my request and we pulled into a service station heading east after about twenty minutes. I figured we were heading towards the Balkan states and I asked him straight out who exactly he was.

"I'm the international version of you," he replied, "or the international arm of your cell and whatever it is you think you stand for."

"I don't work for an organisation. I'm part of a decreasing number of people who are fighting for a cause I don't' really quite understand. I came over looking for answers, a distraction to the mess I had gotten myself into, perhaps redemption, yet all I've seen is misery and chaos – there's enough of that back home. You've essentially labelled yourself as an international fuck up."

"Minx thinks you have some kind of talent for seeing things differently - she also says you're irrational." He drank his coffee slowly, like he was savouring each mg of caffeine. "You think I was wrong to have shot that man, don't you?"

I thought about it for a moment. In hindsight, what would we have done with two captives? They may have plotted, perhaps attempted something – Djemal simply reduced the odds in our favour. "I guess when you choose a life of crime you have to deal with the consequences," I concluded. "They were working a payload of nearly £100,000 or Euros, or whatever currency they were dealing in. They probably did very well out of people's misery, so I'm not sad for him. I was just surprised you acted so quickly."

"You don't trust people. Minx told me that. If I'd hinted at my intention you might not have come along, because you're a cautious man – very English."

I raised my middle finger as I drank. Djemal laughed and started rolling up a cigarette. "Minx is one of the most perceptive people I've ever met: amazing, really, especially since she spends most of her time behind a computer screen. And on reflection … I'm glad you shot him because it sends out a strong message, and it means there's one less trafficker out there."

He waved his completed nicotine stick at me triumphantly. "Exactly. You think London is the only city that has a problem with Ants?"

Hearing Djemal say that word sent a chill down my spine. I hadn't really considered, or wanted to imagine, that the problem might run a little deeper beyond our own country. I guess, considering the way in which a hive works - how a true ant network functions - there are different purposes to each colony. A sea is just an obstacle not a permanent barrier. As a country we tunnelled beneath it and re-joined the European continent. I needed to think about the wider picture, about systems, about supply chains ... I gave a small laugh in my recognition at the fact.

"We can win this, you know," he said calmly. "It's not all going to be down to us, but with your help and sharing of ideas, we can disseminate our knowledge to the people. Grassroots journalism and activism, John: that's how you bring about change. We're working on the biggest case of our lives trying to break down these networks. Isn't that exciting?"

"Yes it is, but it's bloody dangerous work. How many people have you lost?"

Djemal was silent for a moment. "Too many. Close friends, loved ones - I am also on a personal journey of salvation, John. I need to make every moment count from now on."

"I'll drink to that," I said. I made some kind of an attachment with him at that point. I thought that maybe I could even trust him.

We headed back on to the road and the weather turned bad. Rain began to fall heavily. I asked where we were going and Djemal said he would wake me when we got to Italy. I was pleasantly surprised. I imagined that the coffee would be even better on our arrival. Despite the events of that night I took up his offer and managed to get some sleep.

I've never been to Italy before. Djemal woke me just before he pulled up outside a small café near the main port of Genoa on Via Magazzini. The cosmopolitan streets looked like how I imagined them: vibrant and buzzing with rich colours and packed full of olive-skinned beauties. The café had canvas chairs outside with blue livery and the coffee was much better than I expected. It was to be our base for the next two hours whilst Djemal met with 'contacts' who spoke passionately with him. I was merely an observer, eating pastries and referred to with a look or a nod and a smile from each visitor that arrived, which included: a well-dressed woman in her forties with a large greying beehive; a Nigerian priest with a heart-warming smile; and then the more wayward types, haggard looking men who had scars and telling tattoos that indicated they may have been part of a criminal gang. Djemal was clearly gathering and sharing information at a community level.

When we got back into the van he asked me to drive. I had half hoped he was going to take me to a pizzeria but instead he told me to head towards the main road. We were heading to Slovenia.

"How long does that take?"

"If we're lucky, we should be there in six hours."

My heart sank. When we hit the motorway I started quizzing him about the many people he had met in Genoa.

"Some were old friends, others new acquaintances, and then there were those like you and I, John."

"I wish you'd stop saying it like that. You make me feel like such an outcast."

"Genoa is a hub of activity, in fact all ports are prime sites for trafficking and the exchange of various goods and services, legal and illegal of course. I was getting fresh information about where certain drop-offs were going to take place; I even had a man pray for us both."

"You think if someone is praying for us that it makes what we do much easier to swallow?"

"Not at all. We are all sinners and God would frown on what we are doing, but there is no hierarchy in his eyes: we are all loved the same. I do this for the good of others, except I embrace wrath too easily which is why I must ask for forgiveness. I pray God will give me the opportunity to right my wrongs and I put my faith in him to one day lead me out of this mess."

"I still don't understand how people like us can be saved when we have done so much wrong. It's mad."

"God's grace and love for us is unconditional, John. We are no different to unruly children, and children regularly stray from the path and make mistakes, but a good father will never abandon his children."

I didn't ask any more questions. I was short on theological knowledge and what he said played on my mind. It reminded me of my conversation at the hospital months ago. Then I thought back to the slave trader Robert Peel, a man with a reputation for being a cold-hearted, vicious drunk who traded in misery, in the lives of slaves; one evening during a terrible storm, when all seemed lost, he cried out to God for salvation - and he was saved! God's grace was so amazing he penned a song stating exactly that, Amazing Grace, a song synonymous with our culture and an ability to reflect on one's wicked self. Was I lost and now found? Perhaps God really did want to save a wretch like me. And ironically, Djemal and I were on a mission to rock the boat of trafficking and modern slavery.

Djemal made himself comfortable and I focused on the road, a tear in my eye as I recalled my own personal journey.

We stopped for some dinner just before nightfall, before we crossed the border. My prayers were answered with a real Italian wood-fired pizza. Djemal joked that he had never seen me look so happy after we had passed a small taverna. I did not ask to stop, I just took control.

Djemal disappeared to the toilet to make some calls.

Suddenly I felt the events of the past two days catch up on me. I started yawning and was grateful when Djemal announced he would continue the drive into Slovenia. I had no perception of the country or why we were going, but I started to trust Djemal that he would keep me safe.

By the time we started the van up and pulled away from the restaurant, it was already dark again. I fell into a deep sleep. I dreamt about the people of Grande-Synthe, herded in squalid conditions, waiting to be plucked to a better way of life. I imagined that if I delved deep enough I would find someone like Michael, buried quietly in one of the camps – his tent a mecca of misery. I dreamt of Karl, the man whose life was cut short because he discovered something, got too close; he was also there in the camp, desperately trying to light a fire to stay warm, busily burning papers, piles and piles of journals and documents. When I went to try and read some of what he was burning someone grabbed my arm.

I woke up. The van had stopped. The road was empty and there was little, if any, sign of civilisation. I looked to my left to see that Djemal had gone, but where? The door had only slammed seconds before I woke so I deduced that he couldn't have been far away. I focused on the surroundings, pine woodland bound together in a delicate mist. Nearly a minute passed and Djemal had not returned; the back of the van had remained closed and I had not heard a sound. I plucked up the courage to get out of the van and check for myself. I did it as quietly as possible.

There was a small call box some fifty yards away down the hill, a dim glow coming from within it. I tried to ascertain whether we had driven through a town or we were about to hit one. I pulled out my own phone and looked at it – the welcome screen said Telefon Italia but I was out of range of any signal. Then it dawned on me just how high we were; I found myself breathing in deeply to rouse me from the effects of my slumber. There was still no sign of Djemal.

As I waited I could hear rustling in the trees, not just that of a single branch snapping but foliage being deliberately pushed and shoved aside. I hid on the opposite side of the road, ducking into a ditch and waiting. Three minutes later, two men emerged from the undergrowth, followed by seven or eight women. I watched the men light a cigarette and talk to each other. I'm useless with accents so it was hard to pin down where they were from, but it definitely wasn't Italy. They were pointing at the van, looking and waiting for someone to emerge. It was then I realised why we had taken the van and not the car: these men were traffickers, this was the designated pick up vehicle and they were ready to deposit goods. As I lay on the ground observing, I suddenly felt a torch shine brightly on my face. One of the men had seen me and was reaching for a weapon. I closed my eyes, and in that moment I heard three loud 'pak' sounds and then screams from the women. I opened my eyes again to see the two men lying dead on the road and the women rushing back into the woods. I got up and started running down the hill myself, away from the van, and that's when I noticed a solitary figure, resting against the call box. It was Djemal. He held out his hand and told me not to run any further.

I realised 100% then that Djemal was not like me - not at all - and not from an NGO background and definitely not a reporter; I even doubted he was part of a network similar to ours. He was hardcore. To take two men out, in the dark, from that distance took considerable skill and, dare I say it, practice. As he walked past me, a rifle balanced over his arm, he gave me a playful smack across the neck.

I shoved his arm away, scathing at him, "I thought you were going to start being honest with me?"

"You wanted to see traffickers, I'm showing you traffickers. I didn't promise you they'd be alive."

"And what about the women below, what do we do with them? I guess we just leave them to themselves, let the authorities pick up all your mess like the last lot!"

"Help me move these men off the road, then we'll talk some more." He didn't even look me in the eye as he spoke. I felt like my words were just background noise to him. I felt totally trapped.

I swore at him several times and I shook with rage, or nerves, probably both. We took a man between us and lifted them onto the verge. Djemal searched each of their pockets and withdrew a mobile phone, wallet, some false documents, real passports and a gun before rolling each one into the undergrowth down a steep drop. Djemal threw the money and the documents into one large bag and shouted down to the women before tossing the bag aside.

"What did you just say to them?"

"I told them that if they wanted their lives back that there were passports, cash and a phone in the bag by the roadside. They are free. Come, John, we have one more stop to make."

Getting into the vehicle, I was beginning to feel pins and needles across my body. My head was fuzzy and my chest tight. I was an accomplice to three murders, all within 24 hours, and there was still time to increase Djemal's bloody rampage it seemed.

"I'm not going any further until you tell me what the plan is. If you're going to show me anything more I want to know where we're going, who it is and whether you intend on killing them or not."

Djemal cosied himself up in the passenger seat and casually told me to follow the SatNav, promising me that there would be no more intentional killing, and that if I drove quick enough I would get to see a beautiful sunrise in the south of France.

"And if I don't like romantic sunrises?"

"Then you can stay here and deal with all of this

mess."

I started the engine and began to drive.

I'm glad to say that there were no more planned stops or killings that evening, or the next day for that matter. The sunrise was pleasant but not worth the hardships of the previous day. We refuelled and he had several meetings whilst I sat on the beach and caught some sun, desperately trying to clear my mind of murder.

Djemal drove me back to Calais later that day. We talked some more on our drive towards the port and he told me about what he really did and who he worked for. I can't share that information, but I wasn't so mad at him for being truthful with me. I told him to be careful and said I would learn to pray, just for his sake.

I boarded the ferry on my own.

DJEMAL'S LEGACY

Less than a year later I got a message from Minx to tell me that Djemal was dead. At the time I didn't feel anything, probably because I wasn't surprised - he should have died much sooner but I guess God uses us for a purpose, to put into plan another action to build his kingdom stronger. He was a servant, selflessly fighting the cause of the orphan and the widow. But as I reflected on the news I grew sad. Djemal had entered a world he couldn't find a way out of. I found myself asking questions about my own path in life, most notably: what direction do I want to take? The Donor had given me a choice.

I'm wrestling with that same question today and slowly coming to terms with the fact that I might end up treading a similar path to Djemal if I'm not careful.

I've made my choice.

The plight of women trafficked to the UK and across Europe

Though I don't feel like I have much of a heart left, this topic sits close to what remains of it. Sex slaves of the UK are, worryingly, in abundance. I recall, regretfully, my encounter with Cha-Cha in Crouch End several years ago. It was just the start of a dangerous journey into the unknown and one I sadly still cannot forget. I have tried reckoning my actions and sought forgiveness, but guilt and shame return to haunt me every time I deal with similar situations. Maybe that's what motivates me?

Women from her culture are just one of several who are still widely abused by western men and women. I have seen, first hand, the effects of abuse inflicted on their souls. Djemal's legacy simply made me open my eyes wider, allowing me to see a hidden and dangerous world that expands across the European continent and beyond.

Before his untimely death, I had flown to Croatia and met him once more with other members of his group. We tracked the boats that left port for Italy, watched the African traffickers deal misery into Sicily, and stopped off along other migratory routes from Albania, Montenegro and Moldova to see just how efficient and clandestine the traffickers' operations had become. Sadly Djemal didn't kill any other traffickers during that visit. He did, however, destroy my expectations by arranging a euro-rail trip to Romania where I got to see the birthplace of Vlad Tepes (Dracula); I found nothing but some poorly constructed tourist shops and a lukewarm local dish (the name of which I can't remember) offered in abundance. No vampires and no Ants. It made me realise I was chasing nothing but a relic of Slavic folklore.

Myth.

When Djemal escorted me back to France and dropped me off near Calais for the last time, he warned me that not everyone would see what I was doing as something for the greater good, that if I left messy trails I would be hunted not only by the Ants but by the NCA and other agencies that had vested interests in bringing these men to justice. He said that finding support from those legally working to enforce our borders would be an incredibly difficult thing to do in the online age.

"Finish the job," was his final, chilling line to me as we shook hands for the last time. He had a look in his eye that day. Perhaps he knew more about me that he cared to let on, but overall I felt he had been where I was at some point in his life and it was decision time. I would either grow to become a militant like him or bury myself in books to become a learned hacktivist like Minx.

I was torn either way, and to this date I like to think that I'm a bit of both.

I'm not ready to die quite yet.

THE END?

You, reader, are part of the colony that I have created. I exist both on the surface web and below it, tangled in the darkness of such subject matter; I find myself being looped through Tor nodes and encrypted between PGP keys and OTR messages, all the while negotiating a minefield of trolls and searching for genuine allies like needles in a hay barn. Back in the real world I fight to protect those most at risk of harm from Ants and speak out against injustice.

Firstly, I hope to grow my colony slowly and efficiently, and I want to raise awareness about the horror of trafficking on our doorstep. I hope you will fight for that cause alone. I do not condone violence nor do I seek to instigate violent acts; I have experienced enough that will stay with me for a lifetime.

Secondly, I do not know if I will ever resurface or break free. The queen of an ant colony often remains buried, protected by workers and slowly producing more workers, clones and soldiers fit for purpose. I have concluded that as long as there are those trafficked, exploited and abused by those in society who knowingly inflict such harm then I will continue to produce more workers until I am ready for the process of nuptial flight to begin again and allow members of my colony to create new colonies of their own around the world and fight for a worthy cause.

I am ready. Are you?

EPILOGUE

When I submitted the complete version of this manuscript to my publishers, it was significant for me; not because I felt I was able to correct a stylised version of my life but because in doing so I have received a sense of closure. I would like to give you some closure also.

Rameses is gone. I can't say much more, because I don't know much more than that. It was on a Sunday morning when I got the call from Minx telling me that he'd been taken during an operation. I remember being sat on the end of my hotel room bed, breathing a sigh of relief and feeling a sense of elation and closure. I don't know whether 'taken' was another word for arrested, or incarcerated, or better still – killed. I guess I will never truly know because that was never my official mission, only my personal vendetta against the man who I believe plotted my descent into madness, manipulated Michael along the way and even had a hand in my father's bizarre death in retaliation for what happened to Veronica. Like I said, I do not have any of the details.

Later that same day the Donor, Jo, Minx and I met for a Sunday Carvery at the Norfolk Hotel in London and celebrated with fine wine. Even then, the Donor and Jo were tight lipped about the events but did manage to express some degree of gratitude for my efforts and suffering in bringing the bastard to justice. But I also knew that the meal was more than celebratory – it was in fact acknowledging the end, the start of a new covenant.

In my journey, which started back in 2008, I have finally come to a place where I can walk no further in the shadows of who I was and have to step back into the light as a new man.

The Donor concluded that the cell had served its purpose and was no longer needed. I have been able to talk about my experiences for the first time, slowly drip-feeding them across Tweets in code, and online through carefully edited extracts. This meant, sadly, that my relationship with Minx officially ended in a work capacity. I would like to tell you that we kept our friendship going, but we both realised that a fresh break means a fresh break. This story, or rather the one you've managed to work through, is the official version I will stick to, whereas others seeking thrills and adventure can still hold on the to the idea that I remain October's Son, scouring London to find and eradicate a greater evil.

You, reader, can make that choice about what I do from now on.

There are other cells. I am told this in good faith, and in a selfish way I hope that they have read some of what I have written and take hope in the fact that their mission might one day come to an end also.

Even though Rameses, a man of pure evil in my eyes, is out of the equation, I feel that now I am able to slowly rebuild my life. I do sometimes find myself contemplating who, where and what the other cells - however many there may be – are doing whilst I enjoy this time to myself and slowly reinvent my life. I don't miss the danger and the constant threat, but I did get immense gratification from bringing down key players in the fight against human trafficking in the UK. To this day, I still follow this topic with interest and support key charities and NGOs.

You should do the same.

And so I shall declare this to you: I'm officially retired from the London Vampire hunting business. Everything I started online is to be wound down and consolidated. Active operations have ceased and my written and online legacy has been taken out of my hands, legally signed over to someone else to manage so that I can continue to rebuild my life. I guess this doesn't make me the rebel I thought I was and you may think I'm selling myself out to keep a lid on things. But let it be known, they may exploit what is there but they may also simply let it dissolve, slowly contaminate the genre pool in the hope that it might exact some much needed change from the repeated myth and conventions of vampire horror.

Let it also be known that I had a choice at all times.

I'd like to thank you for supporting me along the way. Some proceeds from this book will be donated to NGOs helping raise awareness and fighting the evil crime that is Human Trafficking. I hope you will be inspired and motivated to raise awareness yourself and support the brilliant volunteers and enemies of modern slavery to help obliterate this longstanding evil.

Regards

JM

MISCELLANEOUS

I don't dream as much as I used to. Perhaps it was because for a long period of time I dreamt about nothing but death. I dreamt that I was the deliverer of death; death was what became of everything that I loved and what I touched. Death was my alias. But after Michael departed from my life I stopped chasing shadows; I started to dream again, about people, faces I imagined I would meet; places I yearned to travel to and experiences I still crave with a childlike heart. Death was just a temporary phase. There is good in this world, it's just getting harder to find. Remember, reader: through death there is new life – I hope that by reading this you can take heart that the most wretched person still has the ability to live and to love.

"The boundaries which divide Life from Death
are at best shadowy and vague. Who shall say
where the one ends, and the other begins?"

-**Edgar Allen Poe**, "The Premature Burial"

THE POWER OF PRAYER

As you may have inferred from reading this book, I used to be an atheist. I never believed in God, simply because I never understood why God would let his people suffer. I did change my view when I came to realise that God was suffering with me and was there waiting for me to reach out to him and be saved.

I resisted for so long because I thought I could fix everything by myself. I'm a stubborn man and it took time. The door had been left open for me to walk through but I chose to keep going through life on my own; turning away from a relationship with my creator. With that I had to accept everything that came with independence: pain, suffering, a sense of emptiness, loneliness. The list is endless. Man was not designed to live as one but to be as one through companionship. When I came to accept that my greatest ally had been carrying me through my darkest years I started to speak with him.

I did this through prayer.

I started with simple gratitude prayers, giving thanks for the times he had provided me with food, shelter and services to get me through the day; I thanked him for the people who were selfless, offering to help me through my darkest moments.

As I grew in confidence, and slowly in faith, I started to pray for others, asking God to help them overcome barriers and obstacles (like I had). I've prayed passionately that he would bring about a dramatic change in the way that trafficking could be fought on a grander scale; I know that he is working behind the scenes to work for good, for his will and not mine. More and more people are opening their eyes to the modern horror that has remained beneath the surface: human trafficking and modern slavery.

MY FINAL PRAYER - PRAY WITH ME:

Father God,
I give thanks for the times you have looked out for me;
providing me with what I needed in my darkest hours.
I'm sorry I hid from you for so long, resisting opportunities to
leave this way of life and follow good according to Your will.

I give thanks that you are a merciful father, perfecting people
through their weakness. And I'm grateful that you've never
given up on me.

I pray that you will free people from the shackles of slavery and
support those in their darkest hour; women, men and children
who are taken as slaves in this world; deliver them just as you
delivered your people out of slavery in Egypt.

I pray for people who are in authority and for the traffickers;
that you will make them seek righteousness and help them
rekindle compassion.

*I pray that you will continue to support the victims, that you are
with them as they walk through the darkest valleys, that your
light will continue to guide them and inspire them,
like it did me.*

*I pray for the readers of this book that they will take a moment
out of their lives to remember the dead, the forgotten, the
sojourner, the orphan and the widow.*

*I pray that you will fill their hearts with compassion and love;
I pray blessings upon those who helped me and those who will
also help them; help people turn away from the idols of this
world and to a life serving others.*

*Father God, restore us, renew us and remind us that you love
us and broke into this world and died for us
so that we could be saved and live a fuller, richer life.*

*We ask these things in the name of Jesus Christ
Amen.*

NGOS

There are several NGOs, both in the UK and abroad, that do amazing work trying to educate people about human trafficking and eradicate the barbaric practice. I am reluctant to provide an extensive list since I fear I may miss some of the organisations off.

Local to you, there are likely to be organisations, churches and other charities that work with the victims of modern slavery and trafficking, so please use the internet to **research ways in which you can help**. Alternatively, you can try contacting any of the following numbers (correct at the time of print) below to find out more and support efforts on a national and international level:

Stop The Traffik www.stopthetraffik.org 0207 921 4258
UnseenUK www.unseenuk.org 0800 0121700 (Modern Slavery Helpline)
www.antislaveryday.com/organisations/
Beyond the Streets www.beyondthestreets.org.uk 0300 3021122
Human Trafficking Foundation 0203 7732040 www.humantraffickingfoundation.org
Oasis UK www.oasisuk.org 0207 921 4200
Ecpat UK www.ecpat.org.uk 0207 607 2136
Hope for Justice www.hopeforjustice.org 0300 008 8000

Alternatively, search #modernslavery or #trafficking and find out about the work people are doing **RIGHT NOW** to combat this heinous crime. Who knows, we might meet again online.

ABOUT THE AUTHOR

John Michaelson remains an enigma.. Yet he is a constant, lurking about the dark underworld that exists below London and creeping across the surface web of modern civilization. We do not know when, where or whether he will resurface and he has given a strong indication that this book offers closure to his former life, that he has since been liberated and reborn.

Burton Mayers Books have no phone number for John Michaelson, just the email address he gives out: thelondonvampire@yahoo.com and his Twitter Handle @thelondonvamp we do, however, manage the content of his website but rest assured all enquiries are forwarded directly to him. If you manage to make contact with him, keep it simple, straightforward and be clear about who you are and what your intention is. We once didn't follow this rule and were snubbed for a whole year!

If you ever get to meet John Michaelson, this is surely a good thing (hopefully) but we have not met John since 2014 when we took pictures for October's Son. John declined the invitation to take further pictures for Nuptial Flight. He says he is now retired from vampire hunting.

The team at Burton Mayers Books would like to wish him the very best in the future and we would like to thank him for taking us all on a very remarkable and painful journey to hell and back.

www.thelondonvampire.com